Lauren Keegan is a psychologist, writer and mother who lives in the Wollondilly Shire, the land of the Dharawal and Gundungurra people. She has worked in public mental health for twelve years, has two young girls and drinks more tea than is sensible. This is her first published novel.

ALL
the
BEES
in the
HOLLOWS

Lauren Keegan

affirm
press

affirm press

First published by Affirm Press in 2024
Bunurong/Boon Wurrung Country
28 Thistlethwaite Street
South Melbourne VIC 3205
affirmpress.com.au

10 9 8 7 6 5 4 3 2 1

Text copyright © Lauren Keegan, 2024

Affirm Press is located on the unceded land of the Bunurong/Boon Wurrung peoples
of the Kulin Nation. Affirm Press pays respect to their Elders past and present.

 A catalogue record for this
book is available from the
NATIONAL LIBRARY OF AUSTRALIA — National Library of Australia

ISBN: 9781923022850 (paperback)
Cover illustration and design by Louisa Maggio © Affirm Press
Typeset by J&M Typesetting
This proof printed and bound in Australia by Pegasus Media

[Dedication to come]

PART I

HIBERNATION

PART 1

HIBERNATION

CHAPTER ONE

1557

Musteika, Alytus County

Grand Duchy of Lithuania

Austeja

The bitter air strikes my cheeks as I stumble from the gloomy house into the snow-dusted field. When I breathe in, my chest expands fully for what feels like the first time in weeks. The pressure has elbowed its way in, sharp and stabbing, since my tévas became sick. Outside the suffocating house, some of that pressure eases. The expanse of forest soothes my aching heart. I glance back: smoke drifts behind the house, sifting out through the vent above the hearth. The door is closed. No one has followed me. I don't know if it is relief I feel or disappointment.

I lift my skirt above my ankles and run. Get away. It's all I can think of doing. Get away from home and Senelė's wails, Motina's solemn and silent expression and Danutė's worried face. I can't be there right now, in that room, with all that sadness. There is nothing we can do.

The waiting is unbearable.

The forest beckons me. The cool air prickles my nose, is sucked in, snags on the lump in my throat. I slow down and skim the edge of the swamp on my way to the forest. It's safer this way. I don't want to look at the iced swamp, but my gaze is drawn there anyway, and I wonder what is concealed beneath. What creatures lie stagnant, stuck? Waiting for spring to crack open the ceiling and let in the light.

The clouds hang low, dark and heavy. With each step, I close in on the forest, break free from the tenuous marsh and into the solid, fixed, pine groves. Distance. The gap between me and home stretches with every heavy tread. The space fills with spruce and pine, lichen and the odd oak. Beech and alder too. Close-knit and familiar, they lean on each other, as my family does now. Only I am leaning away, like the wildflowers in spring that tilt towards the light of the sun. My family are huddled around an ashen bed while I scamper away. Pine needles shake off snowflakes, dusting my hair and coat.

My body is heavy with the bulk of the boots, the winter's-end snow and the weight of grief surging through me. I force myself to focus on the fallow deer footprints in the thickening snow, which sits more densely between the trees than back in the clearing. A capercaillie bird canters, echoes through the forest, and my shoulders tense. Spring is closer than I'd thought. It won't be long before these birds perform their spectacular courtship and hungry beasts awaken from their slumber.

Again, I run, scanning the snow for traces of the deer, but the track vanishes. I crash into the trunk of an oak, falling into the slushy undergrowth, moss and rotten leaves hidden beneath. It is here, leaning into the oak's sturdy torso, that I feel closer to him. It is only with this distance between us, between me and the bed where my father lies, where he wheezes and gasps and mutters, that I feel connected with him once more.

Before the coughing disease, he was tall and strong and solid. Much like this oak. Even as his seasons turned and his leaves fell, he remained standing. Before this illness, he never let me down. Now, however, he lies weak and small, his spirit ready to leave his body. It will drift on up to the High Hill, where he will join my older brother Azuolas, who left us last winter, and my older sister, who left before I was born, and Tévas's own parents and brothers. He will live his life alongside we who remain, but apart. It will never be the same again.

I lean against the rough bark, run my index finger along the lines that tell of his age, strength and survival. I rely on the oak's deep connection to the earth, the roots anchored into the ground below my feet. I inhale the mixed scent of wet earth and must, the smell of my father. I will not walk this forest with him again.

I should pray. I want to. Motina would want me to. The new priest will expect this of us. But the words won't form when I open my mouth. I tighten the linen headscarf at the nape of my neck and glance up through the barren oak canopy to the mottled sky. I plead with the forest; I don't know what. Please. Save him. Keep his spirit here with us. Please.

Beneath the warmth of my coat, a shiver passes down my neck and trickles down my arms. Like an escaped gasp, the breeze sucks in around me. The crisp air constricts my lungs and immobilises me as the snow softens beneath my boots. The trees fall silent but my heart raps like a tree hollow being chiselled out by a woodpecker.

Senelè says the wind, Vejas, is the knowledge of the world. She says it is curious and determined. If it wants to see the bottom of the ocean, it blows the water from the sea and causes a flood. Well, if Vejas is here now in the forest, she is having a breather.

In the silence a cuckoo call echoes. Hoo Woo. Hoo Woo. Hoo Woo.

And the vibrations shatter my body. I squeeze my eyes shut. And then my chest expands, and the forest breathes once more. I slip, no longer held by the sturdy oak torso but shaken off at the foot. My legs are tingly and unsteady as I draw myself up. Home. I must get back, to the cottage, and my family, and the bed. I had been so desperate to escape the den but now my chest aches for nothing more than my family pack. Before it is too late.

I run again; hulking up my dampened skirt, I move as fast as my cold limbs allow me. My ankles are stiff, and I no longer know why I wanted all this distance. I halt at the edge of the frozen swamp. There's no time to skim the edges, I must take the direct route. Slow. Steady. I creep across the tempering ice. This time I do not think about what is caught beneath.

Instead, I think of Tévas. At dawn he told me in his raspy, gaspy voice that he had one final request. I leaned in close with anticipation. His breath was sweet, honey scented. Honey-tea was all he consumed in the days since the mead ran out. His eyes flickered and then he fell into a deep slumber. What if I am too late? How am I to know of his last request? How can I do this one last thing for Tévas if I do not know what it is? If I'm too late, I'll have disappointed Senelè. I shouldn't have left.

Crack.

I stop. I'm almost there. At least I think I am – it's hard to be sure with all this white where the swamp ends and solid land begins. My back foot slides away and my boot plunges into the water. Whoosh.

'Ahh.' Only shin-deep, but the shock of the cold paralyses me. I remain still, and the trickle of water beneath the ice directs my attention outwards. Deep in the forest, a wolf howls, and a breeze follows, sending shivers down my neck. I will myself to ignore the rush of adrenaline within and the worries of what might have happened if the ice had cracked when I was tiptoeing across deeper waters, and what may still happen if the frozen slab beneath my other foot cracks and crumbles too.

I set aside the fears, dust them off as if they are snow upon my coat. My focus is on getting home, to Motina, who will be angry when she sees my sodden boot. It will take near a week by the fire to dry completely.

I pick up my heavy skirt again. My arms reach out to balance as I lift my foot out of the water, and I drag one foot in front of another. Driving forwards. Almost there.

As I reach the cottage, my younger sister Danutè throws open the door. Her face is red and tear streaked. 'Tévas—'

'He's gone,' I say. The bird's call echoes in my ears. The knowledge in the icy wind left a sting on my cheek, and yet I desperately want my sister to tell me I'm wrong.

'How did you know?' She looks down at my saturated dress and boot.

My stomach drops. I push her aside, entering the cottage, and realise I am wrong. My father no longer smells like must and earth, not like the forest at all. The air is thick and heated, and it catches in my throat. Not in the same way of the icy air outside, not in the way that reminds you you're alive. I turn back to the door, but Danutè has closed it. Maybe if I don't look at him, the smell will go away. I can hold on to the scent of the damp forest and the promise of spring, of life.

My stomach falls further, if that is possible, and I drag my feet through the dirt ground. I do not know Tévas's last request of me. It is said that if you don't grant the last wish of a dying person, misfortune will visit the person who ignores it. What happens to those who did not choose to ignore, but simply did not hear?

'Austeja,' Motina says and her low voice catches.

I turn and face my mother. Disappointment is evident in her deeply furrowed brow and the downwards pull of her lip. I have let her down – though she does not understand. I am not like her; I cannot just sit here calmly and watch him leave. I had to move, run, breathe in fresh air.

'Come,' she says, and her tone is gentle. I can almost believe she does not resent my getaway. Almost.

I feel the internal pull to be beside Motina, beside Danutè and my grandmother Senelè, to be at my tévas's bed, but my feet won't move. The chill and dampness seep into my bones. The grief sits heavy in my heart.

I swallow. 'Did Tévas say anything?'

Motina's eyes narrow and her head twitches, and my cheeks flush in shame. It is not the right time to ask. And yet I do not know if this slight movement of her head tells me he said nothing or not to ask this question of her now. I was not with my father when he took his final breath, but I endured it in the forest, alone.

I step closer.

My mother sniffles, Danutè sobs and Senelè weeps. Her weeps become wails, louder and intense. And then she cries with words.

'Oh, my dear son, why did you have to leave us? Oh, why did you have to take a trip up to the High Hill?'

A white scarf is wrapped around my grandmother's plump face. She dabs her nose and eyes with a tattered cloth. Her words are pleading; she sucks in breath. Sobs. Gasps. Tévas is in a very deep sleep, and she pleads with him to wake.

'If only you had a look at your two daughters and wife, if only you had stayed here and brought them up. If only you came back to your old mother. My dear son, do you not hear your mother speak?'

I am drawn forwards to Senelè's lamenting, to my father's bed. His face is no longer strained or pained, but slack. It no longer holds his character, his warmth, his cheerful disposition. His spirit.

'If only you hadn't flown away to the High Hill. Ask the earth to let you go, to open the windows and let you fly. Travel back along the high road and come back to me. Follow the bright sun: she will show you the way.'

Danutè slips her hand into mine. She darts a nervous look between Senelè and me. I squeeze her hand. She's worried the new priest will come. He may not tolerate the old ways like the former priest did. She needn't fear, though; the forest shows no sign of visitors. He will not come today.

'Ask those pied cuckoo birds to lend their speckled wings. Oh, my dear son, fly back to us. Come to the window, so I can see you once more. Oh, we can cuckoo together, maybe that would wake you up. Oh, my dear son, you've forgotten the road. You've forgotten your daughters and your family. You've gone to the High Hill. You've gone to the High Hill without knowing anything.'

Senelè's voice grows weary, and the words cease. She rocks back and forth, her arms around her torso. We stand together around Tévas's bed and yet I feel lonelier than ever. She looks to me, but I can't find my voice or the words, and so silence descends: shame too. I was not here when my father left, and I am not strong enough to carry the ancient traditions.

I look up because I cannot look at Tévas or my family. It is too painful. The roof is made from the bark of spruce. Tévas layered the dried vegetation with his own hands.

He told me of the way he'd collected fallen conifers, including one from a lightning strike, in winter when the moisture in the air was at its lowest. Conifer was the best material, he explained. He selected mostly spruces to keep his mother happy. Senelè once told me that you build a house made of pine for positive energy but to absorb negative energy you build a house from spruce. It seems obvious to me that you build a house that radiates positivity. Why would you build a house that allows bad things to happen at all?

My gaze sweeps from the hardened dirt floor to the clay and rock, compressed to leave no gap where the first log lies and all others stacked up on it. Will the gloom in the air be absorbed by these spruce logs?

A thud on the roof and a melodic call. Hoo Woo. Hoo Woo. Hoo Woo.

Senelè's gaze darts to the window.

Danutè gasps. 'Cuckoo!'

I bring my gaze to Tévas and wish he were still here to make us whole again, to connect us, the trunk to all us branches. Without him we are not joined. If Tévas were here he'd laugh off this cuckoo, but he is not and I'm afraid I'm the only one to sense the shift in the room. Danutè closes her eyes and tilts her chin up. To her the cuckoo will signal Tévas's receival in heaven. Senelè will see her son in the cuckoo's call and will think she can convince him to come back from the High Hill.

I know it is just a bird, making a sound, just as it did in the forest. It does not know what has occurred within the timber dwelling beneath its claws.

Hoo Woo. Hoo Woo. Hoo Woo.

Or does it? It is sometimes said the cuckoo's song freezes the actions of people, turning them to fate. My family are in mourning, and so mourning will be our fate for the year to come.

I don't need a cuckoo to tell me of this misfortune.

Motina's frown lines soften, and she no longer cries. Senelè squeezes her shoulder, thinking she believes the cuckoo is her husband communicating with them. But I know Motina: I see the way her lip twitches, and I know how she thinks. To her, the cuckoo's call does not freeze her in mourning, nor is it a message from Tévas.

To Motina, the bird call is the first sign of spring. The cuckoo is here to sweep away the last of winter. She's thinking of the work that lies ahead. The work she will now do alone.

With renewed encouragement, Senelė's wails erupt again. They slice through the room as cleanly as Tévas's axe into a felled pine.

'Oh, my dear son, stay here with us. Ask the earth to release you from the High Hill and come back.'

Motina looks down at my father's hand, clutched within hers, but I can't pull my gaze from her face. The cuckoo has given Motina hope. There are now two reasons for my mother's impatience for spring's arrival. The first is to bury my father's body in the thawed earth and let him rest in peace.

The second is to welcome the bees.

CHAPTER TWO

Marytè

Upon her husband's death, there is only one place in which Marytè feels compelled to go and that is to the hollows. She is not absconding, in the way of her daughter. Marytè feels sick knowing Austeja was not there for her father's passing, but it also does not surprise her that in that final moment of need Austeja thought only of herself. No, Marytè does not flee. While her mother-in-law wails, Danutè sobs and Austeja's heart fills no doubt with guilt, Marytè finds the strength to rise, disentangle her fingers from her husband's cool hands and do her duty. There is always work to be done.

The master is dead and so she must tell the bees.

Marytè marches through the dense woodland until she arrives in a clearing and heaves the rope higher on her shoulder. It is around one hundred feet long, heavy but durable. Flax fibres retted, hand-twisted and spun by Marytè herself. A small woven basket is attached securely to her waist to carry her trusted tools: carving knife and hand axe.

The river remains frozen but crackling sounds echo through the forest. It is unsafe to cross. Austeja's sodden boot is evidence of this. She should've known better. Marytè gathers fallen branches and clusters them together, positioning them across the frozen river to the opposite escarpment.

She is pleased with her makeshift bridge. It is no medgrinda, wooden road, but it will allow her to safely take passage. Her bridge, a kamšos, is a less expensive, simpler version. She's heard the men of Darželiai, a village six miles north, are building medgrindos stretching for miles and wide enough for carriages to pass, for the arrival of the Duke and the new priest. Winter's end is not a safe time to travel through Lithuania because of the numerous wetlands: rivers, lakes, marshes and swamps. In winter it is like a freeway, a direct route across the ice, but in spring, travel is more treacherous.

It was three springs ago the Duke last visited them and so he'll want to be here for the beginning of bee season, she presumes. Her chest tightens, as her thoughts drift to her husband Baltrus and how he will not be here to greet the priest or the bees. There is some relief buried in her chest too. Baltrus is no longer in pain or struggling to breathe. He is now at peace.

At first, Marytè steps cautiously across her makeshift bridge but her pace quickens as she nears the other side. Putting distance between herself and the river, she enters the ancient part of the forest. A mile from home, where the trees are centuries old, there is little human interference. She breathes in clean, fresh air. She knows she has made the right decision to come.

It was not easy to leave the cottage or meet her oldest daughter's outraged expression. Austeja looked at Marytè with those grey-wolf eyes and silently pleaded with her to stay.

'They are šeima,' Marytè said.

Austeja lifted her chin in that way she often does now when she believes she knows best. 'No, Motina, *we* are šeima.' We are family.

Marytè was in no mood to argue with her daughter, and besides there was no time. It is her duty as a beekeeper to extend the news of Baltrus's death to their bee family. Austeja knows of the consequence if Marytè fails in this: if she does not awaken the bees, they will fly away with Baltrus to heaven. Or worse, they will die of heartbreak, Senelè would say. And what will happen to her daughters then?

Marytè cannot see how her daughter can have been part of this small but active community for seventeen winters and not know the importance of their work. It has been in Marytè's family for many generations, and in her husband's for even longer. It is in her blood to be a beekeeper, and yet Austeja turns away from it.

It reminds Marytè of the unpleasant odour emitted by the black and white striped Hoopoe bird to deter threats. Only it's not a bad smell that Austeja emits, but a bad attitude to their precious way of life. Austeja is this way with any responsibility that she has not chosen for herself. Why can't she see? Marytè is a beekeeper, and so, through marriage, her daughters will be too. This is the way they do things.

15

Marytè sighs as she wrangles her way through the forest. Perhaps Austeja will change her mind when she marries. Marytè just needs to find the right son-in-law – when the timing is right, of course.

When Austeja became of marriageable age, a Marti, Baltrus was keen to take in a son-in-law, but as his health declined it became a lesser priority. Austeja, from what Marytè could gather, was keen to marry too – the prospect of finding her unique purpose in life enticing – but she rejected every potential candidate among their bičiulystè, beekeeping comrades, in Darželiai, to the north. Senelè insists they make a match for Austeja from a different village. Laima, the goddess of fate, blesses these types of marriages and sends misfortunes to pairs who come from the same village. Marytè doesn't allow herself to be too caught up in Senelè's superstitions, but she also does not want to tempt fate, particularly on the eve of her first beekeeping season as a widow. Whether the son-in-law joins their family from near or far it is only customary that Austeja finds a suitable husband through bičiulystè.

While Baltrus had been training Azuolas to continue their traditions, Marytè passed her knowledge on to Austeja. A woman, as she has come to learn, should not rely solely on her husband for her livelihood. Embodied in her future hopes she'd woven the word austi into her oldest living daughter's name, meaning 'to weave'.

Unlike Danutè, Austeja is steadfast and will make a good beekeeper, if only she lets herself become one.

Sometimes Marytè does not know what her daughter wants, and she wonders whether her daughter knows either.

The snow is thick in the depths of the forest but there is birdsong, somewhere, in the white-dusted pine needles of the spruce and pines. They stand bulky and firm among the lofty, bare-canopied birch and lindens. Like her, the forest is poised for spring.

Marytè pauses at a lime tree and glances up at the first hollow. The hole is covered with a piece of wood to protect the bees and honey from animals. Bears and woodpeckers are the main threats to the hollows.

She runs her fingertips over the marking her husband engraved on the tree. Axe bites, two lines with another overlapping, to signal that this hollow is owned by her family. More than fifty trees in the forest bear the same mark. She wishes he were here: that they could be together for another season.

It seems only fitting, with the cuckoo's call and Marytè's struggling thoughts of potential bridegrooms, that the lime tree be the first she will climb with her grave news. The lime, or linden, is the sacred tree of Laima. This is where she makes her decisions as a cuckoo.

'Hello,' she whispers, leaning her cheek against the smooth surface.

The hollow is six metres above ground and so she prepares her rope, doubling it over and wrapping it at waist height around the base of the trunk. She winds the end through, pulls it firmly and then repeats the process at shoulder height. On the lower loop, she secures her right foot and pulls herself up and then slips her left foot into the higher loop. She is now three feet from the ground and her muscles work hard to keep her body upright, with one arm wrapped around the trunk for balance. Her feet are protected by her well-worn boots with a stiff wooden sole. She is the only woman, wife, in Musteika to climb the trees. Marytè was taught beekeeping by her own father, and when she married Baltrus, he always encouraged her to use the skills she'd learned. After all, it made for quicker work at harvest time. It is the reason they could manage more hollows than most of the other families in the settlement.

Smilte, having three grown sons, none of whom have been wed, will now have the advantage, given there are no men left in Marytè's home. She does not feel envious of her friends, though; she has no doubt Smilte will send her boys around to help if needed. It is the way of bičiulystè. Like the bees in a hive, the families in the settlement work together, respect each other and put the needs of the community before their own.

Marytè feeds the rope over her shoulder until she has enough slack to whip it around the trunk at her new shoulder height. Again, she loops and tugs the rope, then slips her right foot in, levering herself up so that she creates a foot-loop ladder up the trunk of the tree. Her blood pulses through her body, the familiar rush of scaling a tree, rising above the forest, the same as men. It is almost as intoxicating as Baltrus's honey mead. Thinking of Baltrus and his mead-making reminds her of another responsibility she will inherit. Honey, wax and mead are how they paid their taxes, and if they don't pay their taxes, they will lose their right to tree beekeeping. They will lose their livelihood, not to mention their traditions.

A shudder erupts through her body. No, I will never let that happen. She would not allow her daughters to feel the same kind of despair and hopelessness she felt following her own father's death.

By the third loop, she is eye-level with the hollow. The wood covering will be sealed shut by the bees but she prises it open so in spring they can take flight. Marytè's chest feels lighter as she reflects on her role as a beekeeper. Inside the hollow, there remain the bark and moss she left after removing the honeycomb they harvested last autumn. The extra padding keeps the bees warm in winter.

The bees are still here, humming evenly; the sound of their chatter is beautiful to listen to. She ignores the ache in her thighs and arms as the heaviness in her chest gives way to coming home. She doesn't take too long to bask in the sound of her family: she has an important message to deliver.

Marytè taps on the hollow three times. 'Bee family, your master has left.' Her throat tightens and she draws in a cool breath. 'I am your new master, and I will care for you.'

She exhales, slowly, feeling some of the burden ease. And this is when it dawns on her. For the second time in her life, first at the death of her father, and now with the death of her husband, Marytè will inherit the hollows. A wave of panic and exhilaration pulses under her skin. She has never been good at relying on others, but Baltrus made it easy for her to learn. She will mourn her husband for the rest of her life, but she will not let it consume her. Her daughters and their future are too important for that. Beekeeping is like the blood in her veins: it keeps her alive and functioning.

She may undergo another change in name, from Marytè wife of Baltrus to Marytè widow of Baltrus, but she will always remain a beekeeper.

Perched upon the branch, Marytè spies a dark-headed figure in the pale landscape. And she knows that figure and his well-worn coat, but she does not know why he is in the forest now. The bees have not yet taken flight, and so she cannot think of any particular reason to explain the presence of the Hollow Watcher.

CHAPTER THREE

Austeja

As night falls, I worry. From the log-house doorway, I scan the shadows, but there is only forest in these shapes and none of them are Motina. She has been gone all day.

'Keep the door shut, Austeja. You're letting out the warm air.' Senelè stresses my name, so that it heats and crackles as if it were the fire in the hearth. Another quick sweep of the forest, but there's no sign of movement, so I shut the door on the crisp air and my mother. It's a familiar sensation, closing myself off from Motina. It happens deep inside me, even if it's the last thing I want.

Sometimes it happens when she moves towards me, arms open and welcoming, and I turn away. Or when her voice softens, gentle and caressing, when she sees me in a low mood. My voice is harsh in return.

My body rigid. I don't know why but it feels good in that moment to see her composed face crumble. But after that my stomach coils and my thoughts return to that moment, churning it over and over. Considering all the ways I could have responded differently but didn't.

It was never like that with Tévas. Everything was so easy. I knew where I stood with him, and he knew where he stood with me. The only emotion I can be certain of with Motina is her persistent frustration with me and mine with her.

I am a terrible daughter.

Just this morning, Motina announced that she was off to tell the bees. There was a brief pause, anticipation buzzed in the air like her beloved hollows, but I avoided eye contact. She turned and left; unspoken words hung in the air. There are more than fifty hollows in the forest with our family mark. More than fifty trees to climb. I know Motina and she'll stay out there all night until the work is done. My throat feels thick. Perhaps I should have gone with her. Then again, she did not ask me to come. I suspect this is the kind of task she prefers to do alone.

I return to my straw-weaved bed and pick up the needle and thread. A moment passes and then there's stomping outside the door, the loosening of snow on boots. Motina's boots. The door swings open and when I see her face, tired and slack, I want to run to her and bury my head in her chest. Tell her I've been worried about her. I've missed her.

Danutè launches herself into our mother's arms, but I remain where I am. A younger version of myself would've given in to this temptation.

But I am not a little girl anymore.

I miss Tévas.

Motina lets out a low cough, as if something is wedged in her throat. It reminds me of Tévas's cough last winter.

Her movements are stiff and laden with fatigue as she pulls off her coat and dusts it down, hanging it by the door. There is something else etched into the creases around her eyes – something other than fatigue.

'Ow.' The needle pierces my fingertip. It tastes sweet as I press it against my tongue. I hold up the white flax linen that is to be my new dress. I have outgrown the one from my brother's mourning and so Danutè will have it, with some alterations. Senelè insists I make this one myself: focus my attention on the repetition of threading needle and not on Tévas. It makes no sense to me, as this dress, this white dress, will forever remind me of him.

There is a blood spot on the corner.

I sigh. I am no good at this.

'You are getting better at this.' Motina pauses at my bedside. She peers closer, eyes narrowing on the bloodstain. She presses her thumb against her tongue and then swipes it across the linen. The stain weakens in colour but swells in size. My jaw clenches. She has taken one vivid speck and made it bigger and horrible.

She doesn't look at me, doesn't want to see my agitation, or doesn't notice it's there. She adds a log to the fire. It hesitates and then rears up, crackling like a threatened aspen.

I press my bloodied thumb against the spot Motina has paled, to revive it. But the blood smears on the damp linen, swelling beyond the parameter in a way that reminds me of the riverbanks in early spring. If Motina thinks my sewing skills are good now, then what does that say about my earlier efforts? Why must we do these things when we are no good at them? Why can't we focus our attention on things we do well?

'Austeja,' Senelè says, watching me from across the room. She is sewing the shirt and pants Tévas will wear at the burial. 'Head down.'

And so, I put my head down, because Tévas is dead and everyone is sad, and it is best to do what is expected of me.

A sob erupts from my sister's bed. Danutè is lying facedown, her shoulders shaking. I lower my thread, but Motina is there first. She whispers something in my sister's ear and caresses the back of her head, running her pale fingers along Danutè's loose hair. Irritation rises again. Motina never comforts me in this way. Would I let her?

It is not Danutè's fault: she is young, and she needs her mother. I am old enough to be wed, to be a wife, a woman of my own household. I do not need my mother in this way anymore. But how long has it been since she ran her fingers through my hair? Was I eight winters old like Danutè? I cannot picture the moment in my mind, but there is a vague memory that pulses through my veins, a memory of how it feels to have a mother's soft touch.

I suppose I am no longer her youngest daughter. Danutè will always hold that title. I am not the youngest daughter, and I am also not the oldest, but born in the shadow of a lost daughter: I am the second, the middle, not earliest, not latest, somewhere in between.

The oldest has never lasted long in my family.

Tévas remains in bed, in a deep sleep, now cocooned in blankets.

Tomorrow our bičiulystè will visit. The priest has not yet arrived in town. There is rain to come and so he will be delayed. Tévas will soon be moved to the threshing barn until the coffin is built and the earth is soft enough to dig.

Worry. That is the emotion etched on Motina's face: the creases are deeper now that she sits beside my sister. Did she see something in the forest? Will spring come soon, or not soon enough? I hope the bees do not take flight as we put my father to rest.

'This is enough for now.' Senelè sits on my bed beside me. She unstitches the last few lines and sets it aside. 'Come back to it tomorrow morning with fresh eyes.'

'Senelè?' I pose the question before I can think it through. I steal a glance at Motina, but she isn't listening. 'Did Tévas say anything, anything he meant for me to hear before he left?'

'What happened in the forest?' she asks as if she has not heard my question. 'When your father went to the High Hill?'

'The forest?'

How can I explain to Senelè what I felt when I do not understand it myself? Senelè clings to the old ways, but it is discouraged. Our family is Christian, and we must hold on to our faith, especially now. 'I don't know. Perhaps God sent me a message?' I say, but my voice is weak and Senelè frowns.

'You didn't answer my question.'

I swallow. 'I needed fresh air, to be in the forest. I just wanted a break; I didn't mean to be gone when he—'

Her hand rests on my leg. 'It's okay. Go on,' she says.

25

'I was running, following the fallow deer marks in the snow and then I fell ... into an oak tree and ... it's like the air stopped moving. Everything was still. Quiet. And then ...' I look to Motina, who does not like to hear of the old beliefs. Tévas would've laughed. I do not mention the cuckoo. 'And then the forest breathed again. I think I knew then, in that moment, and I ran all the way home.'

'Vejas,' Senelè mutters under her breath. 'I always thought you would have the gift.' Her smile is strained, and she eases herself off the bed. Gift? I want to ask her about this, but I fixate on the pull of another thread.

'Wait, Senelè,' I say, and she turns. '*Did* Tévas say anything about me?'

She pauses and inhales through her nose; when she exhales it whistles. 'He did not say anything to me,' she says, turning from me and climbing into her bed.

I lie on my back, waiting to feel relief. Instead, the worry etches in. Senelè didn't exactly answer my question.

CHAPTER FOUR

Marytè

Her husband's body remains within the cottage, but his absence couldn't be more palpable, Marytè reflects, in the darkness, from her bed. Marytè felt herself pulling away, putting up walls around her heart as Baltrus's health declined. She was making preparations. As the scale tipped from her dependence on him to his dependence on her, she began to live life as if he were already gone.

She misses him, of course, but her husband has not been her husband in many, many months. Now his spirit is gone too, and Marytè realises just how present he was in the family. His absence is felt most strongly by his mother and his daughters.

She thought a tragedy such as this would bring her closer to her daughters. But she cannot find the right words. The maternal instinct to nurture and embrace her daughters, which came so naturally in those early years, has deserted her now.

Danutè is young and vulnerable and Marytè feels most at ease in comforting her, but it is Austeja she worries about the most. She presents as strong and independent, much like Marytè at that age, but she does not fool her mother.

When did it happen? When did Austeja stop looking at her and when did all that adoration turn to loathing? Or was the adoration never there to begin with? When Marytè thinks back, it was Baltrus Austeja gravitated to; she followed his footsteps through the snow in the forest. She stood at the base of her father's trees at harvest, even when he'd been intent on training Azuolas. It was Baltrus to whom, when Austeja could walk, she would run when she grazed her knee or when she wished to avoid her chores. Danutè, on the other hand – it was easier with her. She'd always leaned towards Marytè, complied with the way of things, sent clear signals about what she needed from her mother.

Marytè thinks now that maybe she and Austeja have always had their signals mixed up. Is it too late to set them straight?

It is silly to think of such things when there is so much work ahead. She yawns and her back groans with aches and pains.

Sleep eludes her and so she gets up, tiptoes to the hearth. Observes the crackle and wave of the flame as she adds more firewood.

Senelè is very precious about keeping the fire going. It is not a tradition from Marytè's family; after all it is now outlawed. But out here in the forest, within the home, in winter, who is to question this fire's longevity? An eternal flame. A living reminder of the old ways.

The ones, as good Christians, they were meant to forget. They were not meant to worship the goddess of fire, but God himself.

Austeja whimpers from her bed. Scanning the sleeping faces of Danutè and Senelè, Marytè crosses the room and examines her oldest daughter. Oldest living daughter. Rasa, the first, breathed for only three weeks before she slipped away to the High Hill. After Austeja was born, Marytè had spent every night of the first year watching Austeja as she slept, fearful she'd stop breathing too. Marytè supposed the habit to check on her daughters in the middle of the night stemmed from this fear but is now maintained merely by superstition. Something might happen if she stopped. Now she can't help herself: it comes as naturally as her own breath. Marytè rests upon the edge of Austeja's bed, pulls the wool blanket over the arm that has wrestled free. Since she was a baby she slept with her hands above her head, as if she were ready to start the day, stretching out long. She brushes aside the strand that falls across her forehead.

Marytè cannot put her finger on why it feels natural to do this in the dead of the night, when there are no watching eyes, and why she cannot bring herself to be close to her daughter when the sun is high in the sky. There are many things about motherhood, even after more than twenty years, which she does not understand. She supposes this is why she loves her bee work so much. It is often said that bees are good judges of character. Marytè supposes, now that she is master, if the bees stick around, it will say something about her.

CHAPTER FIVE

Austeja

The women arrive with loaves of bread. Ruginė Duona, dark rye bread, wrapped in linen and cradled against their bosoms before the women of the settlement reluctantly part ways with their baked creations. Smilte and her sons are the last to arrive. She makes the sign of the cross as she steps inside and, upon seeing this, Senelė sniffs and returns her attention to Tėvas. Our families share the south-eastern forest; our homes are closer in distance but separated by a more dangerous journey, fraught with marshes, swamps and rivers, all of which are unpredictable at this time of year. Senelė does not care for Smilte's disregard of the old ways, but still, she is here, with her sons and her bread. Smilte places the bread on the table beside Tėvas.

Aldona and her husband Liudvikas, who live on the south-west of the forest, in the direction of the church, arrived earlier this morning. Not much remains of their bread, as we have all taken chunks as offerings for Tévas. Aldona fusses over Danutè in excess and Motina glances in their direction with narrowed eyebrows. My sister throws herself at Aldona like a fly on honey.

Aldona's two daughters married many springs ago and joined their husbands' families in Darželiai, expanding the beekeeping community to the forest's north. She had two sons too but neither survived beyond being weaned. Senelè says those years, before my birth, were particularly wet and cold. With no children at home, it is no wonder Aldona fusses over Danutè, braiding her hair and smothering her with kisses. She does the same to me when I let her.

Liudvikas busies himself with my father's duties, bringing firewood stored in the threshing barn into the house. He says it is to lessen our burden, but I saw the look of pity he gave Motina. I know they are making space in the threshing barn for Tévas to lie until the funeral. I shiver, thinking of how cold he will be in there all alone without fire.

Elena and her husband Dominykas come mid-morning with several loaves and five children aged ten down to a few months old. They live along the marshland, the boggiest spot, closest to the church. Dominykas does not stay long; he must return home to complete the coffin. He takes the oldest two boys with him to help, leaving Elena to watch the three little children who scuttle about the room.

Smilte and her sons fill the log-house with towering, broad-shouldered bodies. Petras is the youngest, Jonas is of a similar age to me and the oldest, Tomas, is taller and leaner than his brothers. They are like oaks in a forest of pines, padding out the space with a solid presence. There is no space to breathe, and I cannot look at them and their manliness: it reminds me too much of the absence of men in my family.

'Oh, Austeja, my dear. How are you?' Smilte asks, tucking a fair strand of hair under her white scarf. I readjust mine too.

I smile, and her face blurs as I blink back tears.

'Oh, my dear,' she says again, pressing the palm of her hands upon each side of my face. They are warm and soft, wrinkled. Her eyes are filled with compassion. She has always been a kind presence at church and takes the time to seek me out at the festivals in spring and autumn. 'It is a great sadness to lose your father at such a young age.' She glances at the bed. Senelè is gathering the women, ready to lament once Aldona completes the hymns. 'You know, your mother, she lost her father at a similar age to you. She took it very hard.'

'She did? Yes, I suppose so.' It is strange to think of my mother once the same age as me. She has always seemed so strong, and old. Untouched.

'Here.' She breaks open her loaf. It is dark, darker than the others. An amber-coloured crust, which is perfectly intact, no splitting like Elena's, who I suppose, with such young children, hasn't the time to let it sit before baking it in the stone oven. The smell is strong, a touch of sour. I place the offering on my tongue and close my eyes. The rye has a deep flavour, like the taste of earth. It is chewy and crusty; there is a hint of caraway. The spices tingle my tongue. My jaw aches with each chew. There's just the right texture on the bottom crust – an achievement only to be had with a stone oven. It tastes just the way Smilte's embrace feels: hearty and comforting.

'This is delicious.'

She smiles. 'Be aukso apsieis, be duonos ne.' One can manage without gold, but not without bread.

'Thank you.'

'We'll make sure you're well looked after, don't you worry,' she says. I think of all the food and delicious rye she will bring to keep us fed while we mourn. It was an effort to lie down and sleep last night, a struggle to boil the water, difficult to rise and dress this morning. My body feels so heavy and weighed down, that the thought of someone taking care of us makes me feel a little lighter.

Then I catch the way she nods at her middle son, and as I swallow the rye it leaves an unpleasant taste in my mouth. Jonas. We were childhood friends, but I didn't see him last spring harvest as he was travelling with his father. He has grown and returned a man. He is the same height now as his older brother, Tomas. His gaze pierces me, and I turn away. Senelè wails and I take my place by the weeping women.

There is no time to wonder about the type of care Smilte really has in mind.

It rains for three days and three nights and on the fourth day the sun hides behind darkened clouds that cast out deluges at random intervals. We have all been within the confines of the log-house, waiting for a break in the weather. Tévas was moved to the threshing barn by Liudvikas on the evening our bičiulystė visited. My father's absence is felt like a heavy weight upon all of our shoulders, but the smell, had he stayed, would have been unbearable.

I want to visit Tévas. Senelė laments. Danutė sighs and groans. Motina is restless. Spring is delayed.

'There will be more rain but no more snow,' Motina announces to herself.

I join her at the door. I will the sun to show herself. Don't be shy. My nose tingles. The temperature is at its lowest today since Tévas left.

'No,' I say. 'There will be snow, too.'

Motina frowns and ducks her head further outside to inspect the sky. 'You think so?'

'Tomorrow,' I say. My breath quickens, waiting on a rebuke, waiting for Motina to question me. But she does not.

'Hmm.' The sound vibrates at the back of her throat, and it is unclear whether she expresses doubt or agreement. She turns away, but I continue to stare at the sky.

The clouds do not part for the sun, but the fresh air allows my lungs to breathe more freely.

Danutė and I shovel snow from the doorway.

'I miss Tévas,' she says.

'So do I. What was it like when he took his final breath?'

'It felt like my last breath too,' she whispers.

I think back to what I experienced in the forest. Was it Vejas, the wind goddess? Or something else? Perhaps it was nothing at all.

'You must have felt it,' she says. 'Didn't you?'

'What do you mean?' I ask, skin fizzing. I dump a shovelful of snow aside and look at her.

Her eyebrows are drawn in and she looks older than she did a few days ago. 'That's why you came back, isn't it? You felt it in the forest. I heard Senelè tell Motina.'

I suck in a breath. 'Senelè told Motina? Why? Motina doesn't like to hear that nonsense.'

'So, it's true?' Danutè asks.

'Of course not,' I say, harsher than I intend. I place my hand on her shoulder. 'Danutè, I came back because I felt sad, and I wanted to be with Tévas. That's all. We shouldn't talk like this. It's unchristian.'

I flinch, sounding like Motina, not liking the tone or how my sister's face drops when I rebuke her. Senelè may be nonchalant about her talk of the old ways and the magical power of nature but Motina has taught us to be cautious about what we say and to whom.

In other settlements, such speech has been condemned as witchery and the punishment is death.

'Come,' I say, and she falls into my chest. The layers of clothes are a barrier between us, but I run my hand through her hair and then cup her cheeks. 'Danutè, can I ask you something?'

Her eyes are wet.

'Did Tévas say anything? Before he ... before he went to the High Hill?'

'Tévas is in heaven.'

'Danutè, did he say anything?'

Her eyes flicker to the house. 'He could barely breathe let alone speak.' She pulls away and runs inside.

I should feel relief. Reassurance. There are no final words from Tévas that I must follow.

Only, I don't feel reassured. I feel dread. Senelè and Danutè have not been honest with me. Perhaps Motina too. What could Tévas have possibly said that they'd want to keep from me?

I am torn. I could ask Motina again, but I still feel shame for running away. If I ask her what Tévas said then I'll have to acknowledge my absence and I don't feel ready for that either. There was a moment earlier, when we woke to snowfall, I'd thought Motina would be angry. It'd be longer to wait for the bees. Instead, I spied a faint smile on her face, and I felt my face flush. I could not look at her.

I consider following Danutè into the house, but I'm tired of being indoors. Besides, there is someone I want to see.

I kneel beside him. Tévas's skin is translucent, his body wrapped warmly in blankets. I touch his cheek. It is cold as the snow powder on the barn roof.

Oh, Tévas. Why? Why did you have to leave us? What did you want from me? The questions swirl around my mind and I wish I had it in me to sing them, like Senelè. When I open my mouth, the sound is strained, and it catches in my throat. I am useless. I cannot continue the traditions of Senelè. I am not made for beekeeping like Motina. What will I do without Tévas? He is the only person who doesn't ask me to be someone else. The only person who sees me. Saw me.

A sob escapes and my body shudders. I did not think there were any more tears left to shed. But, just like spring, the drying of the well is holding off a bit longer.

Footsteps. Someone clears their throat. A man. The cold air sucks in, funnels down my throat and tightens my chest. Tévas?

When I look, I see it is not Tévas, not quite a man. Not a boy either. 'Jonas?'

'I'm sorry, Austeja, I did not mean to interrupt.'

'What are you doing here?' I ask. I try to pull myself up, but my legs feel heavy. They have forgotten how to hold my body upright.

'Here, let me help.' He moves quickly before I can protest and one sturdy arm links beneath mine and I am up on my feet again. He steps back, catches my eye and then glances away. His cheeks are flushed. He must have walked here on his own. 'My mother asked me to come and offer my help. Your mother asked me to collect some firewood from the barn.'

My gaze flickers over the log pile in the corner, neatly stacked by Tévas in autumn. 'I need some fresh air,' I say and push past him to step out of the barn.

'I am sorry about your father.'

My gaze is fixed on a spot above. One white puff in an otherwise blue sky. I'd forgotten how vivid white clouds can be after a winter of grey. I draw in a breath. Is this how it will be now? Will it feel like my breath is stolen from my lungs whenever I think of my father?

'Are you okay?' His hand brushes mine but I step away, fighting the instinct to move closer. To be comforted.

I look at him. His hair flops across his forehead. I remember that from when we were children. We would run through the forest at harvest time, when all the families came together. One time we came across a bee and he stopped. 'What are you doing?' I asked.

'It is gone,' he said. 'We must bury it.' Together we dug a small hole beside a nearby wildflower.

'What do you think happened to him?' I asked.

'It may have been his time.' Jonas shrugged and hair flopped across his eye.

'Maybe he stung someone?'

'I hope not,' Jonas muttered.

'Me too. It would mean we have an unsavoury person among us.'

He looked at me with a conspiring expression. 'Indeed, and we do not want that.'

Jonas plucked a flower and sat it beside the bee.

'He will need it in his afterlife.' He grinned. I felt a flush of warmth for him then.

'Are you okay?' he asks me now.

I shake my head. It is the first time in many days I've felt any peace. 'Yes, I just remembered something from when we were kids.'

He smiles but does not question me further. I realise I have missed him, my childhood friend. But I don't really know him now. He was away for military training for a while and the older children do not always come to harvest. Jonas is there whenever he can be; as the second son he is learning to take over the trade from his ageing father.

'Everything is wrong now,' I say.

'Yes.' I expect him to say more but he doesn't. He waits.

'Your mother was very kind to me when she visited. Her rye was delicious.'

He chuckles. 'It is the best in the settlement.'

'She said she would make sure I was taken care of,' I say, tentatively. 'So, you must thank her for the rye and for sending you to help with the firewood.'

He tilts his head and his lip twitches. I want to provoke him, test the waters. But he does not take the bait. 'Of course; we are bičiulis.' Bee friends.

The cloud has drifted behind the canopy of the only tree in the clearing. My Scots pine. Tévas taught me to climb it once I learned to walk. The loss of the cloud sits upon the other losses stacked upon my chest. Why does everything disappear?

'Have you heard about the new Duke?' Jonas asks.

I frown. New Duke?

'Your mother didn't tell you?'

'Tell me what?'

'He'll arrive any day now, with the new priest. Plans to stay for a while.'

'To collect his taxes in person?' My stomach knots, my anger waning momentarily. A new Duke and a new priest? Poor Motina. 'This is not good,' I say. It is not good timing at all. Motina will have to deal with the Hollow Watcher too now that Tévas is gone, and she has never liked him.

'They make money from it,' he says. 'Honey was never a commodity. It is distasteful. Not the Lithuanian way.'

'What do you mean?'

'They take a portion of our honey and wax and then they export it. Did you know there are now three wax kilns in Kaunas?'

The cloud is visible again beside the canopy of trees. It has changed shape. From a small blob it has stretched and grown, from child to woman.

'I should take these logs in for your mother.'

'Of course,' I say but I don't want him to go. He is the only person who has spoken to me properly in days. This moment with Jonas makes the pain easier to bear. I follow him inside and brew him honeyed tea.

CHAPTER SIX

Marytè

She almost forgets he's there until he breathes heavily beside her. Marytè picks at the cuticle on her right thumb. She shifts uneasily on the oak bench chair and steals a glance at Margusz, the new priest. He has a pointed nose and a weak jawline. He speaks in a gentle but confident tone: someone who is used to commanding the attention of the people. Marytè eyes him warily. He is younger than their last priest, Albertas, who was an integral part of their community. He may have serviced three villages aside from Musteika, but he was approachable and compassionate. She leaned on him for support when Baltrus's health declined. He listened.

Margusz is a talker. He's delivered his sermon and is now basking in the silence of his echoing voice, so Marytè's thoughts drift off.

'Death ends all sorrow, sickness, suffering, sadness and tears,' he said. 'God will wipe away the tears and there shall be no more sorrow, sickness, suffering, crying or pain. All of this has passed away.'

She misses the familiarity of Albertas. He knew their people and he was good with people. He understood the kinship rules among the beekeeping families in Musteika. Albertas cared about the people on this land. He cared about *her*. Margusz cannot care for them, as he does not yet know them. Marytè does not really care much for him either. To care about those outside her family, her bees and the community is too much weight to bear. Grief has already settled upon her shoulders.

Marytè picks at the cuticle on her other thumb. Sitting here is doing her no good. Can't he see that? There is no time to sit and reflect upon her loss for there are so many things to do. Collecting more logs for the fire is one of them. Senelè gets riled up when the wood gets low. The floor is in need of sweeping and it won't be long before supper will have to be boiled on the hearth. Supplies are running low this winter. Spring cannot come soon enough. Not to mention there is a funeral to arrange and a spring festival to prepare. A funeral and a festival? It seems outlandish that both will occur in the coming weeks.

She will find peace with her loss by continuing with her duties. She hopes it will help her daughters heal too: she sent them out upon the priest's arrival. Keeping her daughters busy and going about their usual duties will help the long days without Baltrus pass more easily. It may seem like punishment, but she only wants to help them.

She did not miss Austeja's snarl as she stomped out the door, grumbling about being put to work in mourning. By the time she and

Danutè have tilled the last of the winter rye back into the ground, ready for their spring crop, they will be too weary to be angry at her.

Marytè aches to be with her daughters, working the land, driving the fatigue out of her arms and legs. Instead, she sits, waiting until the priest is satisfied he has done his job. Senelè is asleep in her cot by the hearth; she's barely moved since the priest's arrival. Marytè hasn't heard the usual grunts and snorts her mother-in-law emits when she's sleeping deeply. Marytè suspects Senelè did not wish to meet with the priest.

They sit by the door, the priest and Marytè, very close to boots she could pull on to return to her duties. She doesn't want to be rude, though. She lets out an unsteady breath.

The priest's eyes flicker open and Marytè snaps hers shut. She waits a moment before opening them with feigned drowsiness. Margusz's eyes are dark like the leathery paw of a bear cub. His gaze is set on her with visible expectation, as if awaiting a round of applause.

'I feel much better,' Marytè says and makes to stand.

The priest beams. 'Shall I continue?'

'Oh, no. No. I have things to do.'

He is crestfallen. It reminds her of a young Danutè's expression when she once toddled about with wildflowers in the spring. A gust of wind and the petals fluttered away from the flower head, leaving it bare and her heart empty.

'It's just that I no longer have the assistance of my husband and all of his duties fall to me,' Marytè says.

'Of course,' he says. 'I will take my leave.'

Wouldn't it be nice if he said 'How can I help? Shall I peel these turnips?' as Albertas would have done had he been here. But of course, Margusz is not a thoughtful or helpful man.

Sigh. 'Thank you.'

'I will be staying with this settlement for a few weeks, for business. I will visit you again before the funeral.'

Marytè will welcome his visits because she is a good Christian. Her late parents, keen to separate from their pagan heritage and show their dedication to the church, had taken Marytè and her two younger siblings, who later perished due to illness, on the long trek to Vilnius to be baptised. Her parents were given shirts and woollen clothing for their efforts. Marytè wanted to follow in the footsteps of her father, a skilful beekeeper, and so became a dedicated Christian to gain his approval.

While she no longer needs his approval, being a good beekeeper is always in the centre of her mind. She steers clear of Senelè when she speaks of the old ways. She attends church when she is summoned, and she follows the ten commandments because this is what a good person does. After all, the bees only stay with good people. If she follows all the rules, the bees will be good to her. And with no husband, two daughters and taxes to pay, she desperately needs a good harvest by autumn.

Yes, she will mourn Baltrus in her own way, but she will also allow Margusz to do his duty, as she will do hers. This will be her greatest tribute to Baltrus: being a beekeeper worthy of the bees.

As she sends him on his way, Marytè mulls over the priest's declaration. He will remain in the settlement for a few weeks for business. Business? This seems odd. What business does a priest have in Musteika? Alytus is where all the 'business' takes place. What has brought him here for several weeks at that? Albertas would stay no more than two weeks in Musteika before circling to the next village under his service. She suspected he'd have liked to stay longer, as no other region in the south produced such bountiful honey as they did in Musteika. Albertas had a particular affection for sweet honey and Marytè secretly relished being the beekeeper harvesting his favourite.

Marytè picks at her cuticles again, then drops her hands to her sides. She leans against the doorframe, waiting. Waiting. A buzzing within her chest, rattling around, waiting to soar. She imagines the bees feel restless too, impatient for the weather to be just right, the temperature warm enough to leave behind the safety of their winter cocoon. In winter the bees hibernate but so too does Marytè's soul.

Standing by the doorframe, the crisp air pinching her nose, Marytè wonders again about this business Margusz must attend to. Something flutters deep within her, and it is not an anticipatory anxiety for the bees. No, this is something else. Fear. She cannot quite grasp the origin of this fear, though visitors to their community, a community she is extremely protective of, do make her feel ill at ease.

Uncertainty. It always unsettles her. Her entire life is guided by the seasons of a beekeeper. The structure is containing, but the changeable timeframe is not. She knows spring will come, her husband will be buried, and the honey will be harvested, but *when* exactly is not within her control. It is in the hands of everything around her. The forest, the sky and the earth. Deities. God.

And as if being widowed is not enough change for her to adjust to, the Hollow Watcher has emerged early from his winter dormancy, the Duke will be here and his presence always makes her nervous, and the new priest has business to attend to. There's also the matter of her husband's funeral. Why does the latter bring her a sad sense of peace and the former two make her feel on edge?

'Come,' Marytè calls to her daughters as she sets her sights on them. Danutè and Austeja have returned with some salvageable rye. She waves them inside as if to save them from the threat of a thunderstorm. According to Senelè, Perkūnas, god of thunder, is yet to descend upon them.

The girls stomp snowy mud from their boots outside the door and duck past her, warming their hands over the hearth. Senelè, now awake and spritely, joins them.

Marytè can no longer see the priest. The sky is a vivid blue: not a dark, storm-inducing cloud in sight.

CHAPTER SEVEN

Austeja

A bill-clattering sound echoes through the canopies. I glance up. The sky is clear blue but for two large white shapes soaring overhead in the direction of our house. One takes a playful dive while the other has a furry rodent, or rabbit perhaps, hanging from its long narrow beak.

Motina will be pleased. I am grateful she allowed me this fleeting distraction before we lie my father to rest. I should be helping her with preparations, but she noted my restlessness.

'Go. Go to the forest,' she said. 'But don't be long.' The unspoken words hung in the air. You won't be able to do this forever. You're getting too old to roam through the forest.

Senelè eyed me warily, as if she were inspecting me for this gift she speaks of. Motina hurried me out the door.

And now I have some good news to report. Spring's first white storks have taken flight and they have found themselves supper. My belly rumbles. We've been surviving on stew, boiled vegetables and grains but by winter's end our supplies are now low. The last three winters were long and cold and the springs were wet. This led to small autumn harvests and smaller food stores for each subsequent winter. Winter has been lingering again, but the clear sky is a good sign for this spring.

The storks disappear from sight. Danutè will be disappointed she missed them. It won't be long before there will be gigantic nests scattered among the treetops and squawking baby storks nestled upon them.

Distant bird calls fade away and in the calm I hear something crack. Ducking behind a tree I scan the woodlands. The ground is almost visible but there are no footprints but my own. Bright new foliage appears on the beech trees; leaves are wrestling out of darkened timber. Shrubs appear above ground where only weeks ago it was covered in snow. The forest smells damp and there's a chill in the wind.

There's another crack, this time closer. It could be the ice cracking over the river, but, no, it's not cracking ice but boots on crackling undergrowth.

Someone else is in the woods.

My heart thumps against my chest. I focus on my breath to slow it down. It's hard to make out the sounds of the forest when the thumping echoes in my ears. Could it be a bear? It's a little early but it could be testing out the early days of spring. Or a wolf. They can be very protective of their cubs, who remain with their mothers for two summers. I shove my trembling hands into my coat. It's nothing to worry about.

The tree shields me as an outline emerges between two pine trees. It is no bear or wolf, but a man. A young man. Tall and lean like a young linden tree. But not as tall as our men. He must be a Pole, or a Russian.

Who is he?

He gathers sticks fallen from nearby trees and tucks them under his arm. Surely he is not collecting firewood? Any idiot knows that conifers are too moist to burn. He moves about jerkily like a rabbit. He is not at ease in the forest. City-born, then. If he is not careful, he will lure the wolves with his fear.

I want to remain hidden from the intruder, but he reaches for a stick that is attached to a trunk.

'Stop,' I say, rising from the shrub.

The rabbit startles.

'You cannot take that,' I say.

'Who are you?' He speaks Lithuanian, but his diction is poor. Polish, then.

'Austeja.'

He frowns. The young man is not dressed correctly for the forest or the weather. His dark trousers and dark coat aren't made for the snow and his cheeks are flushed red.

'I am collecting firewood.'

I study him, head to toe. He does not look like the one who should be fetching the firewood. He looks as if he would have people who do that for him.

'That wood is a living tree,' I say. 'An oak, no less. You are lucky it is me and not the elders who have caught you.'

49

He draws up, and he's even taller than I first thought. 'What are you talking about?'

'The oak tree is sacred to my people,' I say before I can stop myself. My words are the echo of my grandmother's and yet there's potency in them. I swallow back the lump in my throat. Speaking of the old ways is prohibited.

'In some villages, the sacred trees like this are felled,' he says, but not cruelly.

'I don't mean it is the sacred tree. All trees are sacred. In particular, the hollows.'

'Hollows?'

I point skywards. 'A bee family lives up there. They have been there for three generations. This is my family mark.' I show him the axe bite on the trunk.

He glances up and the mention of honeybees brightens his face. 'Ah, well, then a sacred tree hollow must stay. And why can I not take a branch?'

I hesitate and he smiles kindly. I should hold back but I feel a sudden protectiveness for the forest. 'It is a bad omen to hurt an oak tree. Or any living thing, for that matter.' Unless it's for sustenance, of course.

He tilts his head; the earlier jerkiness has subsided. 'Thank you for warning me, Austeja, was it?'

I nod and his gaze lingers on my face.

'And where does your family live, Austeja?' he asks with friendly eyes but a slight edge to his voice.

'Over the bridge,' I say, which is the safest way to cross if not a longer route home. His shoes are not fit for our kamšos across the river. 'South of the church.'

He steps closer. 'I see.'

'I must go – I have somewhere to be.' I have a strange urge to move towards this young man and yet flee at the same time.

'Where?'

'The church.' To say goodbye to my father.

'Ah,' he says, and I wonder whether he intends to be there. Is this someone known to my father? Did they meet on his last trip to Alytus?

He interrupts my thoughts. 'Well, where can I collect wood without disrespecting the forest?' he asks, with a hint of amusement. No longer rabbit, but cheeky fox.

I peer through the pines, where the church lies beyond. Motina told me not to be long but a few more minutes shouldn't matter.

'Come,' I say. 'I will show you.'

CHAPTER EIGHT

Marytè

She stumbles from the church and gasps for air. With her hand at her throat, Marytè breathes in the forest, the openness. Her daughters' hands curl around each of her arms and they carry her forwards and she allows them to, because moving forwards is what she must now do. She glances back at the wooden church, camouflaged against the forest. She remembers when it was first built, months after her son Azuolas had been born. Baltrus and the local men were enlisted to fell the tallest, straightest and leanest pines for the construction of the church. When complete it looked alien in the forest.

Though she often finds solace in the church, today she is relieved to no longer be indoors. The ecclesial room inside mimics the forest; its pillars and columns simulate the tree trunks of the pines that surround it. Heavily shadowed, brightened only with the beeswax candles she'd moulded herself and donated at the beginning of winter.

The solidness of the church is usually comforting, but today she feels closer to God, and Baltrus, with her feet upon the earth and an uninterrupted view of the sky.

She hoped the forest would take this clearing and its building back somehow, but the encroaching growth is swept away whenever the priest arrives in town and so the forest remains where it is, and so too does the church.

Outside, smoke fuses to her nostrils: the smell of candles being blown out as the mourners exit. Or is it?

She sniffs again. 'Can you smell that? Is it smoke?'

'No. Motina, come.' Austeja tugs on Marytè's arm.

The men, young and old, carry her husband, enclosed in the pine coffin. Dominykas has done a good job with it. Baltrus, were he here, would've admired his craftsmanship. Marytè is grateful for the kinship of their community. The men assuming the heavy labour and the women carrying the emotional load.

Marytè, not one to succumb to her emotions, willingly accepted the help of the women – Smilte, Aldona and Elena – to bathe and dress her husband. The weeks in the barn had weathered his appearance, despite the cold temperatures. She couldn't bear to do it alone. Finally, the earth thawed enough to bury her husband and send him peacefully to his afterlife.

Marytè walks with her daughters and Senelè through the church grounds, across the church cemetery where the clergymen are buried

53

and up to the High Hill where the deceased of Musteika are laid to rest. Despite the weight of the coffin, the men do not falter: they take one long stride followed by another. At the High Hill, the coffin is lowered into the prepared earth. When Dominykas flips open the cover, revealing Baltrus's freshly washed face, Senelė drops to her knees and wails. The other women fall to the ground too.

Senelė laments the loss of her son, her last remaining child. She pleads with him to find his father and brothers. She pleads with him to reunite with and care for his daughter, Rasa, and his son, Azuolas. At this, Marytė drops to her knees too, the weight of the grief too much to endure. She grips at her chest and holds on to the last speck of light, the sunset filtered through pine trees. She thinks about how her husband will now be with their deceased children. Their daughter, their son and the unborn babies who never took a breath outside of her womb. Marytė cries for all of them, all of whom she has lost. She gives herself this one small indulgence.

Marytė does not take much notice of the priest delivering yet another sermon, or the children dressed in white running around the High Hill with their relatives in afterlife, or of the formally dressed men who stand apart from the townsfolk, on the precipice of this tight community. Their presence is odd, but she has no energy to dwell on this now. Instead Marytė draws strength from her community, her people. Her bičiulystė.

When the wails ease, Marytė pulls herself up and reaches into her pocket. She pulls out the things her husband will need in his afterlife: honeycomb, his well-worn knife and a mug of mead. She places these upon Baltrus's chest. Strokes his cheek, where her own tears have fallen. She makes a silent promise. Baltrus, I will do everything in my power to care for our daughters and our bees.

The priest and the outsiders fall into the shadows, and it is the beekeeping families who surround Baltrus and make their offerings. Marytè smiles through thick tears, pleased by the generosity of the community and the rich afterlife Baltrus will have from this day on.

With a nod to the priest, the lid is closed. Dominykas nails it shut, just enough to keep it secure. Marytè squats to the ground and scoops up damp soil and scatters it on the coffin. Senelè, her daughters and the remaining mourners do the same. Dominykas shovels a little more on top. The coffin sits shallow in the ground and there is only enough soil to cover it so that the earth will not weigh too heavy on her husband.

She turns to her daughters, tucking their white headscarves in so her shaking hands have something to keep them busy. She brings her daughters close to her chest and breathes in what is left of her family. Austeja stiffens but Marytè ignores her protest and holds her closer, and Austeja's body softens against her. Marytè closes her eyes and thinks, I can do this. I can be both Marytè and Baltrus. Both mother and father. I can give my daughters what they need to survive in this life.

With her daughters tucked in close she makes her way back down the High Hill with her bičiulystè entourage, back towards the church with its four walls and skyless roof. And with one last backwards glance at the High Hill, she imagines nothing will stop Baltrus climbing the trees in the dense woodlands and tending to his bees, not even death. It was always the one thing they shared.

Marytè ignores the stench of smoke engrained in her nose and the niggling feeling in her gut and, as one of four white-scarved women Baltrus left behind, she enters the church to share a meal prepared by all, to be eaten by all.

CHAPTER NINE

Austeja

The delicate rise in temperature teases me. It caresses my skin, but the chill doesn't sow deep into the bones, not as in the weeks before. There's warmth in the sun's gaze now. Finally, she's waking up. Soon, from the damp earth, stems will surge upwards, buds will form, and petals will soften and unveil a sometimes creamy yellow centre. Pollen and nectar. Motina has been on edge all morning.

The bees will come soon.

A stork passes overhead, flapping big pale wings through the clear blue sky. I take a deep breath in and close my eyes. The air sticks in my throat and I splutter. My hand on my throat, I glance up again. Take another breath. There is something in the air that is not a sign of spring. It is the smell of something charred. Burned. Rotten.

Like a wolf on a scent, my nostrils flare and I dart through the forest, scanning the area for the source. At the river, I pause. The makeshift bridge is sodden and partly submerged.

'Austeja!'

I spin around, heart pounding. I forgot I wasn't alone. 'Danutè, go back.'

'No.' She folds her arms over her chest, and I turn away from her, the smoky scent pulling me north. Over the coming days and weeks, the river will defrost and the water will spill over the banks, doubling its width. It will be impossible to cross then but there is still time now.

'Motina doesn't like us to cross the river alone.' Danutè's voice shakes.

'I'm not alone,' I say, glancing back at her. My stomach drops. She is afraid. 'You should go back. Tell Motina she was right.'

Danutè frowns. 'About what?'

I swallow but there's a lump in my throat. A lump of guilt. Motina complained of smoke after Tèvas's funeral yesterday. I dismissed it even though I smelled it too. I didn't want her to worry. Motina shook her head, wearily, and muttered something about not being able to think clearly. She collapsed on her bed.

I said nothing.

Now the breeze filters between the pillars of pine trees and blows out towards us in the open river clearing. The scent is stronger here and I now know where it originates.

'She'll know,' I say to Danutè. 'Go.'

Danutè's eyes widen and there's something in my voice that she must take seriously. She takes off, back through the forest, towards home. I shiver. Without my sister here, I feel less certain. Am I making a mistake? Crossing the river at this time of year is dangerous. Motina forbids it.

Motina, who is usually so strong and in control, who broke down at the funeral yesterday. Who sobbed, collapsed on her bed and fell into a deep slumber. Motina cannot do this herself. I am here, I can do it and I must be certain before I raise a wider alarm. Motina has enough to deal with, after everything I have done – or not done – and this is something I can do for her.

I gather branches and fallen pine leaves – anything large and bushy. Throw them upon the bridge Motina made weeks ago for the bees when she came here on her own. I was selfish to stay behind.

I am doing this for the bees too. Motina will be proud once she gets past her anger. When my bridge looks compact, I take a couple of tentative steps from the riverbank. My boot sinks into the stream and I leap back. The river is melting and I cannot risk being pulled beneath. What would Motina do? I search for something else. Something bigger, sturdier.

I throw more branches and rotten foliage onto the molten river-edge. I come upon a log. It is heavy but I drag it to the river, throwing it forwards. Pushing it as far as it will go. It does not sink, so the middle is still frozen solid. At least the log will provide buoyancy if I fall.

Stepping slowly upon the branches, close to the log, I cross the river. The same sodden boot plunges into the water on the other side. Still, I surge ahead. I reach the banks and I breathe out deeply. Leaning

59

forwards, hands on knees, I draw in the next shaky breath. I can do this. I'll be okay.

The relief is momentary; as the sweet, smoky breeze tickles my nostrils it wraps its cool hands around me. I tremble. Will it be as I fear? Have we lost a hollow? Have we lost them all?

With the image of Motina's weary face in my mind, I press on. The smell is stronger here. I'm going in the right direction. I follow the wind and Vejas shows me the way.

And then I see it. The smoke rising from an oak, its bare canopy obscured by the haze. A solid tree, much like the one I leaned against as Tévas passed. A sturdy oak that withstands rain, hail, snow and shine. But fire? A shaky breath escapes and I take a few steps forwards. And then I can see the hollow: the smoke is definitely thicker there. The fire comes from within the tree. My stomach twists. Motina will be so disappointed.

The hairs on the back of my neck stand on end. Why would there be fire at winter's end? When the ground is wet, the air is moist and the trees are dormant and water-laden.

I flinch as another stork batters through the sky and I see now it is not enjoying the clear day as the one prior but fleeing from danger. At the base of the trunk is a furry heap. The surrounding snow is bloodstained. I bite my lip, fighting back the urge to flee. To batter through the forest in the same direction as the stork. To get far away from the danger.

Instead, I scan the woods, looking for any predator that may still be nearby. The beast won't have got far. The scent of new death is strong. My back is rigid and my legs shake, but I move forwards to see more closely. I must inspect the damage. Motina will want details.

Every nerve in my body is on alert, telling me to run. To flee. Because that's easier, isn't it? Only, I did that last time, and I missed my father's passing. Now Motina will never look at me the same way again. Another log of disapproval to stack upon my frame. I focus on my feet: one dry boot overtakes one wet boot, one dry and then one wet. I continue until I know that if I hold out a conifer branch, I'll be able to touch the red-stained snow. I look up.

No.

I fall backwards, sinking into the snow. I scuttle back, away from the mauled body. Blood. So much blood. I am deafened by silence as the forest goes still once more. All is quiet but for the thumping of my heart and my panting breath. The scent torments me but it is my vision that betrays me. It must have. I force my gaze back upon the body to refute the image seared in my mind.

No. I did not imagine it.

It is not an animal.

It's a mangled, bloody human body, insides scattered outwards in the snow. He is slumped against the trunk; his swollen, bruised face hangs upon his chest. Despite all the blood, I recognise this man.

The Hollow Watcher.

CHAPTER TEN

Marytè

Her hands grasp the plough's handle and Marytè slowly steps back, dragging the pointed tip to scratch a line in the earth. After the third row, she places one hand on the arch of her back and eases herself upright. Her body has fatigued over winter, but she trusts it will wake up in spring as the warm sun massages her muscles. Today there's an easing of winter, bright sunlight and white cloud puffs peppering the sky. Birdsong in the trees. It's her favourite time of year.

The snow is all but gone in the clearing around the house and so it is time to plant the parsnips. She fetches the bowl from the top shelf above the bread oven – it is the first on the left, in order of use. The bowl, hand-carved by Baltrus from a birch tree fallen in a wild storm four springs ago, and the flaky seeds it contains swell her chest with pride.

She collected them last winter by rubbing the seed heads between her hands to separate each of them.

With care, Marytè scatters the seeds in the prepared rows by the house. Her daughters aren't keen on this particular root vegetable but when harvested in late autumn and throughout winter it gifts them with a fresh and hearty addition to the light meals they consume in the colder months. With last autumn's early frost, the parsnips this winter have been exceptionally sweet. Even Senelè didn't complain. Unfortunately, they used the last of their root vegetables many weeks ago. They were boiled and mashed in an attempt to get Baltrus to eat something, anything. In those final weeks, he preferred mead, and when that had all but run out, he drank honey-tea.

Marytè sent the girls out into the pine forest to look for any signs of new growth. Something to add to their supper of bread and broth. They'd need their strength in the coming weeks. She can't imagine they'll find much out there today but they might enjoy some birch sap. Danutè loves its sweet and sticky taste. For Marytè, nothing can compare to honey.

Marytè lifts her skirt and kneels on the ground to cover the seeds with soil. She works in a rhythm that comes naturally with repetition. To harvest and reap the rewards, one must sow and do the hard work first. Once every seed is concealed, she stands and dusts the damp soil from her knees. She supposes she could have fetched the kneeling board Baltrus made for her last spring, but she'd been too eager to begin. There is so much to be done now her husband has left. Besides, she welcomes the distraction. Waiting on the bees can be agonising; her stomach twisting in both excitement and anxiety.

Marytè examines the rest of her plot. She should plough more rows for the seeds she'll plant in mid-spring, but she decides this can wait until tomorrow. Her legs have gone tingly from kneeling down and so she limps back towards the log-house. She rests by the Scots pine; its height far exceeds the thatched roof's. It sprouted from the melting snow many, many springs ago. It was a particularly wet year and the root crops suffered but in spring the seedlings sprouted like a plague in the clearing. The Scots prefers an open space like this with no competition for the sun. She'd summoned her husband to pick them all out, but he'd missed this one and Austeja was fascinated by its growth with each season that passed. It was the tree she first climbed, and Baltrus hadn't the heart to chop it down. His sweet spot for Austeja was something she learned, in time, to use to her advantage.

It relieves her now, to lean on this tree as she catches her breath. She glances down and sees something near the twisted exposed root. A tiny green and blue fleck in the earth. She peers closer. There are masses of them. Small olive-green leaves on petite stems, crowned with tiny clumps of dark blue and purple flowers. Zibutes! The first flowers of spring. And so close to home. Marytè is very pleased indeed. The bees will be practically knocking on her door. Her little family will soon take flight.

Marytè glances up. The clouds are moving across the sky like rabbits fleeing from a fox. Austeja told her there will be no more rain and Marytè would like to believe her. She takes a deep breath of the early spring air and closes her eyes. She feels Baltrus's arms around her waist, and she imagines him here, basking in the sun and admiring the change of season. For this brief moment she can pretend nothing at all has changed.

Pounding footsteps tear her from her daydream and she looks beyond the house.

Danutè skirts the marshland. At first Marytè thinks she's come with happy news of the bees but then she sees the frantic look on her daughter's face and drops the plough by the foot of the Scots. Marytè curses the swampland for taking her daughter further away from her before she can get any closer. Marytè rushes forwards, ignoring the throbbing sensation in her knee, and Danutè crashes into her chest.

'Motina,' she cries. 'Something bad has happened.'

'What?' She smells it then. The faint smouldering scent and her ribs stiffen around her heart. Oh no.

'Where is your sister?'

'She wanted to cross the river. I told her not to, but she never listens to me!'

Marytè's gut twists. 'Silly girl.' She knows Austeja will want to know the truth of it. She likes to dig deeper at these things. She is like Senelè in that way. A shiver runs down Marytè's spine. Her need to dig at things – her mother, their way of life, and whatever else she's becoming passionately averse to – unsettles her. Sometimes it is best to just let the soil settle.

'Danutè,' Marytè says, grasping her daughter's shoulders. 'I need you to go to the church. Go directly there and get the priest. Tell him to meet us at our hollows. Send them over the bridge into the clearing

65

where the oak and lime trees grow. Tell him it's urgent.'

Danutè wipes her nose on her arm.

'Now,' she says. Danutè sniffles and stumbles to the west. Marytè moves too. Around the swampy marsh, into the forest, she weaves between towering pines, and she does not stop until she reaches the river. Marytè sees that her makeshift bridge has been improved. She tests it with her right boot. It is sturdy enough. If it has supported Austeja's slim frame, then it should support Marytè's slightly stockier build. She pushes away the irritation at Austeja's flouting of her rules because she is rather impressed by what the girl has achieved in this short time.

On the opposite escarpment the scent leads her to her hollows, to something bad. She is short of breath. The snow is thicker here and it requires more effort to lift her heavy boots with each step she takes. She stops when she sees the oak tree and the smoke seeping out from the crown. Her heart sinks.

One hollow gone. One family gone.

She scans the canopies. No other smoke: no other hollows appear to be affected. She exhales.

She sees the body then and bile rises from her gut. She recognises his coat. His long mane as black as a raven's wing. What is he doing here? Why?

The job of the Hollow Watcher is to take care of the hollows, particularly those on the outskirts of the settlement in the grounds of the modest manor, these days occupied, if rarely, by the Duke. He had once spent the warmer months here with his family, but his wife died in childbirth, and then he moved to Alytus. The Hollow Watcher is responsible for collecting the taxes for the Duke.

She scans the woodlands. There's a rustle above and Marytè looks up. She finds Austeja perched on the branch of a linden tree. Marytè exhales. She is safe. She is for once relieved that her daughter can scale a tree as well as any man. Even better than her mother.

'He's dead?' Austeja asks.

'Yes.'

'What do we do now?'

'Danutè will notify the priest and he will bring Dominykas, perhaps Liudvikas too. You need to keep moving and stay warm,' Marytè says. She motions for Austeja to join her.

Her daughter drops into the snow and Marytè notices the wet boot and coat. Austeja shivers.

'Come,' Marytè says and Austeja hurries towards her. She rubs her back to warm her and then holds her face. 'You'll have to go to Smilte's. Round up the boys and bring them here. We'll need something sturdy to carry him on to the church.' Marytè looks to the sky; the sun has tipped west. The day is getting behind them. 'They may need to stay at the church overnight.'

'Okay,' Austeja says.

Marytè frowns. Submission is at odds with Austeja's nature, but Marytè is grateful for it in this moment.

Her gaze returns to the smoking tree. 'It was probably a bear,' she says but her voice wavers. She does not want to worry her daughter, though she has handled this rather gruesome scene rather calmly.

Austeja's eyes narrow. 'It was not a bear.'

Marytè studies her daughter.

'Motina, look at him.' Austeja points and Marytè does so reluctantly. 'A human did this.'

Her daughter stands tall and confident. She suddenly looks older than her years. She trusted her instinct and she was right: something bad has happened. Is Austeja right about this, too?

'How can you be sure?'

Austeja points at the Hollow Watcher. 'His intestines have been pulled out and twisted around the trunk of the tree.'

Marytè frowns, her thoughts still stubbornly on how a bear could have quite easily made such a mess of a person.

Austeja speaks again, her voice low. 'It is punishment.'

Marytè's stomach fills with dread, her gaze upon the smoke filtering out of the hollow. Her hollow. She nods and when she speaks her voice is barely a whisper. 'This is punishment because he harmed the bees.'

CHAPTER ELEVEN

Austeja

The forest is different here. It's more dense, less marshy and swampy than near our home. Smilte's house is somewhere in this untouched space. Lofty trees huddle close together, claimed with their family axe mark. They have a lot more hollows than us. I suppose they'll need them. With three sons they will need bee families to take with them as wedding gifts when they leave their family home to join their brides. Except the second son, of course. Jonas will stay home and take over his family's hollows.

It's been a long time since I've come this way. Smilte's house is the one furthest from the settlement: they have the longest to travel to church and it's not an area of the forest that is journeyed by travellers. They tend to stay further west, where there are fewer dense thickets and marshes to battle.

I follow the faint track, trampled shrubs and molten snow, where the family must have trekked on their recent visits to our home and the church. When the river melts the trek is longer, but with a sturdy bridge further downstream to the west, it is far safer in the warmer months.

There's movement from the corner of my eye and I dart behind a beech tree. Could the person who took the Hollow Watcher's life still be nearby? The figure comes into view. It's just a fallow deer. Our eyes meet and I step out from the tree. It could be the one I was tracking the day Tévas passed. Its ears flick back and forth, its head is held high, but it doesn't move away. It doesn't see me as a threat as I tiptoe past it. How does it know I'm not a threat? Is it the way I look? My smell? What if a threat could remain hidden? Below the surface like the water creatures in winter. If someone killed the Hollow Watcher for hurting the bees, there can only be one kind of person responsible. A beekeeper. And there are only four beekeeping families here in Musteika. Our bičiulystė.

Who would do something so horrid? The Hollow Watcher wasn't well liked but no one would wish him ill. And it makes no sense that he would hurt the bees. His job was to protect them. He may not have respected the bees in the way our community does, but he respected what they produce: honey, wax and mead. Especially mead. We've always paid the price, that's what my parents agreed to when they moved here. In exchange for honey, the beekeepers receive half a volok of land.

Why would he harm the bees? And who killed him for doing it?

I step out from a wall of pines and there it is. Looming above at three times my height is a cross made of pine. Beyond, is Smilte's house which is larger than ours, with windows and a taller door to accommodate her towering boys. They have two barns and livestock. A pig, a cow and a sheep. Tévas was never fond of keeping animals he'd need to serve up as dinner. He would barter our honey stock in autumn to secure us meat for the winter. He was too sick last year.

My stomach stirs now, reminding me I haven't eaten anything since oats for breakfast. Earlier, I stopped by a small lake to drink water, but after another hour of walking my mouth is dry and parched.

I spy an outline of a man in the threshing barn. He is hunched over and shorter than his sons. I waver. Smilte's husband, Krystupas, tends to keep to himself. He attended the funeral out of respect, and he comes to church when the priest is in town, but he stays away from most other social occasions. I don't even recall the sound of his voice. He mostly grunts and nods.

The cow bellows and I jump. There are boots on gravel behind me and I spin around and find myself facing three tall men.

'Austeja?' Jonas's face lights up in surprise. His brothers Tomas and Petras peer at me with curious expressions.

I open my mouth to speak but nothing comes out. My mouth is so dry, and I don't know where to begin. How do I explain what I have seen?

Jonas frowns. 'Are you okay?' He looks around and realises I've come all this way on my own. 'What's happened?'

My voice is husky. 'It's the Hollow Watcher,' I say. 'He's dead.'

The boys exchange a glance and Tomas strides off to the threshing barn towards his father. At that moment Smilte swings open the front door of her home and rushes out to us.

'Motina,' Jonas says. 'Austeja has some grave news. The Hollow Watcher is dead.'

Her hand flies to her heart and the colour in her face drains away. 'What happened?'

I lick my lips. 'I found him in the forest, near our hollows. The hollow was smoked. He was at the base of the tree, and he had been ... Mutilated.'

'Oh.' Smilte makes the sign of the cross. 'Vardan Dievo Tėvo, ir Sūnaus, ir Šventosios Dvasios. Amen. You poor dear,' she says as she gathers me into her broad embrace.

A deep voice behind us bellows. 'Bear?'

I pull away from Smilte. Why is bear the first to be accused? A bear has not killed a grown man, or woman, in all the time my parents have lived here.

'No,' I say, facing Smilte's husband. 'It was one of us.'

Krystupas's eyes narrow and his gaze lands on each of his sons. Then he nods. 'Tell us where he is, and we'll go. Has your mother sent for the priest?'

'Yes, but I'm not staying here. I'm coming with you.'

Smilte clucks her tongue. 'Austeja, you must be exhausted. Please stay here tonight. Your mother will want you to rest.'

'I want to return to Motina.'

She frowns. 'Well, at least come in and warm up by the fire. I will give you some water and food before you travel again.'

Every muscle in my body aches and so I accept her offer. Once I relay my mother's instructions to the men, I follow Smilte inside.

The feeling in my hands and feet has barely returned when the men arrive at the door. I have not been inside Smilte's home since I was a child. It has been a long time since I ran through the forest with her boys. It's no longer appropriate when one comes of age as a Marti.

'We're ready, Austeja,' Jonas says.

I thank Smilte for her hospitality and kindness and join the men outside. They've constructed a makeshift stretcher from pine with rope woven around it so that the Hollow Watcher's body will be secure for the journey to the church. The men wait quietly, and it is only Jonas who meets my eyes.

I can see why my mother adores this community so much. I've often felt stifled by the smallness of it, but for Motina, it is security. Even with all the rules and regulations – such as a young woman being in the presence of a man, or men, alone – common sense prevails, and they do what needs to be done.

I take a deep breath, lift my chin and lead the men back into the forest.

CHAPTER TWELVE

Marytè

There's a hum of anticipation from within the church walls. The people of Musteika gather as the sun's rays rise above the horizon. Senelè woke Marytè in darkness, her husky voice tickling her ear. 'The morning star has risen.'

Marytè does not care much for talk of gods or deities other than their one Christian God but when she dragged off the woollen blankets, pulled aside the loose wooden flap on the doorframe and peered through it, she found her mother-in-law was correct. The deity of dawn had indeed risen and soft yellow streaks filtered between the pines, brushing her fingertips across the front of their house.

Marytè tried to dress with stealth but Austeja, who'd had a restless night, woke as she was pulling on her boots and insisted she come along too. Together they gathered food for Smilte's boys, oats for their breakfast.

At the church, Marytè is swayed to tell the women of the Hollow Watcher's demise so many times it has made her nauseated. She wishes Baltrus were here. He'd know the right thing to say. He'd speak with ease and calm and make their people feel safe again. With him gone, she feels as if she's a laima tree, hollowed out, and devoid of bees.

Smilte's husband and her sons stand aside, murmuring. Smilte, the only one from the community absent, will be disappointed to miss out on all this excitement. There is unease in Marytè's stomach and she berates herself. Do not think of our bičiulystè in this way. Last night, Smilte slept alone, she reminds herself, far away from all the other houses in the settlement. She must have been afraid. While Marytè did not have Baltrus, she did have his mother and her two daughters to keep her company. There is something comforting about warm bodies around a fire under the same roof.

All she can do now is hope the priest will resolve this, bring peace before the bees take flight. If it is not cruel enough her bees have suffered the loss of their master, the Hollow Watcher's death will draw more negative energy to her colonies.

Marytè draws in a breath and observes the room. Who could be responsible for the Hollow Watcher's demise?

Her daughters are kept amused by Aldona's younger children, who are running back and forth along the pews. There are dark shadows under Austeja's eyes. The Hollow Watcher's body is in the small barn behind the church. The children are no stranger to death, but even this is not fit for their eyes. It is not fit for her own.

Elena and Aldona join Marytè.

Elena bounces her youngest on her hip. She leans in. 'Tell me again, was it really Austeja who first came upon the body?'

'Yes,' Marytè says. All their gazes fall upon her daughter, who sits on a pew. The room is dimly lit, but Austeja can be seen biting her lip, deep in thought.

'She must have been so panicked,' Elena says, her voice laced with sympathy.

Marytè shrugs. 'She acted quickly and sent for help.'

'She's a sensible girl,' Aldona says.

Marytè makes a sound at the back of her throat and catches sight of the men in deep conversation by the door. Liudvikas and Dominykas have joined Smilte's boys. She yearns to know what they're saying, to be included in their discussion. It is her daughter who came across the body after all.

The church doors creak and groan as they open outwards on the forest. The priest enters and the room falls silent. They all turn to this strange man who has joined their community on the eve of a tragedy. Two tragedies. Margusz's tunic flaps at his feet as he walks down the aisle and the doors are closed behind him. Marytè lifts her chin as he passes but he does not acknowledge her. He approaches the front of the church and clears his throat. Everyone huddles together.

'This is a most terrible tragedy,' Margusz says. 'Most terrible indeed. I have never seen anything quite so ... terrible.'

Marytè shifts on her feet, ignoring the seasonal throb in her knee, as there are murmurs among them. She wants him to address the problem directly and she is concerned Margusz does not have it in him to do so. She wishes Albertas had not left them. He'd know the right thing to say; he would bring calm to their people.

Margusz clears his throat. 'Stanislaw, the Hollow Watcher, is now at rest in the barn. The Duke will make arrangements for his burial in the coming days. He will join us shortly.'

'And what of the matter of the Hollow Watcher's death?'

When everyone looks at Marytè, she realises she has spoken aloud. She fears someone has come to hurt them.

Margusz frowns. 'We will jump to no conclusions. I will speak with you all in turn, but it is most likely an animal attack.'

The rumblings become louder.

Margusz raises his hands and lowers them. 'Let's not become hysterical. The Duke will be here soon and he will not hear of it.' He anxiously glances at the doors, which fling open as if they've been listening.

A young gentleman strides into the church with two older gentlemen on his tail, whom Marytè recognises from her husband's funeral. A horse whinnies from beyond the doors. Elena's baby grizzles and she hushes him.

'What will I not hear of?' says the young man.

Margusz flushes red. 'Please welcome the Duke of Alytus County,' he says and then lowers his voice. 'I have not had the opportunity to advise the people of Musteika of your inheritance.'

'Ahh,' he says, joining the priest and turning to face the crowd. 'My uncle's death can be discussed at a later time. There is another matter to attend to.'

Margusz tugs on his collar. 'As you wish.'

This young man is the new landholder? He looks barely older than Azuolas, had he survived the last two winters. There is so much change to adjust to this season. Marytè feels the nausea resurfacing.

'As you can all imagine, I am utterly devastated by this news,' says the young man. Duke. 'Stanislaw was a trustworthy man in my uncle's employ for a long time and I am saddened that I will not meet him.'

Marytè bristles. Stanislaw was certainly loyal to the former Duke. He'd not been hired for his sensibilities or his way with people. Stanislaw was a forceful man, determined to gather what was owed and deliver it to the Duke. Marytè always felt uneasy around him: his gaze often lingered a little too long on her and at last harvest it lingered on Austeja too.

'And what theories do we have? It has only been one night, and I have heard a few.'

Glances are exchanged but no one speaks. It is unusual to be spoken to by a duke in such a direct manner. It has been many springs since the boy's uncle has come to Musteika – he favoured the city over time in the forest with the peasants. Marytè prefers it that way. Beyond the church, the modest manor lies permanently vacant, with the exception of the caretaker – and the Hollow Watcher, who lived on the periphery in a small lodge.

'I have one.' A familiar young voice pierces the room. Marytè's body tenses. She steps forwards to have a better view of Austeja, who has made her way to the front of the crowd.

A look of recognition flitters across his face, but he hides it well. Has her daughter already met the Duke?

'And you are?'

'Austeja, daughter of Baltrus.'

'Ahh.' His voice lowers. 'I'm sorry for the recent loss of your father.'

'And ...' Austeja continues.

Marytè silently wills her daughter to remain silent. What is she doing, a young woman speaking directly to a duke? What will become of her?!

'... I am also the one who discovered the body of your Hollow Watcher.'

The Duke's head tilts, his gaze intent on Austeja. 'I am sorry for that too.'

'If you've been told it was an animal, you have been ill-informed. His death was caused by a human.'

'How do you know?'

'It was all done too neatly and carefully to have been a bear.' Austeja says and for the first time a flush of shame flickers across her face, but it is too late for her to stop now.

The Duke leans forwards. 'Go on.'

'The gruesome manner of his death is punishment for the destruction of a hollow.'

Grumblings around the room erupt again and the Duke exchanges a curious glance with Margusz. Marytè's stomach coils and she clenches her fists. How could Austeja do this to them? To their family? To their bičiulystė? She has given him reason to suspect one of them. Someone in their community. People she has known all her married life. She trusts them with her life and now Austeja has betrayed them all.

As if sensing the unease, Austeja speaks again. 'It could have been a traveller. Someone passing through.'

Margusz's face has reddened. 'There will be no pagan talk here.'

Pagan? Marytė fumes. How dare he criticise our practices. We are professional beekeepers and rules must be followed. This is how we fill the bellies of city folk with sweet honey every spring.

The Duke raises his hand as if to quieten Margusz. 'Thank you for your courage, Austeja. We will be sure to scrutinise all speculations. Now it is best you all return to your homes. Margusz will visit with each of you in time.'

'Indeed,' Margusz says. 'Let's not panic. Return home and we will get to the bottom of this matter.'

Marytė is the first to exit the church, shame burning her ears, scorching her skin. She was impressed by Austeja's handling of this awful situation until this moment. Now, she is furious. She clutches Danutė by the arm and enters the clearing. Her heart is pounding in her ears but she will suppress the fury until she arrives home. She will not allow herself to lose control here, not at church and not in front of her people. That is not the way of things.

The pounding in her ears becomes louder. She pauses at the front of the group, an ear to the forest. It is not pounding, but humming, and it comes not from within, but from out there, in the forest.

It comes from between the pines.

The tension falls away. The tightness in her chest releases.

Voices of delight enclose her as the community beholds the forest. They are one family welcoming the arrival of another. Marytè's hand presses against her chest and an unexpected smile forms.

The bees have taken flight.

PART II

FLIGHT

PART II

FIGHT

CHAPTER THIRTEEN

Austeja

I woke when the moon was still high in the sky. I jolted upright, my bedclothes damp with sweat. The draught from the door sent shivers down my body. My heart thumped so aggressively, I felt it might leap from my body and flee. The room was soundless but for the low crackle of the fire. Senelè was in a deep sleep, but she'd soon wake to add logs to the fire so it wouldn't burn out. Motina was curled away from the fire, her body rising and falling softly. Danutè's nose whistled when she breathed in. My family were safe in their beds. I was safe. There was nothing to be afraid of.

I'd dreamed of the Hollow Watcher. His bloodied inner workings were splayed across pure snow. His eyes had been pecked by a raven and he was calling to me as blood dripped from his bearded mouth. 'Help me, Austeja. Help me protect this forest.'

I shivered again and for the first time in our forest I had felt vulnerable. Exposed. Four women asleep under one roof, alone. We face all kinds of beasts in the forest – bear, wolf, floods and fire – but we've never feared our own. Never felt distrust for the people in our community. Our bičiulystė.

'Austeja!' A voice calls to me now.

My vision is blurry. I shake my head and take note of my surroundings. I realise I am here, back at the tree where I found him.

'Austeja?' Motina says it again, but this time worry etches into the annoyance. She turns me to face her. 'What are you doing? You just walked away while I was up in that pine by the river.'

I can't remember walking here. I can't remember much of this morning. Only waking in a panic and then later walking into the forest with Motina and Danutė. We took the longer route, crossing the river at the bridge to the west as the river had begun to swell. No more kamšos.

Motina is angry with me for speaking up at the church yesterday, I know it. But she hasn't said anything to me yet. For once, I am grateful she is preoccupied with the bees.

'I'm sorry, I don't know what I was thinking,' I say and follow her back to the pine, where her ropes lie in a heap at the foot of the trunk and Danutė rests on a nearby fallen log.

'Why did you walk off?' Danutė asks.

My head still feels foggy. 'I don't know.'

Danutė shakes her head as if she is the older, wiser sibling.

'Mind your own business.'

Danutè grunts and turns to Motina for support, but Motina has already collected her tools and rope and has looped them around another pine tree further along.

'Hurry,' she says over her shoulder. We need to tend to as many of the hollows as we can today. It must be done this week. It is the part of bee season that I understand the least. It seems odd to check the hollows when the bees take flight but for Motina and the other beekeepers in Musteika it is a ritual. Motina lifts herself off the ground and ascends the tree. Her knee shakes on the second ring but she ignores it and pushes herself up to the third.

'Smoker,' she calls down.

I take the branch from Danutè. It is a glowing piece of wood with resin, leaves and foliage tied with rope around the end, where it smoulders. The moss is strapped around it to keep the flames down. I check there's enough smoke to calm the bees and hand it back to Danutè before climbing the pine ladder Tévas gave me. It is only used in bee season when my hands are full of tools, or else I could climb a tree without it. On the third step, Danutè passes me the branch and I hand it to Motina.

I remain perched on the ladder so I can see Motina. She has barely looked at me since I spoke to the Duke. We'd only just begun to find our feet after losing Baltrus and now we've lost equilibrium again. I do not know what came over me. When I saw the young man walk into the church, I felt a connection with him. I'd commanded him in the forest and helped him find firewood without disturbing the peace. I hadn't known he was the Duke! I'd felt brave to speak my mind and he had encouraged it. But the look on the priest's face, and Motina's and Jonas's too – makes me think I shouldn't have spoken aloud at all. What have I achieved? Besides attention to our community from a young man who does not know the forest, who does not know us, but who has all the power.

I blink away the moisture welling in my eyes. It is best to stay focused so my mind and body do not wander back to the tree with its bloodstained bark. Motina waves the smoker around the entrance to the hollow and even from below I can see the frown on her face. She pulls the smoker away and leans in closer. She glances down at me and shakes her head. The blood rushes to my limbs and my legs feel weak. More death.

Motina takes her time sweeping out the hollows. She takes her job as the bees' housekeeper very seriously, tending to their homes with far more gentleness and softness than she does ours.

Motina drops to the ground, and I join her. 'What did you see?'

'The family were gone. No sign of predators and their food was almost all used up. It means they lived through most of the winter. They must have died recently.'

'So just like the others, then?' I asked. We'd found four other hollows in the same condition, all within a quarter mile of where I'd found the Hollow Watcher. There are still fifty hollows left to us but every lost family makes it harder to harvest enough for ourselves and to pay our taxes.

'Yes,' Motina says and glances up at the vacant hollow once more. 'They must have left with Baltrus.'

A moment passes and I draw in a breath.

'Or,' I say, and Motina looks at me sharply; I stare at my boots, 'perhaps the Hollow Watcher visited here too, before he was caught.'

'There will be no more talk of the Hollow Watcher,' Motina says. 'No more, Austeja.'

'But—'

'No.' She holds up one hand, then she takes a deep breath to steady her nerves. Her gaze flitters across the treetops. It is bad luck to bicker beneath a hollow, though she needn't worry as the hollow is no longer inhabited.

There is nothing here to judge us.

CHAPTER FOURTEEN

Marytè

After she's waited so long for spring to arrive, it satisfies Marytè to make quick work of the dough. She thrusts the heel of her palm into the rye dough, pushing it forwards and then bringing it back together into a ball. While harvesting honey must wait until autumn, the bread will be eaten tomorrow. She prepared the dough yesterday and it has fermented overnight. Like working with the bees, working with bread creates peace and quiet. A pleasant, sour odour wafts through their home.

'Lean into it more,' Marytè says. 'Both of you.'

Her daughters grunt as they tussle with the clay-like dough.

'It keeps sticking to my hands,' Danutè says. She lifts her hands from the table and the clump of dough is attached to her palms.

'You must be quick,' Marytè says. 'Go and wash your hands, then come back and try again.'

Danutè groans but she goes to the pine bucket by the door and washes her hands in the water.

'Do not dry them,' Marytè says. 'Keep them moist and the dough won't be as sticky.'

Marytè watches Austeja. Her feeble attempts to work the dough are not like her own deft movements, which have come with practice. Bread-making is a cherished Lithuanian tradition passed from mother to daughter down the generations. Despite her own mother being busy with a beekeeping husband and several children, Marytè has fond memories of baking bread with her. Her mother would ordinarily prattle at every moment of the day about this and that, hardly taking a breath. Marytè could not see how she had so much to talk about. For her quieter disposition, the chatter was overwhelming. But when they baked bread together, the chatter fell away: her mother, with dexterous hands, worked the dough with the same fixed concentration as a woman uses to support a birth. No words, just presence and expectation. It was her only small glimpse into the true soul of her mother. The side that allowed the quiet to settle in without fear.

Marytè has certainly never been afraid of the quiet and she's always been more at ease in her own company than those of others. Though the grief of her lost babies is a burden on her heart, she is not quite sure how she'd have coped with a house full of rambunctious children like her mother had. Perhaps that's why she was drawn to her father's placid temperament and his work with the bees. It took her away from the busy house and her siblings.

Neither of her daughters has a quiet disposition and it continues to amaze her how children born of her own womb can be so different to her. She supposes Austeja was drawn away from Marytè's quietness to her father's jovial and approachable manner. Her breath catches in her throat, and she loses the momentum of pushing the dough and pulling it back.

It dawns on her that her daughter has lost the parent she was closest to, just as Marytè did. It was at this age Marytè lost her own father, the one person who understood her. The deep pain from her own loss begins to rise from her stomach, but Marytè swallows it back. There is no time to dwell on the past. There is no use in lamenting loss and what could have been. We only have now. We have bread. We have bees. Tomorrow, we have our spring festival to mark the beginning of the season. They will meet with their community at the church and feast in celebration of spring. This is what she focuses her attention on as she finds her practised rhythm again.

Senelè bumps Austeja aside. 'Like this,' she says and gathers the dough into a ball before flattening it out with the heel of her palm. Her fingers dance across the dough: it is an odd style that has always bothered Marytè. She lets her be because the dough forms in the same way as hers and anything is an improvement on Austeja's method.

Austeja's fair eyebrows draw in, but she remains by Senelè's side and watches the demonstration. Marytè shakes her head. Austeja does not seem to mind her grandmother's finical way: it must only be with her mother that Austeja goes into battle with such fervour.

Marytè's gaze drifts to the shelf above the bench seat with the neatly stacked boots. Their supply of beeswax candles is low. She donated some to the church and she'll need a few for the festival. They used too many in Baltrus's final weeks as he wanted additional light in the evenings. She didn't mind as it allowed her to check on him more readily when she kissed her daughters' heads in the hours of darkness. With the longer days in spring, and without a patient to care for, she supposes she won't need as many now. They will rely on the soft light of the fire in the evenings.

'I wish Tévas could come to the spring festival,' Danutè says in a whisper. Her pace increases and the dough is sticking less to her palms now they are moist.

Marytè's chest tightens. It is in these moments she does not know what to say to take away her daughters' pain, when she too feels the pain so deeply within herself. She also misses Baltrus. She misses how he'd bring laughter and ease to their home. Without him it is sombre and tense.

'He'll be looking down on us from the High Hill,' Senelè says. Danutè smiles. Austeja resumes kneading her dough as her mouth curves too. Marytè wishes she'd been the one to say the thing that made her daughters smile. Of course, it's not something she'd say, because she's not certain she truly believes it. Besides, fantasising won't get the dough kneaded and the bread baked.

Marytè focuses on the work. She tries to think only of the feel of the dense smoothness on her hands, the yeasty scent and the faint aroma of cardamom seeds. Austeja insisted they add them so it will be like

Smilte's. Marytè focuses on her rye bread and tries not to think of the shame Austeja has brought on the family. More importantly, she tries not to think of the words Austeja spoke aloud in the church days earlier. How she laid blame on one of their people.

Could it be true? She may not agree with her daughter's brashness, but she cannot deny that the child has good instincts. What if the Hollow Watcher destroyed her hollow? He could have harmed the other five too. There'd been no smoke at the others when they'd discovered him, but he could have visited on the days prior.

No: it makes no sense that he would destroy the bees. Harming the bees would harm the harvest. A poor harvest will reap poor rewards. Did he deliberately wish her misfortune? Wasn't the loss of her husband enough? He was a repellent man, but surely he could not have been so cruel as to destroy the hollows of a woman in mourning.

No. The other bees must have gone with Baltrus. It's the only reasonable explanation. She is certain she heard the hum of bees at each hive she visited to share the news of the loss of their master. She is grateful she did not lose more. The rest of the hollows have chosen to remain. She is their master, and they accept her.

A niggling thought edges in again. Why was the Hollow Watcher in the forest at winter's end? It struck her as odd when she saw him by the hollows. It didn't make any sense. He often complained of the southern climate, having originated from the lowlands. He was Samogitian. His wife had died in childbirth, and he'd left his home and sometime thereafter was employed by the former Duke, who had lost his wife the same way, and took pity on him. He complained Musteika was too cold and wet. Unforgiving. That's how he described it. Marytè often had to hold her tongue in his company. Go away, then, she wanted to say. There was and is nothing more important to her than protecting her family and the forest.

He was counting.

She can see it clearly now. That day in the forest, high upon the lime tree, she saw him flicking out his thumb and fingers as he mumbled to himself. He was counting something in the forest. Her hollows. But why?

'We need more logs.' Senelè interrupts her thoughts. Marytè has not noticed she's left the table to stand by the fire. Marytè imagines her sometimes, staring into the flames, reading the past, discovering clues about their future.

The wood stack is low again. Burning the fire all day and night they have used a lot of their wood supply. But there is no challenging Senelè. As Baltrus was ill, they haven't gathered as much for their stores. It will make for a testing winter to follow.

'Austeja must wed,' Senelè says.

Marytè's attention snaps to her mother-in-law. Austeja gasps.

Senelè clucks her tongue, her eyes glued to the flames. 'It is time, my dear. We need a man here to help.'

Marytè bristles. We do not need a man. We are as capable as any man. She has always been able to do what any man does. Climb trees, care for the bees, haul timber when needed. On the other hand, there is a lot of work to be done. Baltrus's large, sturdy hands have been missed in the months since he sickened.

In the absence of a male relative, or a son, the management of the hollows falls on Marytè but there is always the risk the Duke may rescind their agreement if he thinks they will not fulfil their responsibilities. If that were to happen, they would lose not only their hollows but their home and land too.

She can sense her daughter watching her and her body grows tense. She recalls the way her daughter spoke in church, how she talked as though she had the voice of a man that could equal the Duke's. Her daughter has a lot to learn.

Marytè lifts her chin and fixes her eyes on Austeja as she responds to Senelè. 'Perhaps you are right.'

She has been expecting him, but even so, she is not eager to welcome the priest back into her home. Marytè sent the girls to Aldona's place to help with decorating the church and Senelè has wandered off into the forest, doing God knows what, so that when Margusz strolls up to her in the clearing, Marytè is alone.

'Let's go inside,' Margusz says. He stands aside and waits for her to take him into the cottage.

'It is so nice out,' Marytè says. 'Why don't we take the bench over to the Scots pine and talk?' She doesn't want to be inside the dark house with a stranger. Albertas once shared meals with them in the evenings, but Marytè cannot imagine feeling at ease around the table with Margusz. It has always been difficult for her to accept new people into their community. Trust is built upon experience, and Margusz has only been here a few weeks. Of course, as he is a priest and a servant of God, she should not doubt his trustworthiness. But, even so, it is hard to know how much of the old ways he will tolerate. And Senelè is hardly subtle.

'The breeze is a little cool. I'd prefer we sit inside.'

'Very well.' Marytè turns away so that he cannot see her face and leads him inside. She slips off her boots and Margusz settles onto the bench they shared when he came to talk with her about Baltrus.

She doesn't like how easily he stretches out his legs and crosses them at the ankles. She doesn't like how he seems more comfortable in her home at this moment than she does. The muscles of Marytè's neck contract and she wishes Baltrus and his broad knuckles were here to knead out the knots wedged between her shoulder blades. She admits to herself she has been worried about her ability to climb all the trees on her own. She feels as if she has aged ten winters, not one, in the time since Baltrus began to fade. Her limbs creak and crack in places; sometimes, her right knee spasms and for a moment it feels as if it will buckle and she will collapse to the ground. She cannot afford to lose her health. Good health and a clear mind are essential for beekeeper work.

Marytè places the pot of water onto the hearth; she is in no hurry to sit with Margusz.

'You say it is a nice day and yet the fire still burns. Why?'

Marytè swallows and turns slowly. What does he know of the eternal flame? 'My mother-in-law is old, and the heat makes it easier for her to get about the day.'

Margusz nods and she can feel his gaze upon her as she takes the lid from the wooden jar filled with last autumn's honey. It is the one food they have in ample supply, though less so than in the days when there were no taxes to pay. Now one tenth goes to the church and two tenths to the Duke. She drizzles the dark liquid into the bubbling pot and the pungent smell wafts up. 'Besides, how will you try our honey-tea without fire?'

Margusz's cheeks redden. 'It smells very satisfying. How fortunate you are to have year-round access to such a pleasure.'

'Good fortune and hard work.' Marytè stirs the sweetened drink and removes it from the fire. She pours a large mug for Margusz and a smaller one for herself.

'Here,' she says and reluctantly sits beside him.

He takes a delicate sip. 'Delicious.'

She waits until he has another mouthful of honey-tea. 'So, you are here about the Hollow Watcher?'

Margusz swallows quickly and then coughs. Marytè scowls. He must wait for it to cool slightly. Doesn't he want to savour the rich flavours of her buckwheat honey? The bees worked hard collecting nectar from the tiny white flowers produced by wild buckwheat in late summer.

Margusz grimaces and Marytè looks away. He doesn't care much for the bitter aftertaste. It was Baltrus's favourite honey flavour, and good for sore throats and coughs, so he drank the tea often. Marytè enjoys it drizzled on her morning oats. She misses those simple moments with her husband, eating breakfast together and sipping on tea in the evenings after the children fell asleep.

'Yes. Marytè, tell me what happened in the forest.'

Marytè shakes off thoughts of her husband and tries to focus. 'I have already told you what I know. You must tell me why the Hollow Watcher was at the hollows.'

Margusz shakes his head. 'I do not know.'

'Until you know what he was doing there, how will you know what happened next?'

Margusz purses his lips. 'Stanislaw lived alone. There is no one to account for his whereabouts. There are only the settlers.'

Marytè bristles. She does not like this word, settler, as it suggests that she is a visitor, or a latecomer. Under law, she is. The forest and the hollows were granted to the former Duke in exchange for his military services but the idea that anyone owned the land did not sit well with her. When they had first moved here, Senelè moaned for months. 'First they tell us to let go of our traditional beliefs and now they take the forest,' she said.

It was Baltrus who encouraged her to focus on their important role and to not be caught up in what they could not control. They left behind their own families because this was an opportunity to start afresh. Together they continued doing what they loved, even if it meant honey became barter for taxes – though she had never been able to let go of her resentment. The forest should belong to no one.

'I saw him in the woods before that day,' Marytè says and then wishes she hadn't.

'When?'

'The day Baltrus passed. I went to the hollows to tell the bees and I

99

saw him there. He didn't see me, but I saw him. I think he was counting the hollows. Why?'

Margusz's dark brows draw in and faint lines extend across his forehead. 'I do not know. I will ask the Duke.'

'It was winter's end and the Duke had not yet arrived. The bees had not taken flight. It makes no sense that he'd be at my hollows. It makes no sense he'd be there at all. I've never seen him venture into the hollows except at harvest time. To ensure we pay our taxes, of course.' Marytè's chest heaves and she draws up, swallowing back the rise in emotion. She mustn't speak to a priest in this manner.

Margusz shifts in his seat. 'I do not have answers to your questions, but I do have questions of my own. That is why I am here. If Stanislaw's death was punishment for damaging a hollow, as your daughter says, I must question the owner of those hollows.' Margusz looks sideways at her through narrowed eyes. 'Where were you?'

Marytè clucks her tongue. 'That is old talk. We don't take things into our own hands here. We make decisions as a community. We've never dealt with thieves before but what happened to the Hollow Watcher ...' Marytè shivers. 'No one is capable of such violence here. The bees do not like bad energy.'

'Hmm.' Margusz uncrosses his legs and crosses them again. 'You did not answer my question. Where were you that morning?'

Marytè sucks air in through her nose and holds on to it, fearing it will expose her nerves. 'I was here, sowing parsnips.'

'And the day before that?'

Marytè huffs and stands upright. Her eyebrows draw in and she leans in closer to Margusz. 'Burying my husband.' She holds his gaze until realisation dawns on him.

'Of course, of course. Please, accept my apologies, and my condolences, Marytè.'

'All of my people were there that day,' she says, though she couldn't be sure.

'Of course.'

Boots clomp on the front doorstep and Senelè wanders in. 'Bad things happening,' she mutters as she kicks off her boots and marches to the hearth. She picks up the pot and pours the remaining tea into a mug, her back to the room.

Marytè clears her throat. 'Senelè. Our new priest, Margusz, is here.'

She sighs and turns to face them. 'I was very fond of Albertas. Why did he have to leave?'

Marytè grits her teeth. Must everyone in this house speak their mind? 'Senelè—'

'He was due to move on to other parishes. We must gain experience in different communities, keep people on the right path. Ensure we all keep our Christian faith. Sometimes people become complacent when they stay in one place for too long. We must not be stagnant in spirit.'

Senelè grunts. 'I'm too old to start again with someone new.'

'I hope, in time, your community will be as accepting of me as you once were of Albertas.'

'We'll see,' Senelè says.

'What happens next?'

Margusz sniffles and places his tea on the floor by the bench. 'I have spoken to Aldona and Elena. I collected their husbands on the way to the forest and neither knew anything about it; of course, none of us knew what we were heading into. Danutè had not said much, only that there was trouble, and we must meet you across the river.'

Marytè sits back down.

Margusz lowers his voice. 'How did you know?'

Marytè chooses her words carefully. 'I thought I'd smelled smoke after the funeral, but I'd convinced myself I was not thinking clearly. As soon as I saw Danutè running back from the forest, I knew. The smoke was still in the air. I knew something bad had happened. After all, why would there be smoke, apart from in one's flue, in winter?'

He looks at her with curiosity. Does he think no one outside the church has special qualities or skills? He serves God. Marytè serves the bees. My people are special too. It's what holds us together. We're like worker bees serving our hive.

'I should speak with your daughter, Austeja.'

'No. She has said enough.'

He looks at her sharply. Senelè chuckles.

'I only mean that she spoke out of turn in front of the Duke. It shames me. I am sorry for that. We have told you everything you need to know. Now you must find out what we want to know. What was he doing at my hollows?'

CHAPTER FIFTEEN

Austeja

I wonder what Tévas is doing right now. I am perched upon a log at the edge of the church clearing so the High Hill is in my sights, and my thoughts drift to my father. His absence.

He loved festivals. The singing and feasting and spending time with our people. No responsibilities or hard work, for one night, relishing freedom. While harvest festival is everyone's favourite, spring festival is a close second.

Where is he now? Is he living his life on the High Hill as Senelè believes? Or is it as Motina and the visiting priests say and he has gone to heaven? That he is higher than the hill, up there in the night sky, beyond the clouds, looking down upon us. I like the idea of him soaring up there like an eagle, protecting us. But I'd also want him to be living his own life too. Climbing trees, feasting on honey and in the good company of my brother and other relatives.

It should no longer surprise me how life can change in an instant. When my brother passed last winter, I felt then for the first time in my life a deep sense of loss. Azuolas was more reserved than Tévas, but his absence was like the gaping hole left by an uprooted tree: at surface level it is concealed but the damage is palpable when you peer a little closer. Now with Tévas gone, it's as if every pine in the forest has been wrenched from the earth and tumbled aside. It's as if there's a big gaping hole in my gut that will never be filled.

I liked the way Tévas made people laugh. He had a way of making us feel united. We need that now more than ever.

There is smiling, laughter and singing, but there's an edge to it all. Hurt and quiet simmering away underneath like a winter broth. Without Tévas everything feels different. My relationship with Motina is harder with Tévas gone. I know she is angry with me but she has deliberately avoided talking about the church and the Duke. Like thunder, it rumbles through my body; waves of emotion wash over me at every turn.

Tévas was always like the bridge over the river, keeping us connected even when it felt like we were flowing in different directions. Without his light, everything feels dark and heavy. Motina is distant and preoccupied. She's standing with Elena and Aldona but her fixed smile never reaches her eyes. Two deaths and someone tampering with the hollows have troubled her.

The younger children play games and run around the fire. Staying up late and being free to roam is one of the joys of being a child. I no longer feel like a child, but I don't yet feel like a woman either. I cannot run wild at night at spring festival, but I am also not accepted into the adult conversations. I am not supposed to speak up at all.

I don't know what came over me that day. Only that I forgot he wasn't one of us. I'd seen him and thought of the rabbit in the forest, kind eyes, jittery and submissive. In the forest, I spoke to him like he was one of us, knowing he was not. I spoke of the old ways, and he showed interest. He wanted to learn more. He did not judge me. But maybe I am wrong?

Once I learned he was the Duke, I should have said nothing. I should not have spoken of the old ways at all. Albertas had warned us that the punishments could be harsh. He had always tolerated or deliberately ignored the traditions and beliefs of the old ways. He'd told us about what happened to people accused of witchcraft. As long as we attended church and followed the commandments, he allowed us to do as we pleased. The new priest, and the Duke, may not be so understanding.

I was wrong. The Duke is no rabbit. His eyes, though kind and curious, are guarded too. He stood tall before our community, broad-shouldered and still. The rabbit from the forest was no longer jerky but at ease in the company of men, even peasants. In that building, the church, he was protected from our wild forest. His forest.

He's talking to Aldona's husband Liudvikas now. Their stances are relaxed, each with a mug of mead and colour in his cheeks. Apart from his refined clothes and unweathered skin, an outsider might consider the Duke one of us.

I know I won't make that mistake again.

'Evening, Austeja.'

'Jonas?' My breath catches as he steps out of the shadows of a pine tree.

'How is your evening?'

My heart flutters and I'm not sure why. I am embarrassed by the way I spoke at the church. But there's something else. When we were children, Jonas was always sensible and calm in comparison to his boisterous brothers. Now he is all grown up and he is the same, but he is also different. His dark eyes hold mine and it is as if he can see inside me.

'I've brought you some of our bread.' He smiles and his whole face softens. I could see myself marrying a man like Jonas, if I were not so intent on escaping our bičiulystė.

I take the bread and his fingertips brush mine. The nerves in my hand tingle.

'Thank you.' I sink my teeth into the spicy-sour rye bread. It has been quite the feast tonight. For the first time all winter my belly is satiated, but Smilte's bread is the best I've ever tasted, so I eat more. Trying to fill that other empty hole.

'How are you?'

I am about to offer a frivolous answer about the celebration but when I see the serious expression on his face, I know he does not care at all for the festival. I stare at the bread but in my mind, I am taken back to the Hollow Watcher and the tree and the blood. The dream. 'I cannot stop thinking about what happened.'

'Me too. It is inhumane.'

'Yes,' I say, and I know what we are both thinking. How what happened is too human. Too brutal.

'What do you make of him, the Duke?' Jonas asks. His eyebrows draw in to his pointed nose.

The Duke now speaks with Elena's husband, Dominykas, whose arms are crossed over his chest; he does not look at the Duke as he speaks.

'I do not know. He seems more involved than his uncle. I do not yet know if that is a good thing.'

'He's an outsider. He and his men arrived before the Hollow Watcher met his demise. We must remember that. There are other possibilities.'

'Are there?'

Jonas nods, his gaze drifting back to the Duke.

My skin tingles. I want him to look at me again. I want to forget about the loss and the pain.

When his gaze does settle upon me again, his eyes have darkened. He no longer sees deep inside me. Instead, it's as if I am no longer here. I'm invisible.

His voice is hoarse when he speaks. 'We must protect our people.'

'What do you mean, Jonas?' I ask, but he has already turned and disappeared into the crowd.

The night breeze teases me and a shiver crawls over my skin. I pull the shawl across my shoulders and tuck it against my chest, glancing over to the gathering at the church. My people. My bičiulystè. The only people we can trust.

'I'll just be a moment,' Aldona calls as she disappears inside and then re-emerges at her door with a curved knife in hand. The sun reflects off the steel and a star shape stretches outwards and upwards in the light. Its sharp edge and sturdy handle can cut cleanly through a turnip, chisel into timber or open a person's stomach so their intestines tumble out. *There are other possibilities.* Sweat breaks out on my brow and I wipe it away.

'Is it not made the way you'd hoped?' Aldona twirls the knife in her hand.

'It's perfect. Motina will be so pleased. Thank you.'

Liudvikas had kindly offered to make her a new tool. Tévas had taken his with him and we only had an old-fashioned version that Motina carried with her every day. It was made by her father's hands. What do I have left of my father?

'Liudvikas will be pleased. Harvest will be tough without your father, so we are happy to make it easier on you and your mother in any way we can.'

'Thank you,' I say, but I know there is no more they can do. With no grown children to help them, Aldona and her husband are very much on their own at harvest. We will have to do our best to manage without Tévas.

I once fantasised about leaving Musteika and moving closer to the city. Getting married to someone who is not a beekeeper, even though it would annoy Motina. Now it really seems like a fantasy. There is no way

I can leave. Too much has happened. I do not yet know of Tévas's last request of me; I do not know what happened to the Hollow Watcher; but I do know I must stay until I have found the truth about both those things. Besides, Motina will never let me leave the bičiulystė. While most girls in the Baltics leave their homes and join their husbands', it is different for beekeepers. The men – with some exceptions, of course – join their brides' families. Only the second-born son remains with his parents. If I can prove I am useful then perhaps Motina will not be swayed by Senelè to have me married to a beekeeper just yet. I am not a stork who can be confined to a nest, not when there are truths to be found in the forest. Motina has made it clear I will lose such freedoms when I am married.

'Have you seen Elena today?' Aldona asks. I have been lost in my thoughts, but she has not noticed. She has collected her coat and a loaf of bread. 'I am to visit her now. Would you like to join me?'

'Oh, I should probably get this back to Motina.' I tuck the knife into my pocket.

'At least come by and say hello. Elena will be grateful. Her youngest has a toothache and has kept her up all night long. Not to mention she is anxious about what happened to the Hollow Watcher.'

I hesitate. 'Okay, I will stop by for a brief moment.'

Aldona's face breaks out into a smile. 'Wonderful. It's such a beautiful spring day today.'

'Yes.' And it is. The sky is a gaudy blue with no cloudy blemishes in sight. It's deceiving. 'But the storms will come soon.'

Aldona shakes her head. 'Oh, it's much too early in the season for a storm. Let's not worry ourselves about that. Let's enjoy this nice weather while we have it.'

I nod and look away. She'll see it soon enough anyway. In one or two days, the clouds will roll in, dark and heavy. The earth will rumble, and the sky will light up with sharp spikes blasting downwards. When Perkūnas, god of thunder, visits us, Senelė becomes particularly excitable. Motina is on edge because the bees are irritable. Bees don't appreciate storms, but I do. There's something about the sky in full blight, reminding us that we are small, insignificant. That we are no more important than one lone pine tree in a forest, or a giant stork in the canopies, or a rodent in the undergrowth.

We are all equal.

Thinking of Perkūnas makes me feel brave. Brave enough to ask the questions that Motina wants quietened.

'Aldona, can I ask you about your hollows?'

'Of course, what is it?' She looks at me sideways as we skirt the swampy marsh and then Elena's house comes into view.

'When you inspected them, did you find any of them damaged? I mean, did you lose any bees?'

Aldona's gaze drops. 'Ah, yes, we lost two bee families. It never does get any easier.'

'Oh? You mean you lost two hollows? Were there any signs of obvious damage?'

'One tree had large claw marks in the bark and the wedge had been pulled out. It was quite obviously the work of a bear with a sweet tooth. And the other ... well, the wedge had been pecked and had fallen aside.

It was likely a woodpecker. The bees would've frozen over the winter. That is a thought hard to endure.'

'Hmm.'

'Austeja.' Aldona stops and faces me. We are outside Elena's house. Two younger children are running through the wildflowers beside the barn. 'Is there something on your mind?'

I breathed in, out, in again. 'Did Motina talk to you about the hollow that had been damaged?'

'We spoke at spring festival. She told me she was very saddened about losing her hollow.'

'She didn't say anything else?'

'No. Should she have?'

Why didn't Motina tell Aldona that we'd lost more hollows? These are her friends. There are no secrets here. Surely Motina couldn't possibly believe the bees all left with Tévas? Why those five and not the other fifty and why only those hives near the bloodstained oak?

Maybe, as Motina says, they do sense negative energy. If she truly believes the bees left with Tévas then she won't tell anyone. She's ashamed.

I swallow back the lump of uncertainty in my throat. I want to say more, to tell Aldona the truth. Maybe she would have another perspective, another reason for the loss? But then I recall Motina's face, her hardened face after the meeting at the church, how disappointed she was by my speaking out.

'It's nothing. Motina is just taking it hard. Tévas, and then the hollows. And the watcher, of course.'

'So many losses one upon the other. Log upon log like a wood stack. Your mother is strong, though, Austeja. She will not fall. And you must be strong for her, too. Best not to overcomplicate things. Or say too much.'

My cheeks flush. Does everyone share the same opinion of me? 'Of course – thank you, Aldona.'

I feel more confused than ever.

Elena comes out then and Aldona rushes to her, kisses her on both cheeks and swoops up the toddler on her hip. 'Hello, beautiful one. I hear you have a toothache.' The toddler grimaces and points to her cheek. 'Oh yes, that would be very painful. I have just the thing for you. Propolis and honey to ease the problem.'

'Oh. Aldona, thank you. I have so many things to do today and she won't let me put her down. She's barely slept all night and day.' Elena's face is tired, and she kneads her waist with her knuckles. She sees me then and is surprised. 'Austeja, how lovely to see you.'

'She's accompanied me on this pleasant walk,' Aldona says with a genuine smile, but her tone makes me wonder if I must now take my leave.

'The spring festival was lovely, wasn't it?' Elena asks.

'Yes, it was nice.'

She looks at me and lowers her voice. 'It must have been difficult without your father here.'

My throat feels thick and I cannot speak. I blink back tears and nod. Why did Tévas have to leave us? Why now? If only he'd been here when the Hollow Watcher was murdered, or the hollows destroyed.

He'd know what to do. He'd find a way to make sense of it all. He'd take charge. No one else is doing that. The priest is new and he doesn't know us, and he will do as the Duke says. He wants to dismiss the death as a bear attack and perhaps that would be good for our people. But what if, as Jonas implied, it was not one of our people who hurt the Hollow Watcher? What if it was someone else? I must know. I want them to face the consequences of their actions.

I want to feel safe again.

'Are you feeling okay, Austeja?' Aldona asks. Her pale brows draw in and her mouth puckers out to the side as though she is biting the inside of one cheek.

'Yes, I'm just a little tired. I should make my way home.'

'Of course,' Elena says. 'It was so lovely for you to stop by. Say hello to your mother and grandmother for me.'

'I will.'

In the clearing outside of Elena's house, I start towards the path around the marshes. I look back at the house and see Aldona and Elena disappear inside. I turn my back on the path and take the trail into the forest.

Jonas's words swirl around my head. There are other possibilities. It feels as if Aldona berated me. Encouraged me not to say too much. Am I supposed to dig further or retreat? Everyone but Jonas wants me to remain quiet. Jonas wants me to think on it. I don't know what to do.

Now I'm weaving around pines, circling oaks, until I reach the bridge. By the bridge, zibutes, violas, sweep over the side. I stop upon hearing the familiar hum of honeybees. I crouch down and find them hopping about from one purplish-blue flower to another. Gathering nectar in their tiny leg pouches.

They remind me of Motina. Always working hard, following the rules. She's happy to be confined because she can do what she loves. 'Do any of you wish to break out on your own?' I whisper. They hum in response and I assume they do not. They seem happy enough. I wonder if they are bees from our hollows, or Aldona's or perhaps Elena's or Smilte's. They can travel many miles, especially if they are searching for their favourite flowers.

The bushes rustle and I rise, my senses on alert. It could be a rabbit or a mouse, but then I see its dark green scaly skin and yellow collar. A grass snake. I remain still, knowing it will not hurt me unless it feels threatened, and relieved that it is not a poisonous asp. It's probably a male snake. In early spring they tend to emerge first and bask in the sun. It reminds me of the story Senelè tells of the old times, when the grass snake was frequently kept as a pet. They lived under a married couple's bed or in a special place near the hearth, because they are sacred to the sun goddess. I find it hard to believe that snakes were kept indoors. They aren't the type of animal to remain cooped up in one spot. They like to roam and hunt. Senelè holds on to these stories, but at least she does not practise this belief. I wouldn't sleep well if a snake slept under Motina's bed. An eternal flame is one thing but a pet snake is quite another.

The bushes rustle again as the snake retreats. The bees have moved on and their gentle hum fades. I breathe out slowly and cross the bridge.

Without realising, I arrive at our hollows. At the oak where I felt my father's spirit leave us, the same oak where the Hollow Watcher's body lay slain. Why do I keep returning here? My body is pulled towards the bloodstained oak, only the blood is no longer visible. The snow has evaporated, and all traces of the Hollow Watcher are gone. Except for the images that remain in my mind.

I shouldn't be here. But I need to know. I must know what happened to him. There must be a reason that I was the one who discovered him. Tévas says everything happens for a reason: God plans it that way. Did he plan for me to find the Hollow Watcher? Is there something more he wants from me? Or is it as Senelè says, and I have a gift?

Soft voices trickle through the forest from the direction of Smilte's house. My instinct is to flee but I cannot move my feet. Images flash. The body. The blood. The dream.

My heart thumps hard against my chest.

Two familiar shapes appear. Jonas and Tomas.

'Austeja.' Jonas steps ahead of his brother. 'I hope we didn't frighten you.'

I realise I am cowering by the oak. I spring away and wipe my hands on my dress, as if to wipe away invisible blood. My voice is shaky. 'A little.'

Jonas glances back at his brother. 'I'm sorry, we didn't mean to. We've just been keeping an eye on the hollows.'

'Oh, you don't need to be doing that.'

'My mother promised yours that we'd pass through the area every day. Just to make sure everything is okay.'

'Did my mother ask you to do that?'

His eyes crinkle at the edges. 'No, she did not. We insisted.'

'Well, that's very kind of you. But what do you expect to discover out here?'

He swallows and for a moment he looks uncertain. Tomas steps closer to him. 'Until we learn the truth, we must be certain no one else will harm the hollows.'

The other possibilities that Jonas mentioned. This means they believe the person who hurt the Hollow Watcher was an outsider. The Duke, his henchmen or the priest or someone from far away. It is ridiculous to think any of them would risk their positions to do such evil. Then again, it is ridiculous to imagine any of us executing the Hollow Watcher. Maybe it *was* just a bear ...

'Do you think we're at risk of further harm?' I ask Jonas, but it is Tomas who responds.

'I think it was a worthless honey thief. Stanislaw was just collateral.'

My brows knit together. A thief? That would make Stanislaw innocent.

Jonas rolls his eyes. 'Don't listen to my brother. If anyone outside the settlement passed through the forest, we would know.'

'We must be careful, anyway,' Tomas says. 'We must protect our hollows and each other. There's no need for you to worry, dear Austeja. That's why we are here.' He tucks his hands into his pockets and wanders off, occasionally glancing up at the treetops as though they hold the answers.

My cheeks feel warm. 'See you later, then,' I say and, before Jonas can farewell me, I dart back through the forest to the bridge.

Tomas speaks to me as if I am a child. As if I mustn't worry myself with these grown-up problems. Does he think he's some kind of hero? He doesn't realise I am part of this. I found the Hollow Watcher. I have a responsibility to see this through. To find the truth. Even if it means confronting one of our own.

CHAPTER SIXTEEN

Marytè

She should be up there on the High Hill lamenting with her mother-in-law. She should sink into the earth upon which Baltrus is buried, wailing and weeping. Moaning. But Marytè cannot bring herself to descend into such darkness. It is too deep, too heavy, too painful. She's afraid if she plunges that low, her knees will truly buckle from beneath her and she may never rise again.

Instead, she sits on a log in the company of her extended family. Her clan dances upon the violet wildflowers which carpet the forest floor. The buzzing fills her ears and drowns her worrying thoughts. Orange and black blurs dance from flower to flower, collecting nectar and pollen. They seem very happy to have come across this delicious spread. Others drone above in pursuit of something further afield.

She breathes in the floral scent and for the first time since Baltrus left, the tension eases. It is here she sinks into the tender earth. It is here tears spring to life and trickle down her cheeks. Tears of sadness and joy.

Calm comes over her.

This has always come naturally. Being close to the bees, being a part of them. It's as if her maternal instinct has been woven, like honeycomb, into the lives of bees. Mothering the bees is straightforward. Mothering her children is fraught with complications. There are feelings and personalities to consider. She never seems to get it right. She loves her daughters, with all her heart, but at times she does not know if it is reciprocated. Or whether she deserves their love. With bees there is no guesswork. They are wonderfully predictable and loyal.

Baltrus, on the other hand, settled into fatherhood easily. She always envied him that. It's as if the moment Azuolas, his first and only son, was placed in his arms he instinctively knew what to do and how to do it.

It was not that way for Marytè. Her children's constant reliance on her was unsettling. They look to her for guidance – even now – in ways beyond her capabilities. She can teach them to sow, to bake bread, to climb a tree, but when their eyes are trained on her with uncertainty about the bigger things in life, such as meaning and religion and grief, Marytè is lost. When they come to her with these emotions, these questions, she feels herself close off. She has never been taught herself. She had no guidance after her father's death and so learned to rely only upon herself, and later, Baltrus.

I miss him dearly.

No. She shakes her head. If she dwells on these painful feelings, she might get stuck, unable to move on. She will not become her own mother. She owes her girls this. If they cannot have Baltrus, then they will have the best version of her. Wallowing in her loss will not be good for them.

Without her wanting them to, Marytè's thoughts hop from memory to memory, backwards in time, settling upon a blossom of bleakness. Marytè, fifteen winters old, wailing at her father's grave. Heaving chest, uncontrolled sobbing and her whole body shuddering. Her father was gone, and it was just Marytè and her mother who remained. Her mother kneeled beside her, silent and stony. Numb and detached. She stood and stepped towards Marytè and for a moment she'd thought, hoped, that her mother would embrace her. Allow her to share some of her sorrow, to relieve her, even momentarily, from this pain. Instead, her mother scuffed the dirt back over the indents left by her knees and then staggered away. Away from the grave and away from her daughter. She left and it was as if she never returned. Physically she was there. In her chair, staring at the flame, or lying in her bed, staring at the thatch ceiling. Always staring and yet never seeing.

Marytè had truly lost both of her parents. If it were not for her beekeeping skills, she wouldn't have made a suitable marriage. Baltrus had saved her from desolation, but it was the bees who saved her from misery.

So she does not go to the grave to lament. No, she comes to the bees so she can feel something. Anything else. Because if there is a hum of happiness, then she knows she is still alive. She is still living. She is not her mother.

She must stay strong for her daughters. For her bees. She must continue.

She notices, immediately, the changing vibrations in the breeze. Louder, fitful buzzes around the wildflowers. A gust blows through the pine trees; the air thickens and has a sweet, pungent smell. A storm is coming, and the bees are frantic. Darting about as if calling out a warning: time for the forager bees to retreat. Marytè glances up at one of her hollows, perched up high in a pine tree. There is increased activity outside the hive as her kin vanish into the safety of the hollow.

The pine canopies dissolve into the grey blanket draped across the sky. A deep rumble shakes the ground, and a crack of thunder reverberates along the earth. She scrambles to her feet. 'Farewell, little ones,' she says, as she makes her own way to shelter, passing back over the bridge and around the marshes into the clearing.

Austeja warned her before she left. A storm is coming. Marytè had thought it too early to be storming but it seems Austeja was right. Again.

A giant spark of light knifes the clouds and a tremor passes through her body. She joins her daughters and mother-in-law inside just as heavy droplets land upon her headscarf. The storm has well and truly set in now. The rain will be here for days.

Another thought creeps in. Relief is chased away by guilt as the meaning of the storm dawns on her. The Hollow Watcher's funeral will be delayed. He is meant to be laid to rest tomorrow.

'Motina.' Danutè's voice brings her attention from the wild to the indoors. 'Look what I found by the marshes.' Her hands are enclosed around something green, its scraggy legs hanging between her fingers.

'What have you got there, Danutè. A frog?'

Croak.

She grins. 'Yes, isn't it sweet?'

'I suppose.' Marytè chuckles and tucks a loose hair behind Danutè's ear. Her hair, wispy and thin, is so different from her sister's thicker and longer mane. Austeja warms her hands over the hearth, her hair loose, damp and wavy. She must've just returned from the forest too. Her skin is already bronzed after these early spring days outdoors. It is unnerving how much time Austeja spends in the forest: she's almost wild in nature. It reminds her of Senelè in her younger days, when Marytè first wed Baltrus. With the awful nature of the Hollow Watcher's death, she shouldn't let her roam so freely, but she cannot bear to take the forest from her. Austeja, like her mother, has lost so much already. It is a small relief that Smilte's boys are patrolling the area, even if she was resistant at first.

'You should have left the poor thing where it belongs,' Austeja says.

'But he may be gobbled up by a snake.'

Austeja shrugs. 'That is the way of things in the forest.'

'I don't like it. If I can save a little frog from being a snake's dinner, then I will.'

'Then the snake will find something else to prey on. A mouse, a rabbit, or a pigeon. Will you try to save them all?'

Senelè interrupts. 'Come on now, girls.'

122

It is a debate her daughters have had since they were young. From the moment she could toddle, Danutè loved to find things to nurture, or bring home pets to fuss over. Insects, young birds fallen from a nest or filthy mice from the threshing barn. Austeja believes everything should remain as is. In some ways, Marytè agrees with her. No one should own the forest, and they should do their best not to leave too much of a mark on the earth. But Danutè is gentle with her creatures and really there is no harm done. 'You can keep it here until the storm passes, and then you must release it.'

Danutè's shoulders slump, but she places the frog inside her boot away from her sister's glare.

Thunder rumbles and cracks overhead. There's warmth in Marytè's belly. She has her children and her health, and she has a roof over her head. The girls are bickering about everyday things. Life feels almost normal. *I can do this. Senelè can lament for us all and I can be strong and hold the family together. I can do what Baltrus would have done had he been here in my place.*

Senelè settles upon her bed, in prime position by the hearth. 'Have I told you girls about the god of thunder?' A thunderclap arrives just in time for her performance.

Danutè lugs her boot to her bedside and sits on her cot, knees tucked up under her chin. Austeja lies down on her bed. She does not face Senelè, but Marytè knows she is listening. She has been fascinated by her grandmother's stories, the folklore of their ancestors, since birth.

'There is only one true God, isn't there?' Danutè asks, frowning. Marytè sighs. All this talk of the old ways is confusing for the girls, especially Danutè. And Marytè is still unsure whether she can trust the new priest not to bring down the church's condemnation if the children were to repeat their grandmother's stories beyond the cottage walls.

Senelè clucks her tongue. 'There was a time when all our people looked to many gods. Our people have always been strongly connected to the land, to the earth and sky, forest and the animals. The sun, the moon, the wind and thunder. There are special forces all around us, if only we pay close attention.'

Austeja sits up and Marytè adds a log to the fire.

'But—'

Senelè cuts Danutè off. 'It is true. We held strong for a very long time. Lithuania, the last European country to hold on to their old ways. Until the churches moved in, and we were urged to become Christianised. To believe in only one God, not many.'

'Why?' Danutè asks.

Senelè shrugs. 'Politics. Power? I cannot say. They called us heathens! I do not know why we cannot hold on to whatever beliefs we have. Why must we all be the same? Politics,' she says again. 'None of that should concern us down here in Musteika.'

'We must be cautious of the new priest,' Marytè says.

'We must be cautious, indeed,' Senelè says and looks pointedly at Marytè. 'Putting our trust in those of the church is not in our best interests.'

'So, what of the god of thunder?' Austeja asks. Marytè is surprised by her interest: she must've heard this story a hundred times before. They all have.

Senelè's cheeks swell with pleasure and she leans forwards, rubbing the palms of her hands together. 'Perkūnas, god of thunder, is very powerful. At his disposal he has many weapons. Every weapon you can think of! A sword, an axe, stones and, of course, lightning bolts! He's a mighty man with a long beard and he rides across the sky in his two-wheeled chariot, bringing rain and striking fire. The sound of the wheels often causes thunder. His chariot is drawn by goats—'

'Goats?!' Danutè says.

'Not just any goats,' Senelè continues. 'They are the holiest, most magnificent goats you can ever imagine. He is king of the skies.'

'And he blesses our crops?'

'Oh yes: when he rolls his thunder for the first time in spring – just as he is doing now – having given the earth a good shake with his mighty thunder, the grass starts to grow and vegetation begins.'

There's another roar of thunder and the cottage shakes, just as Senelè predicts. The girls flinch and giggle. Marytè is thankful her crops were sowed early so the storm won't wash them away. They will have a good start to spring.

'But he is not just the patron of fertility. He is also responsible for keeping order and justice. He lives in the clouds, between the heaven and the earth. He commands the thunder and lightning to shake out any evil spirits. It is said that Perkūnas was married to Saule, the sun goddess. They were a beautiful couple. All the deities were envious of them. But Saule was unfaithful. She had an affair with Menulis, the moon god.'

Marytè isn't listening too closely, as she's rubbing a honey ointment onto her aching knee, but at the mention of Saule's infidelity she

125

straightens. 'Senelè, that's enough. Please do not fill their heads with this nonsense. They've just lost their father: let's not talk of these awful things.'

'And their father was as good a man as Perkūnas. He too believed in order and justice. Our girls must learn about the old ways, Marytè, or they will be forgotten. We do not have them written down in a book like the church. If we do not talk about it, if we do not practise them or teach them to our young, it will all be lost. If that is so, we may as well pack up our things and move into the city, attend church daily like the good folk there. Forget about our bees, our way of life. Is that what you want?'

Marytè grits her teeth. 'Carry on, then.'

'What happens to Perkūnas and Saule?' Austeja asks, even though she knows the ending to this story.

Marytè kneads the muscle and ligament around her knee joint. It is worse in the cold and the wet, as if her bones grate against each other, only warming and relaxing under the sun's gaze. Is that how Menulis felt under Saule's bright gaze? When her attention fell on him, he couldn't resist, even though it was wrong?

'Are you okay?' Austeja asks in a whisper.

'Yes.'

Austeja sighs as though she doesn't believe her and turns back to her grandmother. Marytè rubs harder, flinching with the pain, but she continues. The pain keeps her present. She can't risk her mind drifting off with dark thoughts. She does not wish to hear this story. Not this one. Not now. It is too violent. Depressing. And what justice is served in the end?

126

No, it is not good timing for a story such as this, but Marytè cannot argue with the old woman. She'd just speak louder and wave her arms around, energised by any resistance to her performance. Marytè presses her tongue up into her palate. She focuses on the shooting pain in her leg and not on the shooting flames lighting up the room followed by the throbbing, rumbling of the earth, or on the unwanted images, memories, shooting into her mind.

'Well,' Senelè continues, 'he punishes Menulis. Some say he cut him up into little pieces but I believe he'd have been swifter than that. He split Menulis in half with a sword.'

Austeja shivers and Marytè too feels the drop in temperature. She pulls her shawl up onto her shoulders. Her knee is reddened from the massage.

'What happened to Saule?' Austeja asks.

Senelè shakes her head. 'The witch was banished from the heavens and exiled to earth. Homeless and fraught, she still wanders the earth. She can be seen on riverbanks or by lakes.'

'How sad.'

'That is the punishment for adultery. We must trust our gods to deliver justice.'

Satisfied with the austere end to her story, Senelè lies back on her bed and closes her eyes. Soon, she submits to an easy rhythm and her body rises and falls in a deep slumber. Danutè has fallen asleep too but Austeja stares at the birch ceiling. She fidgets with her nails.

As the thunder rolls on so too do Senelè's words, tumbling about Marytè's mind. Infidelity. Evil spirits. Perkūnas. Justice. If it were true and Perkūnas is the one who calls order and justice, how will he do it? Will he hunt down those who deceive him? She shivers. This idea instils more fear in her than it should. It's just a silly story. It's not true.

Marytè lies down in her bed too, but sleep does not come for a long time. She has grown used to the weighted presence of him beside her. She lies awake thinking of her husband. The Hollow Watcher. The priest and the Duke. Two men have left and two have joined their clan. On the surface it seems as if it is an even swap, but for her, it has brought imbalance. Her world is off kilter.

Like too many bees in a hive. Sooner or later, they must split, and a swarm moves on somewhere else.

CHAPTER SEVENTEEN

Austeja

No one knows I'm here, at his home. They won't notice I've crept away from the funeral at the churchyard. Motina is preoccupied. She is like this every spring: she comes down with bee fever. I couldn't stay, though; it is just so soon after saying goodbye to Tévas. I cannot mourn another when my heart is full and heavy with my father's grief. Though I haven't brought myself to lament like Senelè – there is something so raw and vulnerable about begging one to return – I do think about him all the time. I miss him. He is the only one who could have helped me through this. In fact, had he been here, he would've helped plan my escape from the Hollow Watcher's funeral at the church.

He's getting a proper Christian burial and it's a pitiful event. No tears shed. No lamenting. After all, who here will beg for *his* return?

No one liked him, not really. Not enough to wish him back. How could one live after leaving in such a brutal way? No, it is best he flies up to the High Hill. Or perhaps he will go to heaven. I can't bring myself to think of the alternative. The Hollow Watcher, Stanislaw – I remind myself that he does have a name – lived alone. He had no wife and no children. A dreadful, lonely, pitiable man who died in a dreadful, lonely and pitiable way.

But as much as I despised the living version of Stanislaw, I am inextricably connected to him in his death. I can't let go of the raven-black eyes, the bloodstains on the roughened oak bark. The tree would have suffered. What it must've seen!

Senelė's story of Perkūnas stays with me too. She told me once, in another version of her story about the god of thunder, that the oak is the tree most often struck by lightning, but it is sacred to Perkūnas. Why would he strike something so precious to him?

This oak, my oak, as I think of it now – even bloodstained and suffering – is a fatherly figure. It has stood for many generations. It holds knowledge of the forest and of all its surrounds. Justice. I feel impelled to visit, to see if it withstood the storm.

But first, I find myself here: at Stanislaw's cabin.

It is forbidden to go beyond the church onto the grounds of the manor. The young Duke has barely been seen since his arrival: he emerged for funerals and spring celebrations but I've not seen him again in the forest. It seems he's had his fun and now his henchmen collect the logs for his hearth. Stanislaw would've collected a supply of wood from last winter, surely. So why did the Duke deceive me?

His modest manor lies nestled within pines, but much of the surrounding is clear. Nobles feel safer in the open space. God knows why. The trees are gentle giants, swaying in the breeze, protecting us from the cold, reckless winds and brutal storms. I'd feel so exposed living without them.

At least Stanislaw's cabin is surrounded by shrubs and a lofty birch tree with swollen roots that snake under his front door. My legs tremble. I don't know how long I've been standing here but I must hurry or I'll be seen. I can't imagine how irate Motina will be with me if I am caught. I glance around, and, satisfied there is no one about, I reach for the door. It doesn't budge until I shove my shoulder against the solid pine and then it grunts open. My heart beats quicker as I step inside. It is a bright, cloudless day but inside is dark and musty. A cot, cooking supplies and a hearth reduced to ashes. A few jars of honey. A mouldy slice of rye.

My stomach churns and I cover my nose to ward off the stench. Is this bread from my father's wake? No one else would make him bread and there is no oven in sight. These are not the conditions I expected. The Hollow Watcher was always scruffy, but he was employed by the Duke. Is this all you get when you serve the Grand Duchy of Lithuania?

The door grunts and I freeze. A hand closes over my mouth and a large, solid body presses against my back. Warm breath tickles my ear.

'Austeja, it's me.' I inhale and my eyes dart back and forth as if I can will them to look out the back of my head. 'Don't panic,' he whispers as he releases his hand.

'Jonas? What are you doing?'

'I followed you. What are you doing here?'

'I just ... I don't know. I guess we are here for the same thing.'

In the shadows of the cabin, I can feel his eyes on me. 'And what would that be?'

I lift my shoulders and let them fall. 'Answers.'

His hand lightly touches my elbow as he guides me into the narrow beam of light squeezing past the ajar door. 'We don't have long. Let's hurry.'

My heart beats fast. Are we really doing this? Together? I do not know what I expected when I entered Stanislaw's house. Perhaps just a feeling, or an insight into what happened to him the day he died. I haven't got that but I feel a renewed strength knowing that I am not alone in this pursuit. Jonas wants answers too.

Jonas pulls back the blanket on the cot and turns it upside down. I kick the ashes in the hearth but there is nothing there but dust. A large pot on the floor, the remnants of broth and a fine layer of mould over the top. I look into a large jar and there's a woeful supply of oats. Not enough to last him two more breakfasts. Bile rises. A flash of Stanislaw in the forest. Blood. Tattered clothing. His stomach torn apart. There will be no more breakfasts for the Hollow Watcher.

'Anything?' Jonas asks. He's rummaging through the log pile.

'No.' I pull smaller jars off the shelf and bring them back to the light. One is honey. I return it. Another has dried herbs. And what's this? The third one has a knife. I raise it to the light and gasp. The jar slips from my grasp and tumbles to the ground, spilling its secret.

'What is it?'

With caution, I crouch down and pluck the knife from the dirt. I turn it over in my hands.

'A knife?'

'Yes.' The breath leaves my lungs. 'It was my father's.'

We are frozen for ... I don't know how long.

It is the sound of boots on gravel that reminds us to move. When I look up from the knife, Jonas's gaze is on me. I place the knife in my skirt pocket. 'Someone is nearby. Could the funeral be over already?'

'Perhaps. They could be scattered around the church grounds, setting up for the feast.'

I swallow the fear in my throat. It will be difficult to escape the cabin and not be seen. I peer outside and walking along the path, past Stanislaw's cabin, is the Duke. 'Only the Duke. He's heading to his manor.'

'Only the Duke? Austeja, he could have us both punished. Severely.'

I weigh up the options and there is nothing else I can do. 'I will distract him. You escape as soon as you can.'

'Austeja, no. I can't let you do that. Let me talk to him.'

I draw up tall. 'No. You will be punished. A man snooping around a dead man's cabin. But I? Well, I can claim to have been confused and lost my way.'

'Please don't—'

'You needn't worry about me. I'll meet you back at the bridge.'

I push open the door and dash away from the cabin and the manor, along the path. When I hear his footsteps pause, I spin around so it looks as if I am following him on the path. I slow my pace, scuffing my boots along the ground, lost in my thoughts. It is not a difficult performance. Those thoughts are racing. What was my father's knife doing in Stanislaw's cabin? I saw it being buried with my father. Who took it from his grave? I visited yesterday and there was nothing out of place. Though I suppose we don't bury our dead deeply and so tampering with the grave could easily go undetected. This has never happened before. Could it have been Stanislaw? I never knew my father to be friendly with the Hollow Watcher. In fact, he was always quite snarky towards him and he was not like that with anyone else. My father was well liked by everyone. I thought he was just protective, like Motina, of our hollows. Stanislaw was always nosy, wandering about the hollows as if they were his own. But only at harvest time: never in winter.

'Austeja?'

I stop and look up. I had almost forgotten about the Duke. I walk near him and step aside so his back is to Stanislaw's cabin. From the corner of my eye, I see a figure dart from the cabin and into the forest behind it. It will take him back up to the High Hill. I exhale, pleased that Jonas has escaped.

'Duke.' I bow my head because I've never knowingly been addressed by a Duke before. I shouldn't be here alone. What if one of our people sees me talking to him? It would cause outrage.

He glances back to Stanislaw's cabin. Can he see from here the door is left ajar? I clear my throat. 'Oh, I'm sorry to have left the funeral early. I only laid my own father to rest recently. I had to get away. I didn't mean to come this way; I wasn't paying any attention to where I was walking.'

'You mustn't apologise. Besides, it is done. Everyone is coming back to share in a feast. I am fetching my servants to join us. Your people have kindly supplied food for the occasion.'

I blush. Your people. The Duke did not seem like a duke that day in the forest. He seemed normal, or almost. I knew he was different. He dressed and spoke differently, and he was inexperienced in the forest, his forest. I knew we were different kinds of people. But I never guessed he was a duke. 'Why didn't you tell me you were the Duke, that day we met in the forest?'

He has the decency to look sheepish. 'I am sorry for that. I suppose I liked the idea of no one knowing who I was. You did not know me, and I liked that you spoke your mind.'

My cheeks are hot. 'I shouldn't have done that. In the forest, or in the church. My mother is very unhappy with me.'

'I'm sorry to hear that. But I have lived my whole life in a city. Because of my uncle, everyone knows who I am. He owned the land of the honey. You were the first young woman I had come across who did not care who I was or where I was from. It was refreshing.'

An odd sensation comes over me. Part of me is flattered by the way he views me, as a novel woman, with whom he could become someone new. Another part of me feels irritated. The forest is known as the land of the honey? As if we are a strange, isolated community whose sole purpose in life is to deliver honey to their gluttonous bellies. What do they say about us? Do they laugh about the way we climb trees and talk of the old ways? Do they call us heathens, as Senelè said?

The cold knife presses against my thigh.

'Well, I'm glad I could entertain you. I must be on my way.'

'Aust—'

I hurry along the path to the church. I do not look back.

As I come to the bridge, I see Jonas, pacing back and forth across it like a wolf protecting its cubs.

'Austeja.' He runs his hand through his hair, his face wrought with worry. 'Are you okay?'

I join him on the bridge. 'Yes. The Duke did not suspect a thing. Let's keep moving, in case he sends my mother or someone to look for me.'

We walk away from the church and into the dense forest, new growth filling the spaces left by winter. The knife weighs down my skirt and I heave it up as we tread the path that leads to our hollows. Questions hang between us, but neither of us is ready to speak.

We find ourselves at the oak. Relief sweeps through me. Perkūnas has not struck it down.

Jonas clears his throat. 'I watched you and the Duke, from the pines. You seemed friendly.'

My stomach squeezes in. 'We're not friends.'

Jonas makes a small sound of approval.

'I met him in the forest, before my father's funeral. Before I even knew he was the Duke.'

Jonas frowns. 'He was in the forest?'

'Well, it is his.'

'Hmm.'

'I don't think he has anything to do with Stanislaw's death, if that's what you're thinking. He barely knew how to collect suitable firewood, let alone carry out something like that. He was simply wandering about, probably becoming familiar with his land.' The land of the honey.

I grasp the lower branch of the oak and heave myself up, walking my feet up the trunk.

'What are you doing?' Jonas asks, humour in his voice.

'Climbing. Don't you remember how to do it?'

Not satisfied with the height, I pull myself up to another branch and sit upon it. Jonas is broad-shouldered, and his arms strong, but he is not as agile as me. He climbs slowly but steadily until he reaches the branch where I sit. He shuffles across but remains on the thickest part of the branch. 'I remember. It's been a long time since we've done this. Without ropes.'

'I don't need ropes.'

Jonas's gaze is on me again but I keep my focus on the trees around us, aware of the empty hollow that sits above, the crown void of life.

'I suppose you don't. My brothers were always jealous of how easily you could climb a tree.'

I smile. 'Motina says it's the one true skill of a beekeeper.'

'But that's never really been what you want?'

'No.'

'What do you want, then?'

I sigh. 'I don't really know. It's ... changing.' I blush again and hurry on. 'For now, I just want to understand what is happening in the forest. There has never been distrust in our community.'

'No.'

I pull the knife from my pocket. 'Why did Stanislaw have my father's knife?'

'Are you sure it's your father's?'

'Yes. Tévas got this knife from my grandfather. It was very special to him. Motina buried it with him, which is why Liudvikas made her a new one.'

Jonas doesn't respond but he breathes heavily beside me. I'm certain if I pressed my palm against his chest his heart would be quick too.

'What is it?' I ask.

'Stanislaw had *my* father's knife, once.'

I look at him sharply. 'Why?'

Jonas dips his head. 'He gave it to him. It means they have some kind of deal. If he is owed something, Stanislaw takes something of importance as collateral. To guarantee he is given what is owed.'

'What did your father owe him?'

Jonas shakes his head. 'I don't know. But Stanislaw only had his knife for a few days, so the matter was settled quickly.'

'Do you think my father owed Stanislaw?'

'It's possible.'

'But why would he take the knife after my father was gone? Did he want to punish my father in his afterlife?'

I blink back tears, thinking about how lost my father will be without his precious knife. How will he be a beekeeper without his knife? My chest shudders as I breathe out. Jonas places his hand on mine. It is warm and comforting. It feels safe. It reminds me of Tévas.

There are things I do not know about Tévas. I do not know what his final request of me was. I do not know what he owed Stanislaw. I do not know what he hid from his family. Tévas was always open and honest and he protected our family. That Tévas seems like a different person. One I could rely on and trust. This Tévas, this secret one I did not know of, rattles me. If I cannot trust the memory of my father, the one person who understood me, the one person I could rely on, then whom can I trust?

This new understanding flows through me like the venom of an asp. Burning, swelling, agony.

I clasp my stomach. There is no remedy for being struck by a poisonous snake.

CHAPTER EIGHTEEN

Marytè

It is a blustery day. The bees do not like it and neither does Marytè. Her skin feels taut and flaky, as if she is moulting, like a dandelion seed-head being stripped in the breeze. It makes her throat tickle too and a phlegmy cough follows. It reminds her of Baltrus in his final months, his throat thick and full of mucus, as though with each cough he were choking on his own fluids. Marytè stops along the forest path, near Aldona's house, and looks up. White puffs race across the sky. Even the clouds are dry in this wind. Tapping birch leaves, rustling conifers, shuddering aspens: the forest is in movement, but the bees are not. They've taken shelter but Marytè cannot afford to hunker down today. She must keep busy.

She wants to remember Baltrus in their happier times, not the months when he was dying. But when were those happier times? A heaviness had fallen over the family when Azuolas passed in the winter before. Her eldest son, her firstborn: she'd felt she would never recover. It is cruel to take children before they have a chance to outlive their parents. Azuolas was a dedicated beekeeper, and even though Baltrus always had a soft spot for Austeja, it was her brother he'd been training to take his place. But when he left, Baltrus's hefty frame began to hunch and wither and that little tickle in his throat, their gift from Alytus two summers back now, had morphed into something else entirely. She'd known at that moment, only weeks after she'd said goodbye to her son, that her husband would soon join him on the High Hill.

She tried to remain optimistic, as much as her temperament allowed. Even when she could feel him slipping away. But as she nursed his weakening body over winter, she felt her body weaken too. As if she were channelling all her energy into him, willing him to come back to her. The more of herself she gave the more he slipped from her grasp. And, if she is being honest with herself, her mind began to slip too. She began to plummet. Into that scary, dark place where her own mother had once sunk.

She couldn't risk it. Because then where would that leave her daughters? Alone with an ageing grandmother and no security in their futures. No, Marytè couldn't allow that to happen. There may have been one moment when she had been weak, confused even, but she was quick to get things back on track. She'd done what she had to prevent it.

She urges herself to keep walking. Marytè reaches Aldona's house, where smoke slithers out of the chimney and is carried away in the breeze. A man stands in the clearing, wielding an axe and bringing it down on a felled spruce tree with skilful ease. Baltrus?

The man turns. Did she say his name aloud? She darts towards him, her heart pounding; she is heady with excitement. When she reaches him, she pauses, reaches out to caress his cheek. 'Are you real? Is it really you?'

It is Baltrus. Her cheery, handsome husband. He is here. He has returned to her. Oh, how is this possible?

A door closes beyond. The man remains still, a confused expression on his face. Marytè blinks and the blood rushes away from her trunk as if her stomach is plummeting to her feet.

She swallows back the phlegmy lump in her throat. 'Liudvikas?'

He watches her carefully as she withdraws her hand.

'Marytè,' Aldona says, coming to her, clutching her shoulders. 'Are you okay?'

'Forgive me.' She glances at her friend's husband and sees that this man is not Baltrus at all. He's large-bodied and strong like him, but Liudvikas is fair-haired and square-jawed and more angular than Baltrus. 'I don't know what came over me. I thought for a moment there I saw Bal—'

Her voice cracks and she tries to turn away from them both but Aldona draws her in closer. Marytè stifles a sob. Aldona squeezes her tighter and Marytè sinks into her friend's embrace as her legs buckle beneath her. Her friend holds her until she finds her footing and she vows not to deprive her children of this feeling. Baltrus was as large as a bear and when he enveloped her it felt cosy, secure. Her girls loved being wrapped up in his arms. Though hers are bonier and not as long, she must provide that comfort to her girls. Or else they will look for it elsewhere.

'Come,' says Aldona, weaving her arm through Marytè's and guiding her to the house.

'I'm sorry,' Marytè calls over her shoulder.

'There's no need for that. This happens sometimes when we lose someone we love,' Aldona says. 'We want to see them so badly that our mind conjures them up all on its own.'

'I'm pathetic.'

Aldona gasps. Marytè has never been so critical of herself in the company of others before. She really is pathetic.

Aldona sits Marytè upon a bench by the hearth. The fire has recently burned out, but the room is warm and the coldness that has settled upon Marytè's bones begin to thaw.

'I will hear of none of that talk, Marytè. I too have experienced this. For many years after I lost my Ignas, my only son to survive birth, he was with us through two seasons, but afterwards, I would see him in the clearing. Not far from where you stood with Liudvikas. Running around collecting insects, living the life I'd hoped he would one day have.' Aldona sighs. 'But it was not meant to be. There is nothing pathetic about grieving those we love.'

'No,' Marytè says. 'I'm sorry.'

'It doesn't surprise me, though. You hardly said a word at his one-month anniversary yesterday, nor did you shed a tear.'

Marytè takes the mug of honey-tea presented to her. It was true: she didn't sing, or cry, or say much at all. Senelè more than made up for her silence. Though she wanted to be there, to celebrate Baltrus's life and mourn her loss, being on the High Hill is like reopening a wound, one that festers and oozes and will not heal. She couldn't bring herself to lose control, or else end up in that dark place. Instead, she tried to stay strong as her girls wept. Austeja, to Marytè's surprise, was in quite a state. She has been irritable and distracted since the Hollow Watcher's funeral and then on the High Hill she turned away from the grave and sobbed into her hands. She is taking the loss of her father very hard. Afterwards, Marytè lifted her from the earth and guided her back home.

'It is bound to catch up with you,' Aldona says.

Marytè draws in a breath. 'I love my husband.'

'Of course,' Aldona says, dropping to her knees and squeezing Marytè's hand. 'Of course you do, my friend. No one would ever question your loyalty. But we mustn't keep our pain locked away inside of us.'

'I just want to stay strong for my daughters. This next harvest is critical for us.'

'It is. But we are your bičiulystè. We are all here to support you, as we know you would for us.'

Marytè swallows the warm liquid. It is bitter and sweet. 'I know.' Her stomach softens with friendship and a warm drink. Would it be so hard to depend on her friends? To depend on other people? But deep within, there's a voice niggling at her.

Yes, but I'm not sure I deserve it.

CHAPTER NINETEEN

Austeja

I wake to his hands around my throat.

I can't breathe. I'm choking. Shaking. Sweating. Faint.

Thick beard. Large, constricting hands. Raven's eyes.

He's going to kill me.

The air is being squeezed from my lungs, and my vision blurs. He's out of focus. My body softens as if it is sinking through the bed and into the earth. And then there's a pause. A lessening of pressure. Fingers peel away. I gasp, sucking in breath as though it is for the first time, like a newborn baby entering the world, inhaling the forest air. The way Danutè did. When birthed she emerged still and mute, and we were all silent too. Then her tiny mouth opened, and she sucked in the air around us, holding on to it, stockpiling to fill her petite body. And then she exhaled and she was breathing on her own and she was alive.

I am alive, I realise as I sit up in my bed. Blinking in the darkness. There are no hands at my throat. There is no one here at all. My sister and Motina and Senelè are asleep, and there's no threat here. There's no one here who will hurt me. It is just a bad dream. A really bad dream.

They're becoming more frequent.

Since the discovery of my father's knife at the Hollow Watcher's home it feels as if I walk around all day with a heaviness in me. As if I cannot lift my own arms, as if I am dragging my legs, as if I am a weary fallow deer eyeing a wolf with her blood in his mouth.

I cannot explain the knife. I cannot ask Tèvas what he did or what he owed Stanislaw. I cannot even ask Stanislaw about it because he is gone too. The only other person who I know has had a deal with Stanislaw previously is Jonas's father. And Krystupas is not someone I want to approach. He's not at all like his son, calm and comforting. He intimidates me.

I recall the way Krystupas looked at his sons when I collected him from the barn that day. My stomach churns. He did not look at all surprised. Why?

Is Krystupas hiding something? Maybe Jonas knows more than he is letting on.

Why was Jonas at Stanislaw's cottage? He said he followed me, but he stayed to search the house. He was looking for something too. Did he find it?

I have not seen him since, except at my father's one-month anniversary at the High Hill. He kept his distance but scowled when the Duke approached me to offer his condolences.

Birdsong invites me into the forest. I pull myself out of bed, which creaks, and I pause to check there is no movement from my family members. A chorus of breath and the occasional dramatic snore from Senelè, but no one stirs. The fire is low but I cannot risk adding logs to the hearth as the crackle may wake them. I must get a move on or Senelè will rise soon. She has a peculiar knack for knowing just the moment it needs to be reignited before it burns out.

I pull on my boots and coat, as the mid-spring mornings are still chilly. I push open the door and a breeze drifts in, tossing about the flames in the hearth. Before the fire goes out and anyone can call me back, I step outside and close the door behind me.

In the clearing, the sun sits on the horizon, rays straining between the pines in the forest, through their fronded greenery. There are no clouds. The breeze is gentle but it won't become gusty, not as it has been doing. The weather will be calm today.

The swamp glistens as I pass by and so too does the knife I pull from my pocket. I turn it over. The handle is worn from Tévas's grip and it smells of him. Woody, sweaty and sweet. The knife edge is clean and that is disappointing, though I don't know what I hoped to see.

Blood?

I rewrap it in the cloth I tore from my underdress and slip it back into my pocket. I know I must return it to Tévas but I keep it close, hoping the answers to this unsolved mystery will come to me. Will the knife speak to me as the oak does?

I find myself standing by the oak once again. I must have been partly asleep as I don't recall walking over the bridge or through the forest. But I am here now. It can be no coincidence that I learned of my father's passing while I leaned against this oak and the man in whose debt he died died here also.

Shrubs and flowers have burst up from the once snow-covered, bloodstained earth. They circle the trunk in an array of colours as if to shield me from the pain beneath.

Beside the trunk is a felled log, but not one that belongs here. It has been cleaned and sanded and upon closer inspection it looks as if it has been polished with wax. I run my hand over it. It's beautiful, golden and shiny, and I know it has been left for me. I sit upon the log and lean my back against the trunk. Not where Stanislaw lay, but next to that spot, and then I look up.

Buds burst from every branch. Many have opened but some are waiting. It won't be long before I will see not a bare-canopied sky, but a tree full of green and life. Birds flittering from branch to branch.

There is only one young man I know who could do this kind of handiwork and understand that it would be meaningful here in this very spot.

My chest flutters as if there is a little sparrow trapped within. I hold my hand over my chest, not quite ready to let it free.

Senelè is waiting for me when I return. She sits beside the Scots pine tree, on the bench Motina hauled out so we can enjoy the last few weeks of the spring weather. She really hates being cooped up in the dark. The cottage door is closed and there is no sign of Motina or Danutè yet, although the sun has risen further and the light will squeeze into the gaps between the logs soon. Then they'll rise too.

'Good morning, Senelè.' I join her on the bench and the creases in her face become more pronounced when she smiles.

'You were up early this morning.'

'Yes, I woke and couldn't get back to sleep.'

'Ahh. Yes, sometimes our thoughts can prevent us from truly resting.'

'I keep thinking about the Hollow Watcher,' I say. It feels strange to say it aloud. I've only spoken about this with Jonas, and Motina does not talk about it, though she does squeeze my shoulder or bring me honey-tea if she notices I'm distracted. She has been trying to bridge the distance created between us. My throat constricts again as that thought turns over in my mind. I do miss Tévas, but now I'm unsure about who he was and what kind of deal he had with the Hollow Watcher.

'Does he come to you in your dreams?'

'Yes.'

'Are they frightening?'

'Yes,' I say. 'They are frightening and confusing. Sometimes he's asking me for help, other times he's hurting me.' I rub my throat where I felt his hands. It felt so real.

Senelè purses her lips together and frowns. 'I'm afraid, my dear, he has left this life feeling disgruntled. There is something unresolved. It is up to you to solve it.'

'Me?'

149

She shrugs. 'You found him. You saw the absolute worst that a human can do to another human.'

'So you don't believe it was a bear or wolf? That's what other people are saying.'

'No. I believe what you believe. That a human did this, possibly one of our own people. A bear is not clever enough to tie a man to a tree and wolves are not foolish – they would not have abandoned meat at winter's end.'

It's hard to swallow. 'So who do you think it was?'

'I do not know. But you, my dear ...' Senelè takes my hand in hers. 'The gods have chosen you to find out.'

'The gods?'

Senelè leans in closer. 'The wind speaks to you and I suspect the trees do too. If the Hollow Watcher comes to you in your dreams, it comes through the oak.'

The hairs on my neck stand on end. 'I don't know what you're saying, Senelè. What do you mean? What am I meant to do?'

The door pushes open and Danutè stumbles out, her wispy hair sprouting in all directions. Motina steps outside too, blinking in the sunlight. She limps down the step into the clearing.

'Shh. We'll talk more later.' Senelè glances sideways at my mother and stands up. She squeezes my hand once more. 'I always knew you were special, Austeja.'

I am left alone with my thoughts as Senelè guides Motina away, no doubt distracting her with some trivial story about the old ways.

What does my grandmother mean when she says I am special? I can hear the wind and the oak tree speak? Could it be true?

I have always felt like an outsider in my family. I am not a beekeeper, but I have wanted to be good at something. To feel good at something the way Motina does when she cares for her bees. The way Tévas did when he dragged logs of wood from the forest and chopped them up into small chunks as if they were loaves of rye. The way Senelè looks when she puts one of those logs on the fire and the flames dance before her. The look of satisfaction.

Now I have something that could truly be mine, that I could be good at … It's overwhelming. It's too much.

I am not certain this is something I want after all.

CHAPTER TWENTY

Marytè

The oak is a hive of activity, its leaves dark green where it absorbs the sun's rays, paler and smooth on their undersides. Green caterpillar-like flowers hang down from the canopy above Marytè where she is secured to its trunk by rope. Boisterous bees flit from blossom to blossom. She chuckles. It is like sticking her head into a bee family dinner: everyone all talking at once with their mouths full.

The bees pay no heed to her as she dusts out the empty hollow and runs her fingertips along the neatly carved edges. Baltrus built their family home with his own hands, and this hollow Marytè sculpted with hers into the perfect home for a bee family. Before they had children together, Marytè had set up most of the hollows because she had been doing it on her own since her father's death. Baltrus had only ever worked within his own family, never as a head beekeeper, so he had much to learn. While the land had been given to Baltrus by the former Duke, she and her husband had always worked in partnership.

She hopes this hollow will replace the nearby oak hollow she lost to Stanislaw, which will likely remain empty until the negative energy surrounding the Hollow Watcher's death dissipates. She imagines a bee clan here. She hopes those buzzing overhead will spread word about the empty residence. A warmly welcomed swarm will weave itself a honeycomb feast for next winter.

'What do you think?' Austeja asks from the ground. Senelè was sleeping mid-morning so she's brought the girls with her. It's usually a task she does on her own but she'd like Austeja to be more involved.

'It's ready,' Marytè says. She sweeps the hollow free of insects and rotten leaves one final time, tidying it for her new guests. It wasn't ready last season, but this time it is.

It's a rather handsome oak. A heavy and well-proportioned trunk with sprawling branches demanding space from the encroaching forest. The crown of the tree was removed a long time ago, presumably by another beekeeper who lived here before the former Duke claimed the land, and so the tree's energy has gone into outward growth.

The tree is broad enough for a hive now. Baltrus's health was failing him last summer and so Marytè took the opportunity to carve the hollow for the bees. She is pleased it has accepted its disfigurement. The last hollow she tenderly prepared for the bees was inhabited instead by a great grey owl and its offspring. This one will be filled with bees; she is sure of it. She drops a piece of sticky honeycomb into the empty space, just to be sure.

In all their time beekeeping they have never lost so many hollows in one winter. There was one year, around the time Danutè was born, when they lost three. That was a particularly wet and dreary spring and remained much the same throughout summer and autumn. The crops were ruined and there was little food for the creatures of the forest. Instead of traipsing the sludgy earth they looked upwards, to the hollows. Bears, woodpeckers and whatever else had their sights set on honey. They lost three complete hollows but another ten were damaged. They were inhabited again in time but it had an impact on the harvests that followed until the new swarms grew and thrived. It was an awful time; the only brightness was the arrival of Danutè – an easy baby, compliant and settled. Unlike her sister, who cried frequently and wanted to be held throughout the day and night. The harvest season after Austeja's birth, Marytè had to strap her to her chest so she could climb the trees to collect the honey.

Now, Marytè finds her footing on the rope and begins to lower herself. Austeja has been particularly sullen in the weeks since the Hollow Watcher's funeral and her father's one-month memorial. She will have to keep her busy – the best way to avoid those gloomy moods. Like a snake's den, you take just a peek inside and before you know it you emerge from the darkness and realise a whole season has passed. She won't let that happen to Austeja. She is too bright to be caught up in the negative energy.

This spring is like no other. Perkūnas, if Senelè is correct, has certainly made the soil fecund. Growth is everywhere. She will be able to provide for her daughters next winter. The crops of turnips, cabbage, beetroots, parsnips and flax have been sowed and will keep them well fed over the cold months. Because that's all they can plan for, one winter at a time. There is always work to be done, always things to prepare.

Marytè cringes as her knee jars on the rope. It has become quite the bother. She presses into a tender spot above the kneecap to distract herself from the throbbing. It's as if she can feel the blood pumping around the joint, keeping the pain alive, a constant reminder of her fragility.

'What's next?' Danutè asks as she steadies her two feet on the ground. Austeja drops down from the lower branch of the oak tree. Seedy pollen powders her hair.

Marytè sighs. 'That is all for today.'

'Aren't there more hollows to prepare?' Austeja asks.

Marytè shakes her head. 'That was the last one of the oaks our predecessors crowned. Later generations decided not to interfere with nature. Hollows will develop on their own within ageing or damaged trees. If they are not chopped down, of course. Which is why we only take wood for our hearth that has been naturally felled by storm or decay.'

Austeja places her hand on her hip. 'Yes, but animals can also live in those felled trees. I once saw a family of dormice in a pine hollow that had been struck by lightning.'

'That is true. But they do prefer breathing trees – well, the bees do at least. And besides, we must collect firewood for warmth and to boil our water and cook our meals. Collecting felled trees is the least invasive approach. That way we can all live in harmony.'

Marytè is beginning to sound like Senelè, and perhaps that is why Austeja smiles from beneath her fair lashes.

'When will the bees move in?' Danutè asks.

Austeja rolls her eyes. 'Not until summer, when they swarm.'

'Oh.'

'Come on.' Marytè loops her rope over her shoulder. The extra weight puts more strain on her knee. She drops her new knife into the basket attached at her waist and wipes the back of her hand across her forehead. 'We must get back to your grandmother.'

'Why doesn't Senelè join in on the beekeeping duties?' Danutè asks.

Marytè shrugs. 'I suppose that was always her husband's domain. She preferred domestic duties and cooking. And storytelling, of course.'

'She's good at it,' Austeja says. 'At the storytelling.'

'Yes, she is.' Too good, Marytè thinks. It is sometimes difficult to know where the truth lies within those stories and what's made up. Justice. Senelè's words come back to her.

Her body is weary, but she focuses on putting one foot in front of the other as they follow the forest path back to the bridge.

Sparrows fly in the canopies overhead, bees buzz among the wildflowers and creatures rustle in the shrubs. There are no clouds and the forest is at ease.

'I suppose it is a cruel and outdated practice,' Austeja says.

'Sorry?' She glances at her daughter.

Austeja blinks and looks at her mother with irritation. 'Decapitating the trees. You should never mess with nature.'

Marytè inhales deeply and then carries on ahead, her daughters dawdling behind her, leaving her to wonder what other dark and strange thoughts are going on in her oldest daughter's mind.

She will have to keep a closer eye on her.

Aldona is waiting outside her home when they return.

'What is it?' Marytè asks, fear rising from her stomach into her chest.

'It's the priest. He has summoned us to the church for a meeting tomorrow.'

'Did he say what it is about?' She exchanges a glance with Austeja. A meeting, not a sermon. Could her daughter be in trouble for speaking her mind?

'No. Only that every family must be there.'

'That's odd.' A little relief surfaces. This mustn't be about Austeja at all. Could it be about the Hollow Watcher?

Aldona huffs. 'Does he think we can simply drop everything the moment he calls? It is the end of spring, for god's sake. We have our crops to care for and our hollows too.'

'It must be very important.' Has the priest discovered what happened to Stanislaw? To her burnt hollow? 'What is he still doing here? I'd have thought he'd have moved on by now.' She supposes he is not as accustomed to navigating the landscape in these conditions as Albertas was.

Aldona shakes her head. 'It is odd, indeed. He asked me to come and tell you and I hoped you would send on the message to Smilte and the boys.' She stops for a wheezy cough. 'It is too far for me to go this late in the day.'

Her daughters were once the oldest children in the settlement. They weremarried during two consecutive springs to second-born sons while Danutè was still a toddler, and moved to their bičiulystè in Darželiai, where Aldona's sisters reside. She misses her daughters, who cannot travel that far south with young children. It is a long and arduous journey through dense forest. It's no wonder the priest has delayed his journey, with spring's swelling rivers and storms in his path.

Marytè's knee throbs as she considers a hike back through the forest. She turns to Austeja. 'Can you make it back before sundown?'

Austeja squints at the sun, which has dipped behind the pine canopies. 'Yes.'

She appears relieved to have a task and Marytè knows she has made the right decision. She glances at Danutè. She should really send Austeja with an escort, but Danutè will slow her down. She's easily distracted by insects and new season flowers and, well, anything.

Senelè passes a cup of water to Austeja, who swills it and takes the chunk of bread on offer.

'Tell them exactly what Aldona has told us and then come back home, immediately,' Marytè says.

'Yes, Motina.'

'Wait.' Perhaps she is being overly cautious but all this uncertainty is putting her on edge. Marytè retrieves the new knife from her skirt pocket and places it in Austeja's outstretched palm. 'Take this,' she says. 'Be careful.'

Austeja's eyes lock on hers. Fear dances in her pupils as she tucks the knife into her pocket. She draws back her shoulders and with an imperceptible nod she turns away. Marytè watches her daughter as she strides along the path through the clearing, around the marshes and out of sight.

It is only when Aldona speaks that she remembers she has company. 'Do you think we should be worried about tomorrow?'

Marytè leans against the doorframe, easing her weight off the aching knee. 'Yes, Aldona. Something doesn't feel right. I think we should all be on guard.'

'Why?'

'I suspect the priest has an announcement.'

CHAPTER TWENTY-ONE

Austeja

'What have you got there?' I call out to Jonas, who is traipsing across the bridge with a rope looped over his shoulder. I meet him halfway, pleased to see him and relieved to avoid his father and the long trip to his house.

His face softens. 'Austeja, I was on my way to see you.' He clears his throat. 'Well, to your house anyway. I'm bringing you this.'

Tied to his rope, he holds up a pine tree cleared of its canopy. 'It was felled in the storm. Lightning strike.'

My thoughts drift back to the conversation I had with Motina and Danutè about not messing with nature. But this tree was felled by Perkūnas himself, and who am I to argue with him?

'That's very thoughtful.' I pause. 'And so was the log chair you left for me at the oak hollow.'

'You like it?'

'I do. It's the perfect spot.' My smile falters as I realise the perfect spot is the place where someone was brutally killed. My cheeks flush with shame. 'I only mean—'

'I know you are fond of that oak. I thought it could help to make new, happier memories.'

'I am, thank you.'

'God knows why. There are so many of them here in the forest!' He laughs and I do too, but it feels as if I'm betraying the forest.

'Shall we take this to store in your threshing barn for next winter?'

I shake my head, remembering the purpose of my errand. 'Aldona came by earlier with a message from the priest. There's a meeting at the church tomorrow morning. He expects everyone to be there. Perhaps the Duke will be there too? You must go back and tell your parents, now.'

He scowls at the mention of the Duke. 'What is this about?'

I shrug. 'I don't know. She just said it's important we are all there.'

He drops the log, the rope slipping from his grip. 'Then it's really happening.'

'What is happening?' The hairs on the back of my neck prickle.

He shakes his head. 'You will find out soon enough.'

'Jonas,' I say, gripping his wrist. 'Tell me, now.'

He faces me, his gaze on my fingertips. 'I shouldn't say. I'm not meant to know.'

'Is this about the Hollow Watcher?'

'What?' He frowns. 'No, it's nothing like that.'

161

'Then what is it?' I release his hand. What does he keep from me?

He sighs. 'They want to raise the taxes.'

My stomach drops. 'How can they do that? They already take so much. Twenty per cent plus the ten we donate to the church. We've lost five hollows over winter; we cannot afford it.'

He looks shaken. 'You lost five?'

I shove my hands into my pockets. I want to retract the words. They're a betrayal of Motina. No one else knows about the other hollows – Motina hasn't even told Aldona, her closest friend. And now Jonas knows. 'Yes, we inspected the hollows near the oak and there were another four lost. No sign of animal damage or smoke either. The bees had perished without explanation.' Well, there is one explanation but I can't share it. Motina will be humiliated if people think the bees left with Tévas.

'I'm sorry,' he says. 'I bet it was Stanislaw.' His voice is thick with resentment.

'Why?'

'Well, it makes sense, doesn't it?' Jonas casts an eye over the forest as if concerned someone may be listening. 'He must've attacked all the hives before he died.'

'And who do you think killed Stanislaw for what he did?'

Jonas's shoulders slump. 'I wish I knew.'

'Me too.'

'I should get back to my family.' He looks at the log by his feet.

'Leave it there,' I say. 'We'll collect it tomorrow.'

'Okay,' he says. His large frame sags as if he were a wildflower whose petals had been blown away in the wind.

'Jonas,' I say, seizing his wrist once more. His thumb caresses the top of my hand and I sway on my feet.

'Yes.' He looks at me intently with a question in his eyes, but I have a question of my own.

'What were you looking for at Stanislaw's cabin?'

He sucks in air and it feels as if I am being sucked into his airways too. As if I am the wind, as if Vejas, the wind goddess, speaks to me. The drawn-in air, the pause, she tells me what I already know. Jonas planned to go to Stanislaw's before he even saw me.

'I had to be sure,' he says, his voice breaking, 'that my father was not involved in his death.'

He breathes me out and my own chest draws in the forest air, expanding and holding on to this new knowledge. I want to hold on to it forever, but it is not meant to be in captivity. It escapes, shakily.

Jonas looks at me from underneath damp lashes. He lifts my hand to his mouth. His lips press against my skin and a shiver travels up my arm, my neck and into my crown. The little sparrow flutters in my chest again and then his words sink in. He has doubts about his own father. Has he suspected Krystupas all along? Is he protecting his father even though he may be responsible for Stanislaw's death?

Is there anyone left whom I can trust in this forest? Not Tévas, not the Duke and now Jonas.

My fingers slip from his grasp. I feel cool at the loss of his touch. I turn away and dash across the bridge and into the forest.

I am at one with the wind.

I wake as the morning star rises. Each morning, Ausrine, the goddess of dawn, prepares the way for the sun. It fills me with hope that I can at least rely upon this when I'm filled with so much doubt. She is faithful in her work and the transition from night to day is necessary in the forest. Nocturnal animals settle down for a nap and for the rest of us our day is only just beginning. I prayed for her to wake me before the sun rises over the forest.

I pull myself up to sit, wrap the woollen blanket around my shoulders. Then I wait.

It is not long before the flames wither and Senelè is getting to her feet. She shuffles to the log pile, scoops up a large piece and feeds it to the hearth. Her pupils glisten in the light. She looks at me, unsurprised to see me awake.

She shuffles back to her cot and sits upon it, securing her blanket as I tiptoe across the room to join her.

'Have you been waiting long?'

'No. Why is the fire so important to you? Why don't you ever let it go out?' I ask, though it was not what I'd planned to discuss in the darkness.

Senelè's eyes crease with pleasure. She loves to speak of our deities. 'Gabija is our fire goddess: she is the guardian of the family hearth. She must be carefully tended. Fine ashes must be spread on top of the sleeping embers at night to prevent her wandering about – you do not want a fire goddess roaming your house while you sleep. But you already know this. Why don't I let it go out? Because if I look after her, then she will look after us.'

I groan. 'Wouldn't it be easier to follow the book of Jesus and not have to worry about pleasing so many others?' I ask, as I am exhausted by it all.

'No,' Senelè scoffs. 'Our gods relate to nature, Austeja, not humans. We can rely on the unpredictability of nature. But humans, well, they are predictably unreliable.'

I nod, finally seeing some sense in Senelè's ways. This is something I am beginning to understand. Not everyone is as they seem. I can depend upon the morning star to rise, the wind to blow through the forest and the fire to blaze under Senelè's watch. But I am losing faith in the people I have known all my life. Still. 'But no one else keeps their fire going and they seem to be okay.'

She clucks her tongue. 'What if the fire went out and then something terrible happened? I could not live with that, Austeja. Could you? We have had such bad luck already. We live by these beliefs because we cannot risk doing otherwise, my dear.'

My face warms as we watch the flames consume the log; dark smoke rises to the stained roof. 'Senelè, do you really think I am special?'

She squeezes my hand. 'Oh, I know it.'

I frown. 'Doesn't that make me a witch? Am I like Ragana?' I shudder. As children, we were told stories by the older ones about the evil witch who lives in the forest.

Senelè bristles. 'Ragana is the goddess of the forest, not an evil witch. She can see visions of the future and can divert it in one or another direction. That is not a power to be afraid of. She could right wrongs.'

I think about that for a moment. 'Is that how you see me? Someone who can change the future?'

'You will become only who you want to be.'

The shadows from the flames dance across the walls.

'I know what you want to ask me,' Senelè says, her voice distant.

'What?'

She raises an eyebrow and my cheeks flush. 'You want to know what your father's last request of you was?'

'Yes,' I whisper.

'Are you sure you want to hear it?'

My throat is dry, and it pains me to swallow. 'Yes.'

'It wasn't a request, but he did have a message for you. He whispered it to me. You may have heard it in the forest.'

'I didn't. What did he say?'

Senelè breathes out heavily and her nose whistles. 'He said, tell her I'm sorry.'

CHAPTER TWENTY-TWO

Marytè

A hush falls over the swarm of people as the priest enters the church, followed closely behind by the Duke and his two henchmen. Margusz insists everyone sit in the pews and Marytè reluctantly abides, though her body is too wound up to be comfortably stilled. Her daughters and Senelè join her. Senelè cracks her knuckles and Marytè's stomach churns.

She's barely slept. She tossed and turned throughout the night and in those brief moments when her body relaxed and her eyelids fluttered closed, she'd hear Austeja rustling in her blanket, also tossing and turning, unable to sleep. She was tempted to boil some water for tea and invite Austeja to share it with her. A warm drink helps ease the nerves, but she feared she would confide her concerns and Austeja has enough to contend with. Despite their shared worries, mother and daughter wrestled with sleep alone.

'How long must we sit here?' Austeja says. 'They treat us like common peasants.'

'Shh,' Marytè says, though she tends to agree with her daughter. It's as if these intruders see them as nothing but settlers.

Margusz and the Duke whisper to one another. Margusz has a deep line etched across his forehead and shakes his head, as if in disbelief. The Duke, on the other hand, holds his chin high and his arms across his chest in a manner of authority. Margusz sighs and then addresses his parishioners.

'Thank you for coming today. I understand there was little time to prepare and many of you may feel anxious about the purpose of this gathering.' He looks sideways at the Duke. 'The Duke has brought some news from Alytus. He has kindly delayed imparting this knowledge on the settlers given the recent loss of two of our people.'

Marytè's fists clench. How dare Margusz praise the Duke for what should be human compassion? And how can he cast Baltrus as the same kind of loss as Stanislaw? One was a beloved family man, an integral part of this community, the other an employee of the Duke, an outsider.

'Thank you, Margusz.' The Duke steps forwards. 'Firstly, I want to thank you all for your dedication to your practice and the quality of the honey products in this region, which is of an extraordinary standard.' He beams.

Marytè clenches her fists tighter, willing herself to remain silent. He speaks as if their sole purpose is to serve him. As if the bees produce honey purely for his enjoyment. Ignorant man. The beekeepers do not choose the bees; the bees choose their beekeepers!

'Lithuanian honey, our honey, is exported around the world. All across Europe, people are enjoying the honey that you have harvested.' He pauses for effect. 'The honey and wax tax under the Lithuania Statute helps our region grow and flourish, and to be competitive with the rest of Europe. We may have been the last country in Europe Christianised but we will not be left behind when it comes to our exports. Honey is integral to our economy. Last year we exported two thousand, five hundred tons of wax!'

Marytè shudders. It is a disgrace to talk of honey as a commodity. The bees will not like it. She can only hope they are too busy in the springtime forest to notice.

'As our society grows, we need more to sustain us. It is our responsibility to serve the Duchy. It is for this reason that I have to increase your taxes.'

A chorus of gasps vibrates through the church. Marytè remains still. Austeja clasps her hand. Senelè mutters something unintelligible under her breath. Raise the taxes? 'They cannot do this. We have barely enough to survive,' Marytè says.

The Duke raises one hand and the disgruntlements are muted. 'I know the past two harvests we haven't seen as much growth here as in other regions, but we have high hopes for this season.'

'What is this young man talking about?' Senelè asks. 'We have more hollows now than we've ever had.'

Marytè shakes her head, feeling rather confused by it all. She finds herself standing, addressing the men in charge. 'Was the Hollow

Watcher counting the hollows and reporting his findings to you?'

The Duke pauses, and upon recognition of Marytè, and a sideways glance at the absence of a husband, he nods. 'Yes, that was one of his tasks. All hollows must be registered with the Duchy.' There are more grumblings around the church. The Duke raises his hands. 'This is not a new practice. Stanislaw would've discussed this with the men in the settlement.'

Men? Why not *all* the beekeepers? This affects Marytè too! And when was this discussion had with her husband? While he was incapacitated in his bed? She cannot think of a time when Baltrus had a discussion with Stanislaw. He did not like the man. And her husband would have told her, had he known, that hollows were to be registered. This is much tighter control over the beekeeping community than ever before. Because if they know exactly how many hollows there are then the beekeepers will have to account for any losses and ensure they pay the *exact* tax at harvest time. The politics and financial pressures squeeze the balloon of delight that crept its way in since the bees took flight. She's never had to worry about taxes and quotas before, but with five lost hollows and a dent in their harvest, how will they survive this increase?

The Duke clears his throat. 'The taxes will increase to half of your harvest.'

Cries echo through the church walls. Marytè's stomach churns and she clutches at her chest. Half? Her one true passion is slipping out of her grasp.

The women stand, the children prattle, and the men remain sitting, surly and tense.

'That is too much,' says Elena, bouncing her youngest on her hip. Her stomach protrudes from under her heaving chest. She is expecting again. 'How will we survive?'

The Duke shakes his head. 'I know it seems like a lot, but really there are so few people here – it is unfair that we keep all of this to ourselves, when there are so many people in need.'

'He's not talking about people in need, though,' Senelè grumbles. 'He's talking about exports!'

'I hear you are good at catching a swarm, so perhaps there will be a more competitive edge come this autumn.' He grins.

Marytè wants to rip his mouth from his face. Competition? She has never thought of her bičiulystè as competition. He tells them to catch a swarm as if they have control over the bees. They welcome bees who take residence in their hollows, and when the bees must expand to a hollow further afield, the keepers work in partnership with the families around them to find them somewhere suitable to live. This is how relationships are built. Not through rivalry.

Tension builds within her body, the pressure mounting to provide for her children through next winter. How she wishes Baltrus were sitting beside her, his large hand over her clenched fist. Calming her.

'Does anyone else have any questions?'

Marytè observes her bičiulystè. Aldona and Liudvikas sit side by side with their heads hanging low in resignation. Elena is shaking Dominykas's arm, begging him to stand up to them. Krystupas similarly ignores Smilte's pleads. Her boys, too, remain curiously silent. Will no one stand up to this intruder? This young man who gives nothing but takes everything? She has lost her husband, her other half, and now he will take half of their harvest. How long must Marytè walk around feeling like half of herself? She'd thought harvest would bring her a sense of wholeness, but the Duke and the priest take this from her too.

'Do you have something to say?' the Duke asks and Marytè realises she stands before him. Her people look at her with anticipation. Margusz glares at her.

Marytè stands taller. She can no longer rely on Baltrus to fight their battles. 'The hollows are sacred: honey is sacred.' Her voice shakes. 'We have cared for these trees and their guests for generation upon generation. We have only ever taken a small amount, never more than we need, and now you want fifty per cent of what we collect. How can you ask this of us?'

The Duke clears his throat, chooses his words carefully. 'Beekeeping is a respected profession and, like any professional, any Lithuanian, we must pay our dues. Everyone must pay tax. You do not need to serve in the military or get a job in the city; you merely have to continue doing what you love. You are in a privileged position. I was sent off to war!'

Senelè snorts and his eyes pass over her.

'Perhaps,' he says, addressing Marytè again, 'it is time to take more than you need. Take what is needed to serve your country.'

'But it is the old way,' Marytè says, in desperation.

There is a long pause as the people wait on the Duke's response.

'Forget the old ways.' The Duke's voice booms through the room. 'Serving our country, and God, is the modern way. This is the way forwards for us all.'

CHAPTER TWENTY-THREE

Austeja

The shock descends on our settlement and we stumble out of the church, one by one, into the clearing. An outsider would think we were suffocated in there, from the way everyone is clutching their chests, their stomachs, each other. Gasping for breath. Panicked.

I'd expect the Duke to go into hiding. Instead, he settles in among the disgruntled and anxious peasants, chatting, the smile never leaving his face. As if he is our saviour. How could I have been so wrong about him? I thought him a fresh face, someone who respects our ways and can bring some novel ideas from Alytus. But, no, he wants to eradicate our ways altogether.

As the Duke approaches me, I consider my escape. I do not want to talk to the man who has angered all the people and either does not care or is completely oblivious. But there are still so many things I need to know. About the Hollow Watcher, and Tévas, and the knife. I promised myself I would get to the bottom of it. Instead of fleeing to the forest, as my instinct dictates, I will stay and talk to as many people as possible.

'Good day, Austeja.'

'Hello.' I peek around the gathering, but no one seems to notice the Duke speak to me.

'This spring weather has been a pleasant surprise. Summer is near, I can feel it. Though it still gets very windy down here.'

I smile. It'd be far windier in Alytus, where there are fewer trees to block Vejas's path. She must wreak havoc on those villages, with no trees to talk to. My conversation with Senelè creeps in, about my gift to speak to the wind. I'm not convinced it talks to me as such, but I do sometimes sense messages in the breeze. Ones I may not be able to describe aloud, but I can feel on my skin, and in my body. I wonder if that is what she means.

'You surprised us today,' I say. 'About the rise in taxes. It's quite the shock to my people.'

He tilts his head. 'Yes, I suppose it will come as a shock to some.'

'Some?' I want to know who, apart from Jonas, knew in advance.

He scratches his chin as if considering his next words. 'Well, as I said, I spoke to the men of the village two summers ago, when my uncle still ruled this region. I have big plans for the export trade and I know you are the people who can bring them to fruition. I've not come across such passion and skill in any other region I have travelled through.'

I think back to the summer when Azuolas and Tévas went to Alytus.

They went to make trades on honey and brought back creamy cheese and phlegmy coughs. We thought it was illness that had them in low moods but maybe there was something more that they'd not revealed. 'Did you speak to my father?'

He pauses. 'Yes. Baltrus was a kind fellow. None of the men were too keen on increasing the taxes, though I didn't propose quite as big an increase then as I have decreed now, but perhaps they kept it quiet. My uncle still reigned and maybe they thought it would be some time before the new taxes would be enforced.'

'Didn't you say this was written in the Lithuanian Statute?'

'Yes.'

'Then why would it matter who reigned over this forest?'

The Duke raised his chin. 'The taxes were due to be raised regardless, but I have to prove myself worthy to the Duchy. I may be young and less experienced than my uncle but I am ambitious,' he says with pride.

I feel sick in the stomach. The Duke is raising the taxes simply because he wants to. 'How can you do this to us?'

A confused expression passes over his face. 'I am not doing anything to you. We will all work together, and I can assure you, you will all be greatly thanked for your service.'

'We will work together? Will you climb pine trees in your breeches and tame the bees with your own bare hands? Or, more to the point, go hungry next winter or the one after when we can't harvest enough?' I do not like my tone but there is something about him that compels me to speak my mind. It may be that he allows it. He does not silence me like Aldona or Motina. If anything, I seem to amuse him, for he chuckles now.

'Austeja, come on. We must all lean into our strengths. My strength lies in business. For your people, it is this place.' He looks up to the canopies. 'It is the forest.'

It is strange how this forest can protect us from threats but simultaneously keep us naive about what is happening beyond the treetops. My rare trips to Alytus or Kaunas as a child were like visiting another country. The city generated curiosity and excitement. As a child, who did not feel a calling in beekeeping, I had been enticed by the sights, the smells and the sounds of the modern people of society. I had been biding my time ever since to escape to Alytus, away from the peasant life, away from the monotony of forest life. But the city the Duke speaks of is even more foreign. A place full of politics, where peasants are used for career and monetary gain. Where people's lives are toyed with for others' gains.

Perhaps I am a girl meant for the forest after all.

The Duke holds up a hand to a beckoning henchman. 'I must go. But it has been a pleasure speaking to you, as always, Austeja.' His eyes twinkle. It's a look I've seen in Jonas before.

'Just one thing, sir.' I lean closer and now his cheeks turn pink. 'You said you spoke to the other men that summer. Who else was there?'

He flashes another grin, as if impressed by my interest in his devious tactics. 'The men of each household. Your father, of course, and, let me see. Those men.' He points to Dominykas and Liudvikas. 'That man too.' He nods towards Krystupas, who is watching us. 'And one of his sons, from what I recall. It was a long time ago now, and I have more than this settlement under my reign, so I cannot recall.'

Every man in this settlement knew about the rise in taxes but from what I can see none of the women did. Why did they keep it from us? Why did Tévas keep it from Motina? It makes no sense. He could have warned her. Saved her from this anger and humiliation. My voice is shaky when I speak. 'Do you remember which son it was? Was it Jonas?' I nod in his direction. He knew about the taxes, but he never mentioned meeting the Duke before he arrived in the forest.

The Duke tilts his head, but he is distracted by his henchman once again. 'It could have been, yes. Although those boys all look much the same, don't you think? They're all rather like big bears. I must go. Let's talk again soon.' He leans closer and his breath tickles my ear.

I force myself not to pull away, but it leaves a taste like sour milk. I am thankful when he dashes off and attends to whatever important business he's needed for. Except that I forgot to ask him about Stanislaw! There has been no serious investigation into his death. Surely the Duke wants a firm explanation for what happened to one of his employees.

I wander away from the crowd to gather my thoughts and consider what I know so far. The summer before last, my brother and Tévas visited Alytus. They spoke to the Duke and his uncle. They were informed that the taxes would be raised. Tévas didn't tell us. This winter, Stanislaw counted the hollows for the register. He did a favour for Tévas and Tévas gave him his knife because he owed him. Then Tévas died. The knife was somehow returned to or taken by Stanislaw. Then Stanislaw died.

My gaze sweeps over the other settlers. What went wrong? Maybe Stanislaw deliberately miscounted the hollows in exchange for something. Is this why Tévas and Krystupas owed him? It's possible that Stanislaw was working both sides. If he underreported the number of registered hollows, then when the taxes are increased the reported harvest would be less, and there would be an excess of honey collected that could then go untaxed. But why would Stanislaw, who was in a paid position working for the Duke, agree to this? I cannot think what my father or Jonas's father could offer Stanislaw that would be more than his wage. Whatever it was, it was bad enough that my father's dying wish was to apologise for it. But why was the apology directed at me and not Motina? I don't know how this all relates to me.

My head pounds as the questions swirl about, the answers just out of reach. If only Motina knew what dirty deals had been done right under her nose. This community in whom she instils all her trust. There are some among us we cannot trust. But who?

The oak calls me; I feel its pull. Just as Senelè had predicted. I close my eyes and I see Stanislaw, bloodied and bruised. Eyes wide open. Raven's eyes.

What happened to you, Stanislaw?

I pull myself up off the log. My legs are charged, ready to thrash through the forest. But I know this isn't what the oak needs of me right now. It needs answers. So I turn away from the forest and join the crowd by the church. The Duke and his henchmen have left. The priest is out of sight too. People are nattering away: their voices heighten and then drop to hushed whispers.

Aldona has broken away from the crowd and is twirling Danutè around. 'I'll make you a wildflower chain,' Danutè says. Her grin is broad as she darts across the clearing.

'She loves making those,' I say, approaching Aldona. Her smile is genuine and the doubts from our last discussion peel away. Aldona has always made time for Danutè and me. She is Motina's closest friend. I can trust her.

'She's such a lovely girl. She's adjusting well to the loss of her father.'

'Yes, I suppose.' Guilt gnaws at me as I realise how little I have thought about Danutè's welfare since Tévas left. I have been so caught up in trying to figure out the riddles he has left behind that I have not considered what it has been like for her. Motina is distracted, Senelè spends more and more time grumbling to herself and I am often on the loose in the forest.

'How have you been? You've experienced quite a lot too.'

I chew on my bottom lip, wondering how much to share. I decide on honesty. 'It has been difficult. Sometimes, I have nightmares about the Hollow Watcher.'

Aldona squeezes my shoulder. 'You are a brave girl. We are all proud of how you handled that situation. You responded quickly and sensibly.'

My cheeks warm with pride. 'But we still don't know what happened to him.'

'No.' Her gaze drifts off to the forest. The canopies sway gently in the breeze, rustling and shuddering with the news brought by the Duke.

'Aldona, I wanted to thank you and Liudvikas for the knife he made for Motina. She was really happy with it, and I think it was nice for her to have something fresh and new for her first bee season without Tévas.'

'Oh, Austeja, it's our pleasure. Liudvikas enjoys making those kinds of things anyway.'

'Perhaps I will ask Motina for one of my own. I will have to help her at harvest.'

Aldona beams. 'That's a wonderful idea. Your mother will most certainly need you to take on more responsibility this year. I know it hasn't always interested you, the bees, but it is in your blood. You were born to do it.'

Her words settle upon me and I think about what Senelė said to me. I have been summoned to communicate with nature. How does this fit with my duty to be a beekeeper like Motina? Is it possible to do both?

'Liudvikas will be happy to have more projects to keep him busy. There was a time there when he had made quite a few, apart from your mother's.'

My stomach flips. 'Do you mean he has made more knives than usual this season?'

'Oh yes, Dominykas's had rotted over those wet seasons and so he carved him a new handle. Oh, and there were Smilte's boys, too. He made one for each of them.' She laughed. 'Then Petras lost his, so he made him a replacement. Kept him busy, I tell you.'

My head aches once more. There is nothing odd about Liudvikas making knives for Smilte's boys, but now that I've learned about Stanislaw holding knives as guarantees of a debt, my suspicion grows. Petras may have lost his knife, or it may have been temporarily given to Stanislaw. Maybe Krystupas took the knife to conceal that his own was missing. I don't know what is going on with that family or whether it is linked to my father's or Stanislaw's deaths. But I'm certain Jonas's family knows more than they are letting on.

'Austeja, are you okay? You're looking rather faint.'

My lips are parched and my vision blurs. 'Yes, I think I've just been in the sun for too long. Excuse me while I fetch some water.'

They are gone the next day.

They broke the news as if they were dark thunderous clouds, bringing a downfall of disappointment and anger. And while we slept and the skies cleared, the Duke's men cleared out too.

Aldona came over early in the morning as I was scooping steaming hot porridge into my mouth. She tapped on the door and, as she caught her breath, she told us they'd left. The carriage had likely rattled over the bridge and through the forest, keeping its distance from Jonas's house until they reached the south-eastern side of the forest, which led to the highway.

Motina was furious but eventually she calmed. 'It is good they are gone. Margusz was due to move on to the next settlement anyway. We do not want to cause any trouble. Who knows what they would come up with next if we did? Austeja, we must keep our heads down and do what we are told.'

'But, Motina, they want to take half of our honey and wax. And what about the ten per cent we must give to the church? They need their supply of wax candles. That leaves us with less than half to see us through four seasons. How will we survive?'

I know I should have forewarned her, but I hoped Jonas was wrong.

It probably wouldn't have helped her anyway.

Motina bristles. 'We made no trades last year and we got through a very dark winter. We will be careful with what we have, that's all. Besides, we have no mead to trade this time. I don't know what your father did with it all, but we're near dry. Only what I've spared for medicinal purposes.'

'I could go.'

'Go where?' Motina asks, exasperated.

'To trade our honey for meat and cheese and whatever else I can find. We cannot trade our honey among our bičiulystė but there are other settlements who will gladly barter for our harvest. Let me go.'

'Austeja! You cannot believe that I will send you, a young woman, a Marti, off to another settlement with a few pots of honey. Alone and unescorted. That is ridiculous.'

I cross my arms over my chest. I didn't expect her to accept my offer, but I do want to help. She cannot do everything on her own. And going to another settlement would allow me to gather information about whether the taxes have been raised elsewhere.

'No,' Motina says.

'Marytė.' Senelė speaks gently but firmly. 'Perhaps we must do the unconventional to see us through another winter.'

'You mean to send her on her own?'

'Of course not, but we could arrange an escort. Surely some of the men will be going to trade soon anyway.'

'Then I shall ask them to trade for us. I do not like to rely on others, but if they are going to another settlement anyway, then I'm sure they will do this for us.'

'As you wish,' Senelè says.

Motina regathers her composure. 'Come, we must be on our way. I have to visit Smilte to inform her of the Duke's departure, and I need you and Danutè to net us a fish for supper.'

'Yes, Motina,' I say. I can't help but carry my mother's worry within me. My stomach stirs. How will we make it through winter with only half of our supplies? If our crops are damaged or there is no meat to eat, we always have our honey. But without honey, we have nothing.

I may have taken for granted the privilege we had as beekeepers. What will happen if we don't deliver to the Duke what we owe? What if we don't meet our commitment?

Stanislaw's face flashes before me. Did the Duke know he had deceived him? Is this what Jonas meant when he said there are more possibilities to consider regarding the Hollow Watcher's death? Could this be what happens to someone who double-crosses the Duke? A shiver runs down my spine.

I collect my boots and my net, forcing myself to focus on what I must do right now. Catch a fish. Provide for my family.

Survive.

CHAPTER TWENTY-FOUR

Marytè

News travels fast. Smilte has already heard about the Duke's departure.

'The boys were in the forest near the bridge and they came across Dominykas, who told them. He and Elena had been up early with their youngest. Terrible sleeper, that little thing. Dominykas saw them crossing the bridge before the sun had even risen. A devious exit if you ask me.' Smilte passes Marytè a mug with a strong scent, smirking. 'We need mead more than tea today, my friend.'

Marytè sips and she likes that it is a strong brew. Richer than Baltrus's and not what she'd typically drink in the middle of the day, but Smilte is right. The Duke announcing a rise in taxes to half of their collection sits heavily upon her.

'Half!' Smilte shakes her head. 'I have three grown boys to feed.'

Marytè cannot imagine having more mouths to feed, but even though a large family would be overwhelming she would give anything to have her house full of all the babes she's lost, Azuolas, Rasa and Baltrus too. It feels as if the branches are dropping from her family and all that will be left is a lonesome, unstable trunk.

'It is unthinkable.' Marytè sips on the mead. It leaves a pleasant taste on her tongue and eases the tension in her shoulders and the ache in her knee. 'We rely on trades when the seasons are wet, and our crops suffer. We are such a small settlement: everything we do is for our bees. How will we survive?'

Smilte shakes her head and then swills the remainder of her drink. 'I suppose I will need to consider suitable marriages for my sons sooner than I'd planned. I cannot keep them all here forever. But I'd like them to be close.' She looks pointedly at Marytè.

Marytè has noticed the way the middle boy, Jonas, looks at her daughter. He seeks her out more than is necessary. He is a hard worker and a sensible boy. But he is second born. It is tradition for the second son to remain in his family home and carry on the traditions of his father.

Marytè cannot afford to lose Austeja to someone else's home, even if Senelè is against marriages within the same community. They need a man to help them and they cannot send away more of their children to other settlements, like Aldona has. There will be no one left to keep up with the demands of the Duke. Senelè is ageing and while she keeps up with the domestic tasks she has been unfit for beekeeping since before Danutè's birth. No, Marytè cannot lose Austeja to Smilte. And without a man at the head of their house, she risks losing her land and hollows too. What will be left then?

'You will marry the eldest first?'

'That would be a sensible choice.'

'I have a hollow that needs a swarm.'

Smilte smiles and Marytè thinks she is going to shake hands with her but her smile falls away as she looks to the door.

Jonas has ducked his head in. 'Just coming in for a drink,' he says.

Marytè can't be sure whether he has heard their conversation. She doesn't want Austeja to hear it from anyone but her. She'll likely be unimpressed by the marriage choice, as she has been with all previous attempts to have her wed, but Tomas is the most viable option. An extra set of hands at their home and one less mouth eating at Smilte's, as well as keeping a strong beekeeper in the settlement. Marytè fears their settlement will end with her generation if she does not do something about it soon.

Jonas fills his mug with mead and swills it.

'Jonas, I wanted to thank you and your older brother for keeping watch on the hollows and on my daughters. And for the firewood too. We very much appreciate it.'

'You're welcome,' he says and glances at his mother. 'But I suppose it isn't needed now that the Duke and his men have gone.'

Marytè sits up taller. 'Jonas, what do you mean?'

He clears his throat and Smilte gives him a sharp look. 'I mean that there was never such violence, or threats to our practices, until that man came to our forest.'

Marytè infers from Smilte's grimace that this is a well-rehearsed conversation, one that she does not entirely agree with. Does Jonas really think the Duke or the priest can be responsible for Stanislaw's death?

'Give my best to Austeja,' he says as he empties his mug and exits the cottage.

'How is Austeja?' Smilte asks.

'As well as she can be. It has unsettled her, losing her father and then finding Stanislaw.' Marytè swallowed back the haunting image of the Hollow Watcher in the forest. 'And now with the taxes ...'

'If there's anything we can do to help you, please tell me.' Smilte collects the mug and Marytè stands; her knee is loose and ache-free. She can see why her mother drank so much of it after her father's death. It relieves one of pain.

'I will. Smilte, the Duke said the men knew the taxes would be increased. Did Krystupas know?'

'No,' Smilte says firmly. 'He says he knew nothing about it.'

'And the others?'

'According to their wives, Liudvikas and Dominykas have denied it too.'

'Then what men did he speak of? Baltrus? He and Azuolas travelled to Alytus two summers ago, to trade. But the other men went too, no?'

'Perhaps the Duke does not speak the truth. He is a young man, even younger two summers ago. He could be mistaken.'

Marytè steps outside. They have no reason to distrust their men, but why would the Duke say it if it is not true?

Smilte leans against her doorframe, scanning the clearing. 'Jonas went with him that time to learn how to trade. Krystupas did seem particularly surly after that trip.'

'Oh?'

Smilte smiles. 'Even more so than usual. Maybe they wanted to protect us from worry over something that may never have eventuated.'

'But it has.' And there was no reason to keep it secret – unless there were more secrets within this one. Something does not sit right with Marytè. She was pregnant that summer, violently ill, and begged Baltrus to stay with her. He insisted on going, as many of the men were travelling at staggered intervals into the city: it was a big season for trade. She lost the baby, the last one she ever conceived, the day after he left. By the time he returned Azuolas was ill, and Baltrus was racked with guilt. By winter Azuolas was gone. Why would they keep this from her? What did he possibly gain?

Smilte leans closer. 'You know, I think the Hollow Watcher knew it was coming.'

'The taxes?'

'Yes. He came around and asked about our hollows. Wanted an exact number. I told him roughly seventy, but he wanted one of the boys to show him. He wasn't a bee man; his eyes were not trained like ours to see. In the end I sent Petras to point them all out.'

Marytè sighs. 'He never asked me but I saw him counting our hollows days before Austeja found him.'

'It's very odd.' Smilte bites the inside of her lip. 'After all that, going out traipsing across the forest, he said to Petras, "Let's just say sixty." Petras was irate. Thought Stanislaw hadn't taken him seriously. We're honest people. He told me he'd pointed out seventy-one hollows. He'd been exact, as Stanislaw had requested. Then he recorded it as sixty.' She shrugs. 'He was always an odd man. Drank too much too. Don't know how he got his hands on so much mead.'

'Indeed.' There are a lot of odd things about what Smilte has shared and as she makes her way through the clearing and onto the forest path, she wonders whether perhaps Stanislaw was on their side after all.

From behind a linden tree, Jonas steps out. Marytè pauses, her heart racing at the unexpected encounter. It is just Smilte's boy: no one out here will harm you.

He kicks at the ground with his boot and then draws himself up and meets her gaze. 'I will get you a swarm,' he says.

So he did hear their conversation. Marytè looks back at the cottage, but it is now out of sight.

'I don't want to work with my father for the rest of my life. I want to make it on my own.' He crosses his arms over his chest. 'And I think Austeja and I are the better match.'

Marytè pats his arm. He is braver than Azuolas. Jonas does share that trait with Austeja.

'When the time comes, let's speak.'

He tries to stop himself grinning, but he does not hide it well. She continues on her way. He is not her first choice, but if she has learned one thing since Baltrus became ill, it is to keep her options open. She must remain resourceful if she and her girls are to survive another winter.

She trusts the bees will choose wisely.

PART III

SWARM

CHAPTER TWENTY-FIVE

Austeja

'I got one!' Danutè springs out of the water, holding the net above her head. A perch is fretting about within. 'I knew I would catch one, eventually.' The water, where it was still, ripples with her absence.

She tips the fish into the bucket by my feet; it joins the one I caught earlier, flapping about in a small pool of water. They are not large, by any means, but it is enough for our small family.

'We'll have quite the feast tonight. Two Žuvis for supper,' I say, untangling the damp strands hanging in a clump by her cheek. I tuck them back under her scarf. 'They'll be delicious with the beets Motina pulled up this morning.'

We've been down by the river for hours soaking up the summer sunshine. The air is still and so the water is slow-moving, making it simpler to catch sight of fish. I netted mine a while ago, but Danutè was resolute to catch one of her own. She hiked up her underdress and treaded back into the water after we snacked on juniper berries and lay in the sun. After some time, and my frequent reminders, she learned to still her body in the stream until her legs and arms reached the same temperature as the water and the fish no longer swerved away. It is her first catch and she'll remember it always.

I was with Tévas when I caught my first little pike. It looked like an ant when he held it in his bear-like hands. He was so proud we took it home to Motina and cooked it immediately. It was as if I were walking on tree canopies in the days that followed: I felt so grown up and it was nice to contribute to the family.

We rarely fished together after that. Tévas mostly took Azuolas. As I grew, it became less appropriate for me to jump about in the river in my underclothes, and so I was often left behind with my baby sister to help Motina and Senelè with the domestic chores. It didn't keep me from creeping along the riverbanks in summer to catch a fish and relive that feeling. I released these catches, but the feeling of pride stayed with me in the days that followed. It is this, being out in the forest, working with the forest and being useful, that brings me immense pleasure. The things Tévas used to do. Not cooking on the hearth or sweeping away the spring dust from the cottage floor.

With no Tévas or Azuolas, it has once more become acceptable for me to catch the fish. Seafood makes up most of our summer diet, followed by berries and mushrooms in autumn. Winter means living off our reserves: smoked fish and dried meats.

With her husband gone, Motina is now accepted as head beekeeper of the household. I know she misses my father but the status also brings her immense pleasure. Why must it take the departure of our men for the women to be accepted in these roles? I cannot imagine a life here where we could do whatever we pleased, regardless of our sex. Imagine a boy cooking or sweeping the floors?!

An image of Jonas kneading rye dough by the hearth slips into my thoughts. Those large knuckles would make quick work of the dough while my petite hands are more easily concealed when hunting fish.

As children, Jonas's brothers may have been jealous of my tree-climbing abilities but Jonas has always shown me respect. The way Tévas respected Motina as a beekeeper. That's what I hope to have in a marriage of my own. I can sense the tension building at home. I will have to marry soon. Senelè is less than subtle about her thoughts on the matter and Motina has ceased rebuking her. At least Senelè has come around to Motina's way of seeing things: she wants me to marry someone in our settlement, someone we know. We really cannot risk another beekeeper leaving us for other settlements. I know Motina worries about how we will survive. I worry too. We do need help. Senelè is getting old, and her cough lingers even on the warmest of days. If something happens to her it will just be the three of us.

'Come,' I say to Danutè. 'Let's find more juniper berries. Motina can crush them up and add them to Senelè's tea. To help with her cough.' And Motina's too. She has ignored any attention I've paid to her cough. She simply says it is the pollen in the air, nothing more. I suspect it is more. What if I lose both my parents? I cannot provide for Danutè on my own. Without a man here, we could lose our property and the hollows. The Duke could give it to another beekeeping couple.

I need to talk to Motina about marriage. It is the only sensible thing to do. I once dreamed of marrying someone far away and leaving behind this settlement to experience life as something other than a beekeeper. But now I can think of nothing but staying with my people, to protect the forest.

Danutè and I pull our dresses back over our slips and I collect the bucket as we walk back along the forest path I've trod every day since I could walk. Sometimes the forest grows over it but mostly the earth senses our impending feet and keeps the path free. Tall grass edges the trail, swaying in the low breeze. The forest is now thick with greenness. Oaks, beeches, ashes and birch all rise, their individual branches barely discernible amid a dense canopy. The foliage is so plentiful, if it were to rain, I think we'd stay near dry.

'The juniper shrub was just over here,' Danutè says, skipping ahead, her boots in her hands and the soles of her damp feet darkening with every step. We found it along the path in the underbrush of a Scots pine.

'Let's go this way,' I call her back. 'I've seen a small juniper grove through here. We can scoop them into our dresses and there will be plenty for Motina to grind up and store.'

Danutè pauses. 'This way?' She appears uncertain.

'Yes.' I guide her through a less cleared path, but one I've used often to cut through to the bridge if I am in a hurry. A few minutes along the path we see the grove.

Danutè runs ahead. 'So many berries!' She starts to pluck them from the brush. 'Ow!' She sucks on her finger where the sharp needles prick her.

'Careful, now,' I say. 'Only take the dark bluish-purple ones: they are the ripest.'

We fill our skirts and knot them around a thumb, eating a few more before we leave. A little spicy but a nice forest treat. They are evergreen but are harder to find under the snow. When we can stuff no more into our mouths or skirts, I collect the bucket with my free hand, and we continue back along the path. Danutè has her boots tucked under one arm and she skips, lopsidedly, back towards the main path which will take us up to the marshes, then the clearing and to our house beyond. When it veers off to the right, Danutè is out of sight for a moment, behind a bushy alder tree.

She yelps and then there's a thump. I hurry forwards, the bucket splashing water over the edges and the fish flicking their tails in protest. I hold my skirt tighter as some of the berries topple out. Behind the alder, Danutè is on the ground clutching her bare foot, sobbing, juniper berries scattered everywhere.

'Snake,' she says, pointing to the long grass where the tail of a young adder disappears from sight.

'Oh, Danutè.' I drop to the ground and the berries cascade around us. 'Did it bite you?'

'Yes, I stepped on it.'

My heart races as I inspect the site. The fang marks are faint. There may only be a little, if any, venom in her blood. 'We must get you home. Grab your boots.' I turn so she can jump onto my back, and I heave her up higher. 'Hold on tight,' I say as I pick up the fish bucket and stride back along the path. I should never have strayed from the main path. She should have been wearing her boots! This is all my fault.

I heave Danutè up higher on my back. Focus. I block out any bad thoughts, any niggling voices that tell me I could lose my sister. I scrutinise the path with each step I take, summoning the forest to protect me and my sister until we get to safety.

Guilt claws at my gut as Danutè spikes a mild fever. Motina had known something awful had happened before we reached the door. Senelè shrieked and called it a bad omen. A snake bite! She grabbed my shoulders and shook me so that my head lolled back and forth. 'Did you kill it?'

'No,' I said, for a moment thinking I'd failed again. Why didn't I think to capture it and bring it back with us?

'Good, good. If you had she'd never recover.'

She released me and I swayed, off balance.

Compared to Senelè, Motina responded in a calm manner and sat Danutè upright so her heart was higher than the bite, and she gave her hot tea, which would do nothing for the snake bite, she said, but would at least calm her nerves.

Again, she guides another cup full of liquid to Danutè's lips. This time it's watered-down mead. Senelè circles the eternal flame, scattering salt upon it and urging Gabija to protect us.

'Shh,' Motina says. 'A snake bites when threatened. Danutè did not see it and trod on the creature: there is no evil at play here. Do not fill their heads with such things.'

Senelè snorts and Motina whispers, 'Please.'

Senelè continues to pace but her ramblings quieten so that Motina can focus on helping Danutè. When Danutè is drowsy from the mead and drifts off to sleep, her breath in an easy rhythm, Senelè settles in her own cot and soon erupts into congested snores.

I have been an awful sister since Tévas left and then I take her off the forest path, where she is inexperienced, and she is struck by a snake. I have been careless. As Motina sits down on the cot beside me, I prepare for her wrath. She'll probably want to marry me off to some hairy old oaf.

Her arm rests across my shoulders and she gently enfolds me into her. I flinch, not expecting her affection. It doesn't feel natural for us, but I think she is trying.

'You did well today.'

I draw back. 'How can you say that? Danutè was out of sight, just for a moment, but she was struck by a snake. She could ... Will she?'

'I think she will be okay. There was a little venom but she is young and healthy. The fever is mild and there's no sign of infection. I think she will be well, Austeja.'

I exhale long and hard, the worry being coaxed out.

'You are calm under pressure: that is a good trait.' She smiles and watches the fire. Calm under pressure? That's what I've witnessed in my mother today. She did not rant and ramble like Senelè: she was proficient and remained in control. Is that how I am?

I've always thought I am more like my father, nothing like my mother at all. Maybe that is because I *wanted* to be nothing like her. I have been rather harsh on her. She can be distant and cold but she too is mourning. She has always provided for us and she does what needs to be done. If Tévas were here he'd have gathered me up in a bearish hug and wiped away my tears, but he'd not have known how to treat Danutè: that would be left to Motina. Maybe Motina knew that nothing could match Tévas's embrace and so she didn't try, until he was gone. Now she holds my hand, draws me in towards her again. I realise what I miss most about Tévas is his gentle touch. I rest my head upon her shoulder. She must miss Tévas's physical presence too.

'I'm worried about our future, Austeja,' she says in a soft voice.

My lungs tighten again. I've felt it for weeks, months, now but it has never been said aloud. She's never shown weakness. She's never shown me that she is not in control. And I realise this is what I've always wanted – for her to be human like the rest of us. Imperfect. But now that it's said aloud, anxiety swells inside of me. If Motina is worried, then she does not have a plan. She does not know what the future holds.

I lick my lips and draw in a breath. 'Motina, I have to marry. It is our only way out.'

'Yes.' She looks at me, her face tempering to relief. 'I think that is what we need.'

'I have someone in mind,' I say, tentatively.

Motina bites the inside of her lip. 'I have spoken to Smilte.'

My cheeks redden and my heart flutters, the sparrow reawakens and

I realise this is what I want now. I want to marry Jonas.

'I'm sorry,' she says; her voice drops as her shoulders slump. 'But you cannot marry Jonas.'

'What?'

'He is the second born; he must stay home. It is Tomas you have to marry.'

My stomach drops and the air is squeezed from my lungs. The flutters burst out, abandoning me. Tomas? 'No,' I whisper. That's not what I had in mind at all. I don't even know him. Can't even conjure up an image of his face in my mind. How can I marry him when I am so fond of his brother?

'I'm sorry, Austeja. I know this isn't the way you wanted it to go, but we must all do our part for the family. I am proud of you for making this decision on your own. Marriage will bind our families and will allow us to continue with our work. We will announce it soon and you will marry next spring after Lent. This is what you will do for us.'

CHAPTER TWENTY-SIX

Marytè

Marytè hacks, phlegm rising in the back of her throat. She swallows it back down but it wedges in her throat, so her words come out strangled.

'In the bucket, Danutè.'

Her youngest daughter is swirling around the plot with two large beetroots sitting atop her head as if the stalks are big floppy rabbit ears. Her shoulders droop and she places them into the bucket. Marytè sighs. She forgets Danutè is just eight winters old. Sometimes it feels as if yesterday she was toddling about and other times it's as if she is on the cusp of being a Marti, like her sister. How can children grow so quickly and yet so slowly at the same time? If Baltrus were here, he'd have propped beets on top of his thick mane and bounced about with her. Austeja would've rolled her eyes, but there'd have been a hint of envy behind them.

How long has it been since Marytè had let go in that way? Or her children? There has been a heaviness upon the cottage since their two men left the family. Heavier still when Stanislaw's body was discovered and the taxes were raised. If her worries were a solid mass upon her shoulders, Marytè would fail to walk. She'd sink into the earth and disappear. But the worries aren't a physical, external thing; they sit inside her, squeezing her gut, clenching her lungs, and compressing her muscles. She coughs again but tries to hide it by turning away from the girls and muffling it against her shoulder. She thought the tickle in her throat would've settled by now. It usually bothers her in spring when the pollen is high and the winds are fierce. But it's summer, now.

Marytè stands, collecting a turnip as she does, and dropping it into the bucket. At least her knee has improved in the warmer weather. Apart from a little stiffness in the mornings, it doesn't seem to bother her much these days. The crops look good. A little rain, but not too much, and plenty of sun. The sky is clear and the air is still. Marytè wants to make the most of this healthy weather. 'Danutè, will you fetch the bread and honey from the cottage? Let's eat beneath the Scots pine today.'

They set up an impromptu picnic in the canopy's shadow and devour honey-drizzled rye bread followed by the juniper berries Austeja collected from the grove. She returned on her own, despite Danutè's pleas to go with her. Austeja has been very protective of her younger sister in the weeks since the snake bite. Marytè hasn't wanted her to stray too far either. Even if she kept her emotions intact, when Austeja carried Danutè home she was truly frightened. But she knew it was no use getting caught up in the panic: it would not help Danutè. They were lucky it was a young snake and the fangs had barely pierced her skin. Next time she may not be as lucky.

Senelè returns from her walk around the marsh: determined to keep her ageing body lithe, she has taken to walking each day. Some days she is gone for so long, Marytè worries she has fallen or taken ill, but then, as if she senses her unease, she shuffles into sight, taking careful steps around the wetland.

When Baltrus and Marytè wed, Senelè complained about the site they'd chosen to settle on in Musteika. They were one of four young couples granted to settle in the area after moving from larger settlements in the north. Had they known they would be at the whim of the Duke they'd have remained in the area where Baltrus grew up. They had both given up their hollows to start afresh.

Marytè liked the marshes. She still does. Sure, they're damp, and biting insects are plentiful, but she enjoys watching the birds and frogs and other creatures leaping around the swampland. She likes that their home is close to the river and the church, but not so close to the church that the priest would be considered a neighbour.

Smilte and Krystupas were the last to arrive and they settled the furthest away. While Smilte enjoyed the company of others, her husband favoured his own. Smilte was pregnant with Tomas when Marytè was due to deliver Azuolas. They bonded over the pregnancies and the little boys that followed. Tomas was a timid child, his father at times overbearing and tough. Smilte quietened whenever her husband was about. It wasn't quite fear, but a watchfulness. Yes, that's it: she was always cautious in Krystupas's presence and so too was Tomas. As more boys came along and Smilte was busy with the children, her confidence grew and the watchfulness became less noticeable. It's still there. Marytè noticed it when Smilte looked at Krystupas in the church to gauge his knowledge of the Duke's announcement.

Marytè has always felt grateful that she found a warm and kind man. There are many men who are neither. She hopes the boys take after their mother and not their father, but she has never seen any violent tendencies or any behaviour of concern. They all seem pleasant enough. Austeja will be well looked after.

'Are you okay, Motina? You sound chesty,' Austeja says, drawing Marytè's attention back to the present. She's been coughing again and forgot to conceal it.

'I'm fine.'

Senelè joins them on the soft grass, dropping beside Marytè with a congested eruption. It is far worse and sicklier than Marytè's and it reassures her that her own is of no concern. Senelè's health, on the other hand, is worrisome.

'That was so delicious.' Danutè licks honey residue from her fingers with a grin. 'Can you imagine living in one of the cities and not having honey every day? Unless you're wealthy, of course. We are so lucky.'

'We are, indeed,' Senelè says.

Marytè's body feels relaxed as she watches the women in her life enjoying the very foundation of their livelihoods. Honey. Warm bread. Fresh air and sunshine. It is the first time in a very long time that Marytè is contented. We'll be okay. We can make a life without Baltrus. We all miss him, but we will be okay.

As if reading her thoughts, Austeja speaks. 'I wish Tévas were here with us right now.'

'Me too,' Marytè says.

'He is,' Senelè says. 'Don't forget he's just up there on the High Hill.' She points across the marsh and the girls look at the forest hiding the church and High Hill from sight. 'He's always here and I bet he's enjoying delicious honey-bread too.'

Marytè wants to believe he is here, but she finds it difficult to reconcile the idea of someone being here without being physically present. She thought she would feel his presence, but she feels nothing. No sense of him at all. She supposes he is in heaven, looking down upon them. Yes, that makes more sense.

'Motina,' Austeja says hesitantly, 'why didn't Tévas tell you that he spoke with the Duke in Alytus? He didn't tell us about the taxes being raised. We could've done something earlier.'

Marytè shakes her head. 'He didn't know. He'd have told me: I am sure of it.'

Austeja frowns. 'But he did know. The Duke told me.'

Marytè shifts to ease pressure off her knee which has spontaneously spasmed. 'The Duke is dishonest. I spoke to the women and none of their husbands knew. Baltrus knew nothing, Austeja.'

Austeja bites the inside of her cheek and turns to face her squarely. 'Jonas told me too.'

'He told you what?' The tension creeps back into Marytè's muscles, digging in deep, gripping her gut and making her queasy.

'Jonas said he and his father met with the former Duke and his nephew that summer. All the men were there. Maybe not all at the same time, but at some point, over the summer. They were told the taxes would be raised the following season, though it was never meant to be as high as half. That was something the new Duke took upon himself. He is ambitious, he told me so – he wants to impress the Duchy.'

'No,' Marytè says more to herself than anyone else. 'No, I don't believe Baltrus would deceive us.'

'Certainly not,' Senelè says.

'He may not have meant to deceive us, but he kept this news from us. Speak to the Duke and Jonas yourself. I believe what they say.'

'You believe strangers over your own father?' Senelè asks.

'Tévas isn't here to tell his side,' Austeja says, her voice on the rise. 'But I think he kept some things from us.' She seems on the verge of saying something else; instead she holds back, and stares out at the forest. There is something about her demeanour and the suspicion she holds about her father, the man she has idolised her entire life, that sobers Marytè. She rubs the tendons above her knee as Senelè launches into a coughing fit and then excuses herself, wheezing and whooping back up to the house.

Danutè, losing interest in the conversation, wanders off in the clearing. She's caught sight of a frog and has crouched down beside the marshes to inspect it.

'When I spoke to Smilte, she told me none of the men knew about the taxes,' Marytè says, thinking aloud.

Austeja looks over her shoulder and shifts on the grass to face her mother once more. 'Motina, Jonas knew. Krystupas knew. The Duke says all the men knew but none of the wives. Why?'

Marytė shakes her head. 'Perhaps they struck some kind of deal with Stanislaw. I think he was under-reporting the number of hollows that were registered under the statute.'

'He was trying to ... help us?'

'It's possible.' Then it dawns on her. 'The mead.'

'Huh?'

'It was barter.' Stanislaw would never do anything out of the kindness of his heart.

'Oh, so that's what Tévas owed him.'

'What do you mean?'

Austeja slumps. 'Never mind.'

Austeja bites her lip and when she releases it a toothy indent remains on her bottom lip. 'And now Stanislaw is dead. There are only a few people I can think of who would not be happy with the Hollow Watcher's behaviour.'

Marytė shivers, the sun no longer warming her skin. The chilling realisation seeps in. Her knee throbs and she coughs. Austeja looks at her with concern, but Marytė ignores her, her thoughts drifting over innumerable worst-case scenarios. The tension she felt earlier has gone: in fact her body feels weighted down with a sense of impending doom. An overwhelming force, extracting energy from her body like a blood-sucking mosquito. Baltrus did not protect them. Stanislaw could not protect them. If they do not produce what is expected of them at harvest, there might be dire consequences.

How far would the Duke go to prove himself to the Duchy? If the men of the settlement could not stop these bad things from happening, then can she?

How is she meant to keep her girls safe?

CHAPTER TWENTY-SEVEN

Austeja

The tracks lead me nowhere.

They were more visible along the soft mud by the river, but once I entered the forest path towards our hollows, they disappeared. The long grass and shrubs that edge the path look undisturbed but I know they've travelled along the ground, as wolves cannot climb. I've never been able to track one but I have seen them on occasion, rounded amber eyes, watching me. I've never felt threatened, though. They're more active at dawn and dusk, which is why Motina only allows us in the woods during daylight hours. After what happened to Danutè, it is critical that I am more aware of my surroundings.

Bear tracks are easier to distinguish against the earth. They aren't as light on their feet as wolves. With strong claws that bury into the soft forest floor, their print is like an oversized human hand with stubby fingers. They remind me of Tévas's huge paws.

At the oak hollow, I don't hesitate to kick off my shoes and clamber up the rough grey-bark trunk, reaching out to the higher limb where I once sat with Jonas. The log seat he made for me sits at the base, dusted with wind-blown leaves. Will I see the wolf from here? Is this what it feels like, to be a wolf? Hiding. Waiting for prey to stumble across the path. I wonder if the hunted sense what will become of them. Did Stanislaw?

I know I won't see one. The wolf that disappeared on light feet is long gone. They travel great distances during the day, rarely staying in one spot for more than a few days. I once envied the ease with which they left behind familiar surroundings and established themselves somewhere new. But I won't leave Motina, or Danutè, or even Senelè. This is my home.

Motina has lost a daughter, a son, her husband: she cannot lose anyone else. And neither can I. She has been distant since our picnic under the Scots pine. That was the first time Motina spoke to me as an equal, listened to the information I presented and treated me as an adult. Something has shifted again. It seems most likely, now, that the Duke or one of his men killed Stanislaw. That's why he was never too concerned with investigating his death.

It is a lot to process. Motina has withdrawn into herself, her usual seriousness clouded with desolation.

A cracking sound echoes from below. I shift closer to the trunk, scanning the forest. Is it the wolf after all?

Deep voices strain through the trees as two men emerge from behind the pines. Jonas. My heart flutters at the sight of him, but then I see he is with his older brother, Tomas. The one I am meant to marry. He is taller and leaner than Jonas. I feel nothing when I look at him. I do not know him at all. It is not his face that I summon to mind as I drift off to sleep.

They do not see me but, as they near, Tomas's chatter becomes clear.

'We can't say anything, Jonas. It will only cause trouble for us all.'

'Isn't the truth more important?'

'Not always, brother.' He pauses near the oak and when he recognises what tree it is he physically recoils. 'Come, let's get away from this.'

'I thought I saw a felled tree around here,' Jonas says. He looks around the clearing and then steps under the oak's canopy. He circles the trunk, and his lip twitches when he spies the log seat he made for me. He brushes away the leaves and then stiffens.

He looks up. Our eyes lock and I hold my breath. I want it to be only us here in the forest, for him to join me on the branch so we can spy wolves together. But his brother slaps the back of his shoulder and Jonas stumbles forwards, our eye contact broken.

Tomas looks up and laughs. 'Are you spying on us, Austeja?'

I shake my head.

'Well, come on down from there. You can't be climbing trees like that when we are wed.'

My eyes narrow and I imagine myself leaning forwards and spitting upon the bald patch on the back of his head. Instead, I shuffle across the branch and climb down the trunk, landing on the soil with a silent thud.

When I turn around, Tomas presents me with a fistful of wildflowers.

He nudges his brother. 'This is what women want as a gift, brother. Not a lump of wood.'

I shake an oak leaf from my hair and take the wildflowers. Jonas looks forlorn, his brother smug. I pull the heads off the flowers and throw them to the ground. Stamp on them with my bare feet.

'Hey!'

I lift my chin. 'Not all women want flowers, and I certainly don't want you.'

Tomas growls at me but Jonas holds him back and this gives me enough of a lead to collect my boots, hike up my skirt and dash back through the forest. My heart thumps inside my chest and my limbs are energised, my senses on high alert, as if I am the one being hunted.

'Why do you think Tévas wanted to say sorry to me?'

Senelè stops scrubbing the pot, just for a moment, before she starts up again. She is probably still annoyed with me for questioning Tévas's honesty, but this continues to bother me. If the Duke or one of his men killed Stanislaw, and Stanislaw had Tévas's knife because he owed him mead, then why did Tévas want to apologise to me? Why not Motina?

'You ask a lot of questions.'

'It has been niggling away at me. What do you think it was about?'

'If what you heard is correct, and your father owed Stanislaw: the mead was running out, as he'd been too ill to make more last August and needed it for himself. I suppose that will be up to you and your mother

213

now ...' She shakes her head as if to dislodge troublesome thoughts. 'He must have promised him something else.'

'What?'

'Not what, my dear. Who.'

My mouth hangs open but no words escape. Me? My father wished to trade me?

Senelè dries her hands on a cloth and then places one on my shoulder. It is warm from the water but it does not feel pleasant. My skin feels hot, scorching, as if I am burning up from the inside out. 'Breathe, Austeja.'

And I do. I breathe in the forest air but it does not satisfy me. I draw in more and my lungs fill, my stomach protrudes, my mouth puckers. I want to take it all so that I am full and cannot think about all the things that have happened since winter. The deals that were made before the snow fell. The betrayals.

'Let it go, Austeja,' Senelè says.

The air listens. It is coaxed out of me on her demand. My stomach curls into my spine, my lungs deflate and my mouth is dry and bare.

'It will do you no good to dwell on this. Your father was ill: he wanted to protect his family. They were desperate times.'

'No, he wouldn't do that.'

She drops her hands and returns to scrubbing the pot. It is already clean. 'We are all capable of these things when we are under pressure. Your father was a wonderful man, but he was only human. He told me in his final days. He was filled with regret that he could not right this wrong before he died. The taxes were to be raised, he knew that, and he, along with the other men, chose to work with Stanislaw to mislead the Duke. He made choices to protect our harvest, knowing he may not be here to help with future ones. Even so, I would not have let you wed Stanislaw.'

I would have run away before that happened. I would not have married him. Tomas is unacceptable, but Stanislaw? That is far worse. Stanislaw is old and vile and conniving.

And dead.

I cannot imagine my father ever agreeing to this. My father was gravely ill, and he couldn't possibly have been thinking clearly. Senelè watches me and her eyes are just like my fathers, Tévas's had been duller in the weeks before he left us. He had been so unwell, barely lucid. But if I'm being honest with myself, he wasn't the same after returning from Alytus that summer. He and Azuolas changed, in body and in mind.

I see now it was the moment they realised our lives and livelihoods would change forever. The hard work we put in season after season would profit people who avoided getting their hands dirty. When Azuolas left us, some of Tévas's joviality still simmered. And then he became ill too. If Azuolas had survived, my father may not have acted in such desperation.

'Anyway, it was not to be. Stanislaw met an untimely death. But one thing your father was right about was the need for you to be wed. It is the only way for this family to survive. He was sorry, and so am I. But we need to look forwards. For Marytè.'

'So I am to wed and that is it? You said we should never marry within the same community. And what about all the things you said about diverting the future?'

'Sometimes the signs point to the simple things. If you marry Tomas, you will change the future. Our family will survive, we will succeed in future harvests, and we will pay what is due to the church and the Duke. There is power in these choices, if only you let yourself see it.'

I turn away from Senelè, biting back tears.

Is it possible to hold all of the power yet, at the same time, feel completely powerless?

CHAPTER TWENTY-EIGHT

Marytè

She thought they would send the larger of the two henchmen. Instead, the Duke made the interesting decision of sending the slighter, weasel-looking man. 'You're the temporary Hollow Watcher?' she asks, an eyebrow raised.

'I am,' he says without arrogance, and Marytè warms to him, just a little. Without the larger man beside him, he's hardly intimidating at all.

'Okay. So what do you need from me?'

'Nothing yet. I do not have much experience in caring for hollows—'

'The beekeepers care for the hollows.'

He reddens. 'Of course. I only meant that one of the roles of the Hollow Watcher is to look after the hollows, keep watch over them. I believe the former Hollow Watcher, Stanislaw, already took detailed information about the hollows from each of the keepers and registered it with the Duke. I just need to confirm the numbers, that is all.'

Marytè places a hand on her hip. So her instinct was right. The Duke did know that Stanislaw had deceived him and now he wanted to know exact numbers of the hollows. She would need to tell the truth or she might put her family in harm's way. She could not risk it. 'I have fifty hollows. There were fifty-five, but I lost five over winter. One, well, that was where Stanislaw was found. And the other four were in close proximity to that tree.'

'Did someone harm those too?'

'There was no sign of interference. It just happens sometimes that when a master dies, the bees go too.' Marytè swallows back the humiliation. She needn't let it get to her. This man hasn't a clue about the ways of the bees or their keepers. He just wants a tally, nothing more.

'I see. These five hollows are empty, then? Waiting for a swarm?'

Marytè nods. 'A few in our catchment, but there is no guarantee bees will take up residence. And even so, we cannot count those hollows in this harvest anyway.'

'Why is that?'

Marytè frowns and the man steps backwards.

'I just want to understand how it all works: that is all.'

She sighs. 'Because the swarm breaks away from the original hollow and leaves behind all the honey and honeycomb. They have to work quickly in a new hollow to weave the honeycomb and store enough honey to last them through the winter. We never take from a new hollow or the bees will die.'

'Ah. No, we do not want that. But they can be harvested from next autumn?'

'That's right.'

'Will you be able to do it on your own?' He makes a point of peering over her shoulder. 'I'm sorry about your husband's recent death.'

'I am not alone. I have my daughters to help, and my friends. Next spring my daughter will be wed so there will be a young man here the following harvest.'

'Okay, good.' He looks relieved and Marytè bristles. 'Well, there isn't time for me to personally count the hollows so I will be back at harvest to see what you've collected and ensure the fifty per cent is calculated correctly.'

Marytè purses her lips. She's imagining the buckets of honey, all their hard work, being divided up for the Duke.

'Have a good day.'

'You too,' she says, and as he walks unsteadily around the marshes and out of sight, she's left feeling a little unsettled by the encounter. She shakes it off. There is nothing to be done. The Hollow Watcher's replacement was inevitable. The Duke will not collect the taxes himself. That is beneath him.

The bees are loud today. They are in love with the warm weather and the abundance of flowers in the forest. She knows it will not be long now. There has been a repetitive, irregular sound coming from some of the hollows in the past few days. Bee hollows are busy environments, and the noise is constant. As the colony builds in strength the noise levels increase.

Marytè closes up the house and trudges towards the forest, around the marsh and over the bridge to be with her hollows. She finds herself at the newly carved oak hollow and wonders how she will climb all these trees on her own at harvest. Not all on her own, of course – Austeja will be there to help. Austeja will climb trees and collect honey too. She has only done this a few times in the past, more for amusement than to truly help. But now it is expected. Harvest typically lasts for days but if Marytè were to do it all on her own it would take weeks. And that is too long. The bees need time to replenish their supplies before they hibernate.

Austeja and Danutè have gone up to the church to donate their share of the crop. Beets, turnips, parsnips and onions. It will feed the priest, the caretaker and perhaps the Duke and his men too. She clucks her tongue. How would these men survive without them?

A roar echoes through the pines. Marytè stands upright, her right ear pressed to the wind. Her heart races and her skin tingles. A swarm is near!

The ear-piercing sound approaches. Two young men emerge from the thick woodlands with not one but two swarms, hanging from spruce branches, likely severed from the trees where they hung. The swarms are magnificent! She has never seen two so near each other and the sound is deafening: she can barely hear her own thoughts.

Tomas stalks over, his head held high in triumph. Jonas is more cautious, his focus on each step he takes, wary not to look out the corner of his eyes at the bees. It is dangerous during swarming. He holds the branch with two hands; it is heavy, weighed down by thousands upon thousands of bees clambering upon one another to form a tight armour around the queen. One big mass falling down to a point, like an upside-down ants' nest. The drones zip around in a frenzy; their primary focus is to find a place to live.

Marytè has just the place. Her gaze drifts up to the empty hollow and she is pleased with the honeycomb sample she left behind. She beckons Tomas closer. Bees zoom around his face and he grimaces. Jonas stands back. She knows he will be disappointed, as will Austeja, but this is the way of things. Her daughter must marry a firstborn son. The bees are wise and they do not choose bad men as their keepers. They do not sting good men.

'Come,' she says. 'Let us be friends. Lend me your little family.' Kinship through bees. The words are drowned out by her new bees, but she doesn't mind. They are glorious.

Bees dart up to the hollow and back to the branch held by Tomas. Back and forth. She imagines them telling their queen and the rest of the family all about the beautiful little home they have found. The size, what type of tree and how they will make it their own. Because they do. They will fill any holes and smooth out the rough edges and weave their honeycomb in the exact same manner they would if they'd found another hollow of a different size and shape. They all know what to do; they all have a part to play. That's how families work.

Tomas shifts the branch within his grip, but it won't be long until the pressure eases. She guides him to the trunk and the bees clinging to the branch begin to walk up the oak. Some of their kin fly overhead. Marytè and Tomas watch as they march towards the hollow. Some fly in and back out again as they acquaint themselves with their new home. Marytè is caught up with the spectacle of it all. It is some time before she notices the roar has dulled as the sound is contained once more in a hollow. She looks around and Jonas is gone. He is a good boy; he will find another hollow for his bees.

Tomas has turned away; he is rubbing at his arms and his neck. Marytè darts to him. She pulls up his shirtsleeve. 'What's this?'

He yanks his arm away from her. 'It's nothing. Just a reaction to nettle leaves I brushed up against.'

But the marks are on his neck too: round white welts with a pink centre. She leans closer and in one of them is a stinger left behind. Marytè baulks and steps away from Tomas. She feels queasy.

Is this punishment for going against the old ways and agreeing to a marriage within their community?

Tomas shrugs away. 'It's done now.'

She accepted his swarm and so the marriage is set as if they have shaken on it.

He turns and disappears the way he has come, scratching at his neck and his arms. Her mouth is dry and it is difficult to swallow as the realisation of what she has done dawns on her.

She has made a grave mistake.

CHAPTER TWENTY-NINE

Austeja

Senelè leads the prayer.

She leans forwards, kisses the soil. 'Žemyna, goddess of the earth, thank you for all your gifts. Mother goddess, please accept our offerings and bless the grassland. Be it bountiful for the bees and bring us a good harvest.'

Motina and Danutè are next: their prayers whisper in the wind. I adjust my headscarf, tucking back wisps of hair.

When it's my turn, I kneel beside the arrangement of rocks at the base of the trunk, tenderly stacked and circling the trunk like a stony boot. I shift my knees to avoid the knobby exposed roots, malformed toes on a giant's foot. For such a sacred tree there's been no attempt to keep the big toe within its rock-encased shoe.

I tilt forwards and kiss the earth. It's faintly damp and the roots, intertwined with the topsoil, smell like deep woodland. I extract the hunk of rye from my pocket and inhale its sweet and sourness. I press it to my lips and then place it beside the other bread offerings.

'Goddess Žemyna, please accept my offering and bless our grassland.'

For we need it. This year more than ever.

I want our sacred oak to speak to me. It remains soundless but for the gentle rustling of leaves. No sign of Žemyna.

From a kneeled position, my gaze travels upwards. The trunk is broader than any other I have come across in the forest. It would take eight men to circle it. It is positioned midway between the church and the bridge, in a clearing, as if the oak giant swung its sprawling limbs about to keep all other trees at bay. It soaks up the sunlight and basks in its gluttony.

I don't know who or how this oak was selected as the sacred tree for our harvest blessings, but it's been this way for as long as I remember. All the women are here and the girls too.

Later, the men will come by and throw the dregs of their mead around its feet, just for good measure.

There's a knothole hollow halfway between the ground and the first limb and another two higher in the canopy. The lower one is likely home to dormice or some other small rodent, and then further up a blue tit pokes its head out as if to see what all the commotion is about. Its muted-yellow chest is visible from my vantage point and I spy a hint of its blue cape. I suppose another bird species or an owl lives upstairs. No bees, though. The oak may sense the need for it to remain impartial: a place for us to come without the family mark of a hollow.

What do you have to say, hmm? Do you talk to the oak across the bridge, the one that lost its hive? My oak? I imagine the knobby roots snaking deep into the earth, spreading out in search of its kin, likely born from its seed. Eager to hear the stories, the haunting tales they have endured.

'Austeja.'

I jerk. It is Motina. 'Time to go to church.'

I groan, pulling myself up to stand. Goodbye, dear oak. Bring us good fortune.

I join Motina and Danutè and follow the crowd led by Senelè. I don't know how Motina copes. How does she find a way to live with the old ways and the new at the same time? I don't know what way I sway. I do feel the pull of the old ways, as if it is written in my blood. As if the knowledge and memories of our past live within my veins, inactive until summoned.

So what happens if I become a full Christian and let go of the old ways altogether? Would all the beliefs and knowledge of my ancestors be erased? We would rely no longer on intuition but on one man. God?

I tuck my hand into my skirt and curl my fingers around Tévas's knife. Even after discovering what he had planned for me, I want to have it close. Something precious to him, as I'd always believed I was.

Tévas was a devout Christian. It's as if he distanced himself as far from his mother's beliefs as possible. The truth is, I can see the appeal in it. The simplicity. Wishful thinking that God, our Lord, has a plan for us all.

Only, I don't want to rely on the plans of someone else. Tévas wanted me to marry Stanislaw; Motina and Smilte want me to marry Tomas. But what do I want? The one thing, one person, I have ever wanted is out of my reach.

The breeze picks up and I shiver, pulling my shawl over my shoulders. It is unusually cool for a summer's day. Or is it just me? I glance about but Motina and Danutė's foreheads glisten with a sheen of sweat. The air sweeps my cheek, like a hand caressing my skin. A woman's touch. I stop and feel my cheek. There's no hand there.

I look back at the oak. All around it the forest is still, the air thick as it is on a heated day. But the sacred oak shudders. The canopy lifts and drops, sways and shakes, as if it's having a sneezing fit while the others lean away.

What is happening here?

A pain in my head, between my brows. I press on it to relieve the pressure. As I close my eyes the image of Stanislaw returns. Why are you still here? I scream inwardly. I thought the manner of his death had been resolved, at least in theory. The Duke, or his men, were responsible. They had to be.

What do you want from me? To take on the Duke?

Well, forget it. I do not want to end up with a fate like yours.

Raven's eyes blink back. A solitary tear trickles down his cheek. Does he have regrets about his past? He never fully recovered from losing his family.

Before he died he had no one. Nothing to lose. He only had his mead.

His face fades away into snow. Red-stained snow.

'Austeja?' It is Motina again. Her brows crumple inwards. 'Are you coming?'

Stanislaw is gone, but the oak remains. Still, stagnant like its audience. As if it had never moved at all.

I shake my head. 'Yes, I'm sorry. I thought I saw something.'

'What is it?'

I should tell her. I want to tell her. But Motina will not believe it. She will dismiss it as she does anything Senelè says of the old ways. I can't tell her the forest speaks to me and I see the image of a justice-seeking dead man. No. I can never share this with her.

'It's nothing; come on.' I trudge past her, up the gradient to the church clearing.

Everyone attends church. Senelè heavily negotiated with the priest. He was adamant that our blessings were true sorcery, but Senelè convinced him they were merely a tradition to welcome a good harvest. She suggested he wouldn't want to be responsible for a bad harvest, would he?

No. Well, the priest agreed upon the condition we all present for church, to pray to our Lord for a good harvest. Senelè grumbled but Motina was pleased to have as many positive thoughts as possible sent in the way of the bees.

Jonas sits near the back with his brothers. He catches my eye and his mouth twitches. I haven't spoken to him since I spat at his brother and ran away from them. I hope Jonas knows that marrying Tomas is not what I want. I want *him*. But I don't know how he feels about me and his duty, like mine, is to stay home and support his parents.

The Duke sits in the front pew along with his two men. I sigh. So they've returned, then. The priest takes a step aside, as if intimidated by the Duke. 'Welcome to our first mass,' he says. 'I know I travel between different districts and we have faced some challenges in the months since we met, but I do want to welcome everyone here, officially. In the Grand Duchy of Lithuania, we priests have a duty to educate the settlers on our good Lord and to shift you all away from the ways of old. So I expect we will have a regular mass, every Sunday, from now on. When I am in Musteika, of course.'

Senelè, at this very moment, chokes on his words and erupts in a coughing fit. He attempts to speak again twice more but Senelè starts up again. The men up front shift further down the pew as if she has the plague.

'Senelè, that's enough,' Motina says in a harsh whisper. We both know her cough is real, but the timing is rather deliberate.

The priest clears his throat and stares pointedly in our direction, before he continues. 'I have a moral obligation to set my people on the right path. This is the future of Lithuania.'

Motina's fingertips dance against each other, as if willing him to get to the point about the bees. He seems to sense our impatience and clears his throat again. Each time he does this it makes his words less believable. 'Right, well, the end of summer is near and so too is our harvest. I know you are all eager to bring in a good harvest, to do your duties for the Duke and therefore our country. Please stand and repeat after me. Dear Lord, please bless our harvest.'

'Dear Lord, please bless our harvest.'

'May the forest be bountiful and the bees buzz with purpose and contentment.'

'May the forest be bountiful and the bees buzz with purpose and contentment.'

'May the parishioners bring in a bountiful harvest to serve our Dear Lord and our country.'

'May the parishioners bring in a bountiful harvest to serve our Dear Lord and our country.'

'Amen.'

'Amen.'

I open my eyes and glance around.

Is that it?

It's as if he has never before delivered a sermon, and most certainly knows very little about the bee harvest. Upon closer inspection, he seems far younger than I first realised. The way he tugs at his collar and pauses and clears his throat before he speaks. He is nervous. Inexperienced. He is in over his head.

Scared?

I would be if I were him, living on the land of the Duke. A Duke who delivers harsh punishments for betrayal. How will this priest walk the fine line of the Lord's will and the will of the Duke?

Perhaps this is a question for us all.

In the clearing outside the church, our people gather. There is much talk about harvest. The air is still, the sky is clear, all pointing to happy bees and good timing for honey collection. It will begin soon. This time, Motina will not have Tévas by her side, but me.

Jonas bumps shoulders with his younger brother Petras in a playful way. Only a year younger than me, Petras seems like a little boy compared to Jonas. Tomas joins them and Jonas's demeanour changes. So does Petras's. Tomas folds his arms across his chest and speaks without any facial expressions, except for the narrowing of his eyes. Jonas kicks at the ground and turns away from his brothers. He looks up and catches my eye, just for a moment, and then his head dips and he slinks away.

He is disappointed, as am I, and that brings me relief. I was not imagining what we shared. Tomas looks at me too, and attempts a smile, but it is more of a leer. His gaze upon me makes the hair on the back of my neck prickle.

I join a conversation with Aldona and Motina. They're discussing their crops.

Smilte approaches. 'Austeja, dear. How are you?'

'I am well, thank you. You?'

'Oh, very good. Very good,' she says, clasping my hands in hers. They are warm and clammy. Her scarf is damp around her face. 'You are a dear girl. I told you we would take care of you, didn't I?' She winks and my thoughts drift back to the first time she said this, at my father's wake. I felt vulnerable and alone and she was scheming a marriage. And even now, my family is vulnerable to the Duke's demands, and she is pleased with her plans.

She leans in closer. 'I know nothing has been made official yet, but Tomas will make you a fine husband.'

I look at the son she speaks of. He has joined his father. They stand side by side in stony silence. Their postures are mirrors but their faces are completely different. He is all Smilte. Jonas is more like his father in looks, but less like him in temperament. Far more appealing.

'Are you certain of that, Smilte?' The words tumble out and it catches both of us off guard.

She presses her lips together and then forces a smile. 'It is God's will. You are exactly what he needs, my dear.' She pats my shoulder and shifts her body so I am excluded from the conversation she joins with Aldona and Motina.

I want to go home. Not to the cottage, but to the oak. To sit on my log chair. I know when I am wed, I will not be able to drift about the forest as I do now. I will have home duties and beekeeping tasks too. I will live in the same home, with my family, but life will be different.

Did Motina and Tévas like each other before they were wed? Their marriage was arranged, somewhat, but they seemed happy. Two different people who worked well together and respected each other. Will it be like that with Tomas? Will I grow to love him?

I steal one last look at Jonas. My feelings come naturally for him, but just as easily as they have come, I will need them to go away. He is not my fate. Motina is right, and so is Senelè. The priest is right too. We

231

all have a duty to serve the Duke and the Duchy. I don't want to think about what would happen if we didn't. Jonas doesn't look my way, but I am being watched. The Duke stands with some of the men, smiling and talking, but his gaze is on me. Neck hairs prickle, again.

How have so many things changed since winter? I do not know who to trust. The wind and the forest pull me in one direction; my family and parish pull me in another. What I do know is that my father deceived us. Senelè did too, not telling me about his arrangement with Stanislaw. I must forget about Jonas. I must forget about what the Duke did to Stanislaw. I must accept my fate. Next spring, when I wed, Motina will finally be able to relax. We will all be okay.

Perhaps, now I have discovered these innate abilities, I can use them to my advantage. The forest can protect me, help me protect myself. To wield some power in this unwanted marriage.

PART IV

HARVEST

CHAPTER THIRTY

Marytè

The stream wraps around her skin, cool and crisp like a linen shawl. It's summer's end and the forest air warms her despite the cool of the water. It is only in summer, when the days are long and the sun bears down with force, that she can fully submerge herself. A wash down from a bucket usually suffices, but not today.

Marytè is preparing for harvest. She rinses her face first and dips her head back in the stream, massaging her hair from scalp to ends. Then she scrubs her arms and pits, her legs and her aching feet. One must be clean and not smell strongly of food or sweat when approaching the hollows, or else provoke the bees to sting en masse.

'Scrub yourselves well, girls,' she says to her daughters, who are splashing one another by the river's edge while Senelè, further upstream, steers clear of the commotion.

They all wear white linen slips, having recently scrubbed their outer wear and left it to dry on the nearby rocks. While they clean their clothes as often as possible in the warmer months, it feels good to wash oneself from head to toe, and their clothing too. Senelė has refreshed their straw beds with herbs, to keep away lice and rodents, leaving a fragrant smell throughout the cottage. It is as if they are all starting afresh, after the grimy months of death and grief and calculating men.

The heat pulls the moisture from her skin and so she sinks into the water and lies to float on her back for a moment or two. A little peace before the real work commences.

Harvest begins tomorrow.

The weather is good and Marytè trusts Austeja's prediction of clear skies, and no damp or windy weather to make the bees irritable. A calm forest and calm bees will make it easier to collect honey.

A change in water pressure rustles Marytè back upright, her feet finding the rocky base to steady herself. Austeja glides past her and then comes close to her mother.

'Motina, how do you feel about tomorrow?'

Motina makes a sound at the back of her throat; she pushes back the tickle and meets her daughter's eyes. 'It will be okay. We'll be okay.'

'I know we'll be okay, Motina,' she says, rolling her eyes. 'I feel excited, but nervous too. And I've never felt anything about harvest before, apart from enjoying the amazing feast at the end of each day.'

It's true, she's always been indifferent. Austeja previously held no responsibility; she was accountable to no one. This season is different. Marytè will miss Tévas's presence at harvest but, if she is honest, she will be kept so busy there will be little time to think about her loss.

It will likely creep up on her at the festival when the beekeepers and families gather to celebrate their collection and re-energise with a hearty meal. When she sees her friends with their husbands and Marytè sits alone – this is when it will unsettle her most.

She and Baltrus were used to spending their days apart and going about their duties, but in the evenings they came together, caught up on things and made plans for the day to follow. These conversations take place in her head now: reviewing the day that was and planning for tomorrow. Sometimes there are so many thoughts in her head she fears they will seep out of her and pollute her daughters. Motina takes a deep breath and swims back to the riverbank.

How does she feel about it all? There is a knot in her stomach like those in the ropes she uses to mount a hollow tree. There is worry sitting there, winding itself tight. There is so much deliberating on the coming days.

But her chest also feels light, pulsing with excitement.

She recalls feeling this way after her father's death upon the first harvest. Grief and sadness and yearning, but also eagerness to distance herself from these feelings and focus on collecting honey. There is something deeply satisfying in bringing in a harvest on her own. Being self-reliant.

Her sopping feet sink into the sandy bank as she tries to walk lightly back to the grass. She finds a smooth rock to lean against while her slip dries. It is lightweight and so it shouldn't take long at the hottest part of the day.

'Motina,' Austeja calls, treading along the sandy bank towards her. 'You didn't answer my question.'

'Oh. My mind was elsewhere.' She laughs softly and takes in her daughter's demeanour. She seems lighter in heart too, so perhaps she has accepted her fate, in marriage and profession. Harvest will be good for her. It will keep her busy too, and thoughts of her father at bay. 'I suppose I also have mixed feelings about it.'

'Hmm.' Austeja sits beside her as they watch Danutè ducking under water and then leaping up like a frog. 'I will do my best, Motina, to make harvest go smoothly for us.'

'I know,' Marytè says. 'I am grateful for your help.'

'We'll do this together.'

A flicker of guilt settles in Marytè's stomach. Her daughter's life has changed enormously since winter. A young woman, soon to be wed. A future planned. But it is sharing her beekeeping knowledge and skills that gives her the most joy. On impulse, Marytè grabs her daughter's hand and intertwines their fingers. 'We'll make a beekeeper out of you yet.'

The sun sits low on the horizon, air stagnant against a cloudless sky. Marytè leads the women into the forest, her daughters in a single file behind her. Boots crack on sticks, leaves and dry earth. Senelè hums to herself at the rear, occasionally breaking the silence with whooping coughs that spill out of her as if she is a hawk ridding itself of undigested waste. She sounds more and more like Baltrus.

With effort, Marytè pushes aside any niggling worries.

She draws in a deep breath, filling her body with positive energy. Paying close attention to her feet, one in front of the other. Stay calm. She coughs too. Hopes that rids her of any negative emotions, leaves them behind on the path, away from the hollows. She needs everything to go perfectly today.

Their lives depend on it.

It's why they all smell fresh and clean and are dressed in light-coloured clothing, though she can't remember why that is a bee's preference. It was something her father once told her.

To outsiders it may all seem superstitious, but these rituals are important to a beekeeper like Marytè. It is these rituals that see her through a successful harvest. This is why she does things in the exact same manner, at exactly the same time, every year. Because it works. And she cannot risk an alternative outcome.

Birdsong radiates from the canopies above. Rabbits dart into the grassland and a fallow deer watches them, motionless, near a linden tree. Marytè knows it is not just her family and the dawn-curious creatures frolicking through the forest, but her bičiulystè too. Aldona, Elena and Smilte will also be up with their husbands and children, preparing for harvest. It's comforting, knowing her people are all working autonomously within an interconnected community. All for the same purpose.

She reaches the first hollow: the lime-tree knothole hollow, the first one she climbed when Baltrus had left and whispered the news of their changing fate. The first bee family to accept her as the new master. Once again, she runs her fingertips over the axe-mark tattooed into the trunk by Baltrus.

It is one of their older hollows. Twenty-four years? Yes, they swarmed in the summer before Azuolas was born. There have been many other hollows full of bees on their allotted land, but this was the first bee family to choose her and Baltrus as their beekeepers. It was a special moment.

Marytè intentionally breathes in through her nose and releases it through compressed lips, letting go of the pain. Freeing her mind of sadness and her chest of tension. She can think of such things tonight, as she feasts, but right now she must concentrate on her bees.

She prepares her rope and secures her foot in the loop before leaping off the ground to rest against the trunk.

'Should I start on the next hollow, Motina?' Austeja asks.

Marytè shakes her head. 'No, you will watch me first. Then we will see.'

Austeja shrugs. 'Fine. I will climb up the back of the trunk.'

'Use your rope,' Marytè says, breathing out the anxiety. There is no need to worry. She will teach Austeja and make a successful harvest.

'It'll be too bulky and get in the way. Don't worry: I can climb up the ropes without a harness.'

Marytè is about to insist she prepare her ropes, but Austeja has already rolled up her skirt and launched herself up onto the rope lassoed

240

around the trunk. She is barefoot. How she manages to balance, Marytè will never know. Austeja has the fingers and toes of a red squirrel, swivelling joints that grip and manipulate any tree formation. When Austeja was young Marytè thought it was just a child's innate agility, but she's never outgrown it.

As they reach the hollow, Marytè ignores the creak and groan of her right knee. Danutè climbs the ladder with the moss-covered branch, smoke billowing at its tip, and hands it to her.

'Come closer,' she whispers to Austeja, who shuffles along the rope and leans against Marytè's harness so she can see into the hollow. Bees buzz noisily around the entrance. Marytè inserts the smoky branch into the hollow and within a few minutes the bees emerge, docile, their buzzes muted as if in a drunken haze. Many have filled up their little pouches with nectar, likely preparing for retreat. But they will not have to go far, or for long, as Marytè swiftly cuts away chunks of honeycomb. She takes one third, hesitates and then cuts off a little extra. The Duke's demand echoes in her ears. Take more than you need. Fine, she thinks. But just a little bit more.

'Are you paying attention, Austeja?'

'Yes.'

'Good.'

Austeja hands her the pine bucket passed up by Danutè. Marytè places the honeycomb into the bucket, attaches a rope to the handle, knots it and then lowers it to the ground. Senelè sets the bucket aside. When it is full, she will take it back to the cottage and load it into the barrels. One for the Duke and one for their family. Marytè hopes Senelè can manage all the walking today. Danutè will have to help her: the buckets get heavy with the weight of the honeycomb.

Marytè hands Austeja a knife. 'Here. I had this made for you. It is about time you have your own beekeeping tools.'

Austeja breaks into a grin. 'Really? Thank you.'

'Now, take your time getting down.'

By the time Marytè has loosened her harness and handed the branch back to Danutè, Austeja is on the ground. Marytè shakes her head. Being cautious is not in Austeja's nature.

Marytè lowers herself down each rung of the rope, loosening the lengths and walking down the tree. At the last drop, she places one foot on the ground, but the other catches in the rope and the grounded leg suddenly twists.

'Ahh.' She moans as her knee buckles, the kneecap slipping off to the side, causing a knifing pain through her leg.

'Motina! Are you okay?' Austeja is by her side, unravelling the rope, and guides her to sit on her backside on the grass.

Motina looks at the damage and then flicks her head away. Her knee is jutting out at an odd angle.

'Dislocated,' Senelè says, voicing Marytè's fears.

It's happened once before, after she birthed Danutè, who was an enormous baby. Carrying the extra weight in pregnancy placed strain on her hips, back and knees. After the birth the weight lifted, but it was as if her knees didn't know what to do with themselves. One moment she was picking up a fallen blanket off the ground and the next she was lying beside it, her knee slipped out of joint. Weeks of recovery. Baltrus had to bring Danutè to her every time she needed feeding. Marytè had resented her failing body then.

And she resented it now, too.

This is my punishment.

She should have been a better Christian. A better mother. Wife. Beekeeper. If she had been better, then this wouldn't have happened.

'We must get her home and set her knee right,' Senelè says to Austeja, as if Marytè is invisible.

'No.' Her voice sounds foreign. 'Do it here. I must continue with harvest.'

There is a pause and Marytè doesn't dare to look at the glances exchanged by her daughter and mother-in-law. No, she will not accept this fate.

'We're taking you home, Motina.'

'No,' she cries, pushing everyone away. 'I must continue. It is my duty.'

Austeja crouches down, as if to speak to a small child. 'You will go home to rest and I will continue with harvest.'

'You cannot do all this on your own.'

'It's okay, Motina,' Austeja says, stroking her face, smiling. 'I will take care of us.'

Marytè is lifted by Senelè and Austeja, awkward and off balance, but they manage somehow. Marytè wants to help them, but she feels like a dead weight. Unable to support her own body, unable to care for her family.

It feels like days – years – have passed before they reach the cottage.

'Go,' Senelè says and Marytè watches her daughters scatter from the room, an emptied bucket in hand.

Senelè fills a mug of mead and encourages Marytè to drink it. The very last of her medicinal supply.

She passes Marytè a chunk of bread. 'To bite down on.'

Marytè does what she is told. Anything not to focus on the pain.

'Okay, on three.' Senelè places firm hands around Marytè's knee.

One. The crunch of rye.

Two. The pop of the kneecap.

Three. Plunging into darkness.

CHAPTER THIRTY-ONE

Austeja

The sun drops behind the tree canopies, casting shadows in the undergrowth. Bird calls pacify as they nestle in their nests and the bees return to their hollows after a productive day in the summertime forest. I carve out the honeycomb from the hollow I'm perched at as the bee inhabitants buzz around in a smoke-induced stupor. I place it in the bucket, now full, and lower it by rope to the ground. It lands with a thud.

'Danutè?'

A moan and a groan. 'Yes, I'm here.' She trudges towards the foot of the pine tree, her face reddened from the sun and her eyes drowsy. 'Can we go to the festival now? I'm hungry.'

'Yes, it's time to go home.'

The forest shifts from day to night. The gluttonous sun animals will hibernate and the nocturnal creatures will prowl about in the darkness. When that happens we don't want to be out here with a bucketful of tempting, sweet honey.

By dusk, only the two of us remain. I sent Senelè back to the cottage a few hollows back when Liudvikas came by to help. He collected from three of our hollows, filling the bucket and carrying it back to the bridge for Danutè to lug the rest of the way home. Senelè coughed and hacked more as the day wore on. It was difficult to concentrate with the constant reminder of her failing health.

There is time, later, to worry about that.

Liudvikas's arrival was perfect timing. With the additional help, I have harvested fourteen hollows on my first day.

It was kind of Liudvikas to help and he said Dominykas will stop by tomorrow afternoon. As if there is an unspoken agreement among the bičiulystè to help and support us. News has travelled fast, probably with Senelè's help, about Motina's condition. Even at the busiest time of bee season, the beekeepers are still generous with their time, blatantly ignoring the encouragement of the Duke to make competitors of us.

As I loosen the rope harnessed around my waist and walk down the tree, one foot and then the other, my legs cry out in pain. Climbing, balancing, lowering, raising, walking and heaving, all day long. My muscles are pleasantly fatigued. It feels good, knowing my body can keep up with the work of any man. That I can contribute to my family. Provide for them.

Hanging from trees has given me plenty of time to think about the fragility of my family. Senelè's failing health, Motina's injury. How has it come to this? My little sister and me, left responsible for the honey collection of fifty hollows?

I place myself with steady feet on the ground. Careful not to injure myself, like Motina.

Poor Motina. She will not be happy to stay at home all day, banished from her beloved hollows. And only just having become a master beekeeper! She does not do 'resting' very well. Busy, yes. Resting, no, that's not in her nature. I did not return home for lunch, instead snacking on chunks of rye and the berries Danutè foraged nearby. But Senelè returned with messages from Motina after she emptied each of her buckets back home.

Use the rope, don't take any risks.

Only take half, no more.

Make sure the bees are calm.

Look after the bees.

Be careful.

This last message was repeated copiously throughout the day. It was as if Motina had spent the whole day perched on my shoulder, chirping away like a sparrow. I know it is hard for her to relinquish control, especially when so much is balancing on this harvest, but I have proved today that I can do it.

'Can we go to the festival now?' Danutè asks for the dozenth time. The festival is always the highlight. Physically exhausted but mentally energised by the satisfaction of harvest, the beekeepers gather to feast. To thank the bees, and the gods, for a successful reaping.

I scoop Danutè in close to me and hug her, kissing the top of her head. 'Thank you for helping me today. I couldn't do it without you.'

'Really?'

'Really.'

She grins and I laugh, still incredulous over the situation we find ourselves in. But proud too.

'Let us taste the harvest.'

Danutè's face lights up. 'Can we? Motina never lets us until the end of harvest.'

I wink. 'It will be our little secret.'

I pull out a mass of honeycomb and extract my new knife from my basket, cracking open the wax with a clean slice. Amber-coloured syrupy honey oozes out. Danutè wipes it up with her index finger and places the lot in her mouth. Her eyes roll back in her head. 'Mmm. This is sooo good.'

I laugh. It is nice to see my little sister happy, indulging in something fun and a little bit mischievous. I sweep some of the honey up and drag my mouth back over the finger. 'Mmm. It really is good.'

'Thanks, Austeja.'

I ruffle her scarf. 'Let's go. Do you think you can carry the bucket?'

A deep scowl creeps along my sister's forehead. 'I'm so tired, Austeja.'

'It's okay. I'll take it.' I loop the ropes over my shoulder, my muscles groaning with the weight. I check my tools are all in the basket tied at my waist and then heave up the bucket of honeycomb. We stumble along the forest path, my muscles begging me to stop. But I must push on. I fear if I do so I may not be able to continue. My sister mopes along the path ahead, scanning the grassland. Wary of snakes.

My heart squeezes with guilt as I recall her brush with death.

Time for thinking later: must push on.

The festival awaits us and I feel more deserving of it than ever.

The herbs tucked into my straw bed have dried out, but their scent lingers. As I lie down, drawing the blanket up over me, my body sinks into the cot and the ache peels away like honey from a comb. Oozing, and relaxed.

I was too nervous to sit at the festival, fearing I may not be able to get back up. My body felt deliciously fatigued and, apart from fleeting conversations with Aldona, Smilte and Elena, who all insisted I reach out for help and sent their best wishes to Motina, I did not speak to anyone else. I could sense Jonas near. Tomas was there too, chest puffed up and bragging about his collection. The Duke made his rounds at the gathering, but I was careful to leave before he could find me.

I was wrong about him. I can no longer pretend he is not a murderer, or at the least the instigator of murder. It is best I keep my distance.

We stayed only long enough to fill our bellies and Danutè, who was sleepy and satiated, did not complain when I ushered her home. It didn't feel right being there without Motina.

She smelled of mead – more doses kindly donated by Smilte – when we returned, her knee propped up higher than her hip. She was dozing, but her eyes fluttered open as we entered. Her words were slurred, but

I could just make out what she said.

'Proud of you, Austeja.'

I am giddy, drunk on praise. Such affirmation rarely comes from my mother. Those words fill me up more than the feast. If it weren't for my weary limbs, aching back and the darkened sky, I'd feel bolstered enough to go back into the forest and continue with the collection.

But I must rest for tomorrow. The work must continue. Motina may be in denial, but I know she cannot see out this harvest on her own.

Just as I'm drifting off, Senelė's cracking feet shuffle across the cottage. My lids are heavy and I cannot open them but I hear her adding a log to the hearth. A crackle and the light behind my lids shine brighter, momentarily, before dulling again.

She half-coughs, half-exhales and then whispers to the fire. 'Goddess Gabija. Forgive me. Protect my family. If you must take someone, take me. I am deserving of it. Take me.'

The words settle upon me, but sleep pulls me under before I can make sense of them.

I wake at dawn to birdsong. It is light, and the fire dances low in the hearth. Senelė snores. Her night-time whispers tease my consciousness, but I shake them off.

It must have all been a dream.

CHAPTER THIRTY-TWO

Marytè

She rouses, groggy and blurry-eyed. A day or two, maybe more, of sleeping and drinking. Brooding and fretting. Dulling the pain in her knee.

In her heart.

Oh, why did this happen to me?

She rolls onto her side, and bile rises up her throat. She swallows it. Moans. Blinks.

Where is everyone?

Sunlight. Darkness. Sunlight. Darkness.

She strains to keep heavy lids raised. Daytime. They'll all be out at the hollows.

Where I should be.

Failure. That's how she feels. She failed her family and failed her bees. She only lasted a few months after losing her husband before her body fell apart and her mind plunged into dark thoughts she so desperately tried to avoid. The mead provokes them, yanks them out of the depths of her mind and parades them around in front of her in her rare waking hours.

Punishment.

I deserve all of it.

The harvest has been taken from her because of what she did when her husband was ailing. It was not her; she was not thinking clearly then. Was not careful. Just as she was not careful scaling the tree and now her knee is a pathetic, throbbing mess.

This is all my fault and my daughters will suffer.

Marytè looks about for more mead. The bittersweet, extra-strength mead bequeathed by Smilte. The bucket is nowhere in sight. Where has that wicked Senelè hidden it?

She pushes herself up onto one elbow, her head spinning and a faint throb in her knee. Just push through. Find the mead and you can sleep away all the pain and hurt.

She draws herself up to sit. Her head spins, as if she were a spotted hawk circling the air for a water bird to feast upon, ascending sharply and then plunging into descent on the hunt. Even when her body is still and her eyes closed, her crown sways at a nauseating rhythm.

She blinks, slow and with force, trying to counteract the queasiness. It is no use. Only mead will fix this. It fixes everything. It eased the Hollow Watcher's loneliness, Baltrus's physical discomfort and now it will take away those dark, guilty feelings she wishes not to wallow in.

She lifts her swollen, bound knee and hangs her legs, one and then the other, over the side of the cot. Her feet rest on the cool floor. They are dirty and she smells of sweat. When did she last bathe? A few days ago. Yes, in the stream with her girls.

The bees will have nothing of her now. Her nostrils flare with the stink.

It is this one thought, of her bees, that makes her buckle over herself. Chest on thighs, arms limp. The shame is so unbearable, so essential, that she can no longer hold her own weight, even while sitting. Her body is useless. Her mind is scattered. What is a beekeeper without a lean body and clear mind?

I am nothing. I am no longer a wife. I am barely a mother, for it is obvious my girls can survive without me. I am not a beekeeper. Useless: that's what I am.

I cannot stand myself.

Mead. It dulls the painful feelings, the mortifying thoughts of worthlessness. Hopelessness. Mead will tempt her into another long, deep sleep, where dark thoughts and pain become background noise. She straightens her spine. Clasps her hands on the edge of the cot, leans forwards to put weight on her feet.

'Agh.' Marytè brushes off the throb in her knee. Does not look at it at all. Steps one shaky foot ahead of the other. Reaches the barrels. One for the blasted Duke, and one for her family. They are filling up quickly. The honeycombs hauled back by Senelè and her daughters have been drained into the barrels. The wax is kept separate. Her heart twists. How hard her daughters have worked to get this far.

In the amber liquid she sees her reflection and in her reflection she sees her mother. Her throat tightens.

How has it come to this?

I have tried so hard to be a different woman, a better woman than my mother. And yet, here I am, stewed on mead. Tears drip into the honey. Salty tears. Marytè pulls away. I ruin everything I touch. Staining even the sweetest things in life.

'Marytè?' A deep, shy voice ricochets off the pine walls. Rattles her body, right into her soul. Fills her heart with hope.

'Baltrus?' She whirls around, her knee rotates and groans. She cringes. Not at the pain, but at the man who stands before her.

'No, not Baltrus,' he says. 'It is me.'

'Albertas?' Her former priest. She glances about the room, but it only confirms she is all alone. There is no one here to witness the shame she bears. 'What are you doing here?'

He ducks under the doorway and enters the cottage, a shadow falling over his face. 'You know why I am here.'

'Baltrus is, he is—'

'Gone. I know.' He taps two fingers to his forehead, his sternum, then the left and right shoulders. Brings his hands together and lowers his head. 'I am very sorry for your loss.'

Her insides coil, tears threaten to spill again, as if her former priest were delivering the news for the very first time. She reaches back for the barrel to steady herself. Puts weight on her good leg. Runs a hand over her puffy, drawn face. Her mother's face.

'Marytè.' He steps closer.

'Why are you here?' she asks again.

He casts his eyes over her limp leg. 'Are you injured?'

Marytè shuffles a little towards him. 'It is dislocated. I cannot complete harvest.'

'Oh, my dear.' He comes to her, takes one of her hands between both of his. They are not warm as she expects, but cool to touch. The way Baltrus's were when he took his final breath.

'I am here for you,' he says, answering her earlier question. 'I am here for you, Marytè.'

She licks her lips, feeling dehydrated and light-headed. 'It is too late. Too late for everything.'

'No, it is not too late for us, my dear.'

'No. He is gone. My harvest is going on without me. There is nothing left here.'

'So come with me.'

She shakes her head.

'We can be together.'

She pulls her hand away. 'No, Albertas. Not this again. What we did: it was a mistake.'

He recoils. 'Please do not say that.'

An intrusive image of Perkūnas and Saule comes to mind, and Senelè's tale of Saule's betrayal of the God of thunder. Marytè's body shakes as if he were here with her, thunder and lightning striking her through the heart.

'It is true. My husband was dying. I was not in a good place. You were my priest. You were there to support me, comfort me. It should never have been anything more.'

'It was always meant to be more, Marytè. You know that. What we have is special. Our connection transcends death. It transcends God. That's why I am here. I am willing to give up everything so we can be together.'

'No! I will not betray my husband. I will not abandon my children or leave my bees. This is my home. You are not my home.'

He sucks his teeth; kindness transforms into fury. 'You will not shame me. I have come all this way for you. I waited, all this time. For you,' he spat.

'You were my friend.' Marytè's mind begins to clear. It all comes back to her now, what she has done, what he has done. What they did together. That one kiss by her husband's bedside. That shared, intimate moment of grief and connection, that one mistake.

She hoped to take it to her grave. She tried not to think of it – avoided it so fervently that she almost believed it had never happened at all. And now here he is, making a bad day even worse. 'But you took advantage of me, a grieving wife. I needed your support and guidance. I no longer need anything from you.'

Albertas towers over her, his build similar to her husband's, his hand raised as if to hit her.

His fury slices through her, as if he were Perkūnas bearing a sword, ready to split her in half. Punish her as he did Menulis.

Or would she share the fate of Saule, the wife who betrayed Perkūnas, and be banished as a witch? Wandering the riverbanks, miserable and alone.

'I saw him in you. Or you in him. I just wanted, in that moment, to have my husband back.' I thought you were Baltrus. I could, in that moment, pretend you were him. You were not sick, not dying, not leaving your family. Not leaving me.

'You have taken everything from me, Marytè,' Albertas says through clenched teeth. 'I confessed what we had and I was sent away. They ripped me away from you and now they have filled your head with these lies.'

'Albertas.' Marytè lowers her voice. Lightly touches her fingers on his hand. Compels herself to remember the kind friend he once was. 'I'm sorry.'

He flicks her hand away and looks past her shoulder at the barrels. 'Perhaps it is time I take from you.'

'Albertas, no—'

He plunges his huge paws into the barrel, the Duke's barrel, and heaves up handfuls of treacly honey and brings it to his mouth.

A bear in a frenzy.

CHAPTER THIRTY-THREE

Austeja

I spy Jonas through the pines as I make my final descent from a linden tree. My last one. Fifty hollows in four days.

The linden hollow's opening was small and it was tricky to pick away at the honeycomb. I've taken less than I am meant to, but it is better than nothing. I don't want to damage the bees' food source for winter.

'Austeja.'

I drop to the ground, loosen the ropes around my waist.

'Can I offer my help?'

I shrug. 'I'm done for the day. I've already sent Danutè back with a full bucket. I just have this, here.' I point to the small honeycombs in the bucket by his feet.

'Oh.' He breathes out heavily. 'I'm sorry: I wanted to get away sooner. I know you've been doing all this on your own. I'd finished my hollows early, but my mother kept coming up with new tasks for me to do.'

I sigh. 'She sent your brother.'

His chin snaps up. 'Tomas?'

'Yes, he helped me with a couple of hollows.' And he was perfectly pleasant. I didn't mind his company, until he spoke of our proposed marriage.

He said, 'You don't need to worry about your mother. We will be well off once we are wed.'

We aren't yet officially engaged so his comment annoyed me. And I will always look out for my mother. I do not need him for that.

Jonas shakes his head. 'That explains why she kept me busy, then.'

'I'm sorry.'

Our eyes meet. 'Me too.'

'Austeja, I've tried—'

'It's okay,' I say, my voice wavering. 'I know.'

A pause. 'I brought your mother a swarm.'

'What do you mean?'

'I overheard her talking to my mother about you being wed. I knew they had Tomas in mind. He is the first son. But I've always wanted to be out of that house. I'm not like them ... I promised to bring her a swarm. And I did.'

'You did? And then what?' I hold my breath.

'Tomas brought her one too. She chose him.'

My stomach tenses. 'She chose him?' I know she takes the bičiulystė

259

rules seriously, but bringing a swarm can create new rules, new ties. She could have chosen the man I wanted to marry, but she didn't. Betrayal tears at my insides. Why would she do that?

'You can't marry him.'

The ropes drop in a heap on the ground and I step outside them, moving to Jonas. 'I don't want to, but I don't have a choice, Jonas. I know this will be difficult for both of us, but we'll have to find a way to live with it.' Finally voicing what we both feel.

He shakes his head, takes my hand. Our hands tell the story of harvest. Scrapes, cuts, calluses, dirt-embedded nails. Warmth. 'You don't understand. He's not ...' Jonas squeezes my hand tighter, drawing me closer. He peers back over his shoulder, lowers his voice. 'He's not a good person.'

I gulp. I feel safe with Jonas, but his words set me on edge. Everything about his demeanour is worrying. Why is he saying this about his own brother? Jealousy? No. It's more than that. He knows something ...

'He's arrogant and, well, not all that likeable, but that doesn't make him a bad person.' My mouth is dry and lumps of unease form in my throat. I have to convince myself it will all be okay because I cannot envision a life that is not.

He sighs, and lowers my hand, but does not let go. Our arms swing in the tender breeze. It feels like the most natural thing in the world. Only, Jonas is not mine. He is not my future.

'Jonas, will you do something for me?'

His hand stills mine but my heart beats frantically. 'What is it?'

I free my hand and step back. I close my eyes for a moment, drawing

260

on what little strength remains after a wearisome day. My hand clasps on the object in my pocket and then I place it in Jonas's hand. 'Will you return my tévas's knife to his grave. Please? I can't bear to do it on my own.'

'Yes, of course.' He pockets the knife and then reaches for my hand again. 'Listen, Austeja, there's something I need to tell you—'

'Austeja!'

We jump apart, heart racing, body on alert. Danutè runs towards me, her face flushed, eyes wet. 'Austeja,' she says again, her voice catching in the breeze. She falls into my arms.

'What is it?'

'It's …' She pants heavily. She must have run the entire way here. 'I—'

'Take a deep breath, little sister.'

Danutè draws in a shaky breath; it catches in her chest. 'It's Motina.'

I stiffen. 'Is she okay?'

Danutè licks her lips and shakes her head. 'I can't explain it. You must come home now.'

'Where's Senelè?'

'She's visiting Aldona. Please, we must hurry.' She points at Jonas. 'You should come too.'

Jonas catches my eye and I nod. Yes, come. I do not know what lies ahead. He hauls up the rope, looping it over his shoulder. I fling my tools into the basket and pick up the bucket. 'Let's go, then. Quick.'

Danutè says no more, only confirming that Motina is alive as she trails behind us on the forest path. I drop everything outside the house and glance back at my sister. She hides behind Jonas and points to the door. He watches me, waiting for direction.

'Wait here,' I say, sounding more self-assured than I actually feel.

I push open the door and the first thing that hits me is the sweet smell of honey. And then I see it. Honey.

Everywhere.

Motina is curled up on the floor beside one of the barrels.

'Motina.' I rush to her side, roll her towards me and am relieved to see the rise and fall of her chest. 'Motina?'

'Austeja.' Her voice quivers. 'Oh, what have I done?'

'Motina, are you hurt?'

She mumbles her response. 'No.'

'There is honey everywhere.' Panic rises, my heart knocking against my ribs. The Hollow Watcher visited earlier, checked the barrels. Marked the honey levels. He knows how much we have and tomorrow he will know we have cheated him. What will happen to us then?

'I could not stop him.'

'Him?'

Her eyes snap open and she throws her arm out, index finger at the doorway. 'Him!'

'Jonas?'

Motina blinks. 'Who?'

I tuck my arms under her armpits and pull her up to sit. She is sticky all over.

She shakes her head. 'No. Not him: Albertas.'

'Albertas? The old priest?'

'Yes!' Her voice rises. 'Who else?! He came here and made this mess.

He was gorging on the honey. Our honey. How could he do this to me?'

I share a worried glance with Jonas. 'Motina, Albertas is not here. No one is here.'

'He must have left; if you leave now, you may find him on the path.'

'We just came from the forest path. We've seen no one. You're not making any sense.'

'He ate it all and he made this mess,' Motina says again, but this time with less conviction. 'He did.'

My stomach drops as I examine my mother. Motina's mouth is smeared with honey, her hands are caked in it, and it's pooled all around her. There are no footprints but her own. Her eyes are bloodshot, and she reeks of mead.

'Oh, Motina. What have you done?'

After her face is wiped clean and her hair combed out, Motina is tucked into bed and immediately falls into a deep, spasmodic sleep. I don't know what she sees when she closes her eyes, but it must be frightful. Why else would she have done this?

And what does it have to do with Albertas?

Danutè shivers despite the warmth holding on to the day as dusk falls. I usher her out of the way, sit her down on her bed and wrap a shawl around her shoulders.

'What am I going to do?' I whisper.

'Jonas said he could help us,' Danutè says, through chattering teeth.

'Yes, but not right now.' I sent him home but he said he'll be back early in the morning. He also plans to tell the others we'll not be feasting tonight. But we cannot miss the final night, tomorrow, to mark the end of harvest.

I can't see what he can do to fix this mess. And I'm ashamed he has seen my family fall apart, my mother at her worst. Motina will hate that *I've* seen her this way, let alone someone outside the family, even bičiulystè. She always keeps things to herself.

I had no idea that it had become this bad. Was it only a few days ago we were bathing in the stream? And in that short time my mother has lost her mind, bathing in honey. I knew she'd taken the injury hard, but I thought the mead was helping her rest. Recover. Instead, she has unravelled and bears no resemblance to my beloved stoic motina.

I shiver too. Tèvas once told me a little about my maternal grandmother, how she turned to mead and away from her daughter – my mother – when her husband passed. How she withdrew and mumbled and talked to herself. How happy Motina was to leave that life behind. How the bees had been her escape.

Now she can't serve the bees. That has been taken from her and she is behaving in much the way Tèvas described my grandmother behaving.

It is scary. Because I don't have someone like Tèvas to look out for me. I have Tomas ... that's if news doesn't get back to him about what Motina did. It would not help us to have knowledge of Motina's decline spread among the community. If it gets back to the Duke or the priest she could be taken away from us. We could lose everything.

I can trust Jonas. He'll keep it to himself. His stable presence gave me the courage to take control of the situation. He makes me feel capable.

I survey the damage and sigh. There is no use moping about those two boys. Right now I need to find a way to scoop the honey off the floor and see if any of it can be salvaged.

A loud gasp from the doorway. Senelè stands there, her forehead damp and her scarf slackening about her face. She covers her mouth; her skin goes pale.

'Senelè, let me explain—'

'Gabija!' She is not looking at the barrels or the honey or even Motina in her fitful sleep. She points at the hearth.

The sacred fire has burned out.

CHAPTER THIRTY-FOUR

Austeja

Light slips through gaps in the walls, the morning star rises, and so too do my nerves.

The honey sits a couple of inches lower than the Hollow Watcher's marks. They will think we stole the honey, and we will be punished.

I cannot tell them Motina lost her mind. That she sabotaged the most important thing in her life, during the most important harvest we've ever had. Imagine telling the Duke! Or the new priest. They would take her away or force us to recompense them for her sins. Or worse. Stanislaw's face creeps in: the blood, the gore. That was punishment. Is this what they'll do to Motina?

I won't let that happen. There has to be another way.

I sit up in my cot and rub my thumbs over the palm of each

hand. They are reddened and raw. Hours of boiling pots of water, soaking cloths and layering them, steaming, over the honey puddles to melt them away. Scraping, brushing, wiping. I salvaged only a little honey from the mess. Senelè and I were up most of the night, though it was I who did most of the scrubbing while Senelè tended to the new flame.

She was irate. Devastated. In despair. Her beloved flame burned out. 'Gabija will punish us,' Senelè muttered over and over again.

How can we possibly be punished any more than this?

Motina was barely lucid through the night. Senelè and I gave up trying to understand what happened while we were all gone. We only know that Smilte's double-strength mead sent her over the edge.

Now, the flame crackles and burns. Senelè has rekindled it, nurturing it throughout the early hours.

Praying to Gabija.

She offered bread and salt. A bowl of clean water sits by the hearth so Gabija can wash herself. I know Senelè will not venture far from the hearth in the days to come.

It's as if everyone has turned mad. Senelè mutters and mumbles in her sleep after circling the hearth for hours. Motina tosses and turns and jerks in her sleep. Danutè lies curled in the foetal position, so that she looks half her size, a crinkle of worry between her brows.

My eyes burn as I lie in wait. Waiting for the forest to give me answers. To guide me. The only answer that comes is to harvest from the new hollows. It is an awful thing to do as those bees will not survive winter. But without the correct amount of honey, will we?

Please, Gabija. Žemyna. Vejas.

Fire. Earth. Wind.

God.

Dear Lord, please help us. Please.

Silence. Then the crunch of boots on earth. Footsteps.

I throw aside the blanket and pull the door open. There stands Jonas. A large pine branch rests across his shoulders and hanging from each end is a timber bucket. His face glistens with sweat. He stops when he sees me. A weary smile.

I put a finger to my lips to stop him from speaking and fetch my coat, pull it over my nightdress and step outside, carefully closing the door behind me. I tiptoe to him, bare feet on dewy grass.

Jonas has lowered the branch and the buckets to the ground. The smell of pine resin drifts up, and something sweet too. I look into the buckets.

I gasp. 'Honey?'

'Yes, it's for you. For your family.' He shrugs. 'To pay your taxes.'

My hand clutches my chest. 'Oh, Jonas. I can't take that from you. What if the Duke finds out? You will be punished for cheating him. You must keep it to pay your own taxes.'

He glances around and steps closer. 'You must take it. It is not from our hollows anyway.'

'It's not?'

He shakes his head. 'After our trip to Alytus that summer, I learned of log hives. Fallen trees with carved-out hollows that can be hung on a low branch of an upright tree or at ground height. Easier to harvest and

268

less travelling. I began to collect my own. My father had no interest in them: he's stuck on the old ways. I knew the taxes were to be raised, so I have been keeping them in secret. Far from our own hollows. And a few of them swarmed last summer.'

My mouth drops open slightly. I am lost for words. Log hives? I have never heard of such a thing. 'But if the Hollow Watcher doesn't know about them, what did you plan to do with them?'

He shifts on his feet. 'I planned to leave.'

My stomach drops. 'You did?'

Our eyes meet. 'That was before we began to spend time together; then I thought I could bring them here with me if we wed. But now you are to marry my brother ...'

'Oh, Jonas, but why would you leave?'

'I cannot stay here.' His voice deepens and rumbles, like thunder. 'I cannot live with my parents for eternity. I know that it's my duty – it's expected of me. But my father and I do not get along. My mother has always favoured Tomas. I want to have a family of my own, do things my own way. I want to break free of them.' He steadies his breath. 'I cannot see you wed to him.'

His words vibrate through my body, his pain twisting my stomach in a knot. I too had dreamed of escaping, moving to the city, leaving behind beekeeping, for good.

But now things have changed. And then changed again. I could not possibly leave Motina the way she is. Or Senelè. I couldn't abandon Danutè.

I must stay.

'But if you give this honey to us, you will have nothing to take with you.'

'Don't worry about me.' He reaches for my hand. Hardened and yet soft, callused and tender. Calming on my burned palms. 'You must take this honey and pay what you owe. I cannot live with anything happening to you or your family.'

I draw in a breath. 'I will take it,' I say, because I have little choice. 'But I will be in your debt.'

Relief washes over his face. 'Let's get this inside before anyone sees us.'

He follows me in, and I close the door behind us. Everyone is still asleep. The hearth is high in flame again, a freshly laid log on the fire. Senelè's eyes are closed, and her chest rises and falls. She does not snore.

'Which one is for the Duke?' Jonas asks in a whisper. I'm grateful he doesn't question me about Motina. I wouldn't know what to say anyway ...

'This one,' I say, pointing to the barrel on the right.

Jonas heaves up one of the buckets and pours it into the barrel. It rises to the line marked by the Hollow Watcher. I release my breath; my heart slows down.

He tops it up with the second bucket which brings the levels above the line and then empties the rest into our family barrel, scraping the sides with his knife.

'Try some,' he says, holding up his knife, the tip swathed with a chestnut-coloured syrup. 'It's flaxseed flavoured.'

I scoop up a dollop on my index finger and press it against my tongue, to catch the remaining honey. It is nutty and sweet. 'Delicious.' Jonas grins and my smile wavers. 'I am so sorry to take this from you. I feel awful.'

'It'll be okay.' He taps on the Hollow Watcher's mark. 'You'll get through this harvest now. We all will.'

'Thank you.'

Jonas's lips glisten with honey and all I can think about is tasting them. I swallow the dry lump in my throat. Lick my lips. He watches me. The air tightens between us, as if the wind is pulling us together.

Senelè hiccups in her sleep and I flinch.

'I should go,' he says, his sweet breath tickling my cheek.

'Yes.'

At the door, Jonas pauses. He begins to say something but then shakes his head, his cheeks red.

'Bye, Jonas,' I say into the wind. He strides across the clearing, two emptied buckets in tightly gripped hands.

The pine resin smell tickles my nose. He has left the branch. I pick it up and inhale it. Woody and barky and smelling like Jonas. I rest it against the side of the house and when I look up again, he is gone.

CHAPTER THIRTY-FIVE

Austeja

As the sun descends into the canopies, there's a different kind of buzz in the air. It is the final night of harvest festival. The big one, when everyone gathers, exhausted and relieved, ready to celebrate another successful collection.

And it does feel like success. The Hollow Watcher and his helper retrieved our tax barrel and half our wax without any complications; the priest took his ten per cent also. The wax will be sent off to the ovens in Kaunas or Vilnius. My hard work to be exported across Europe, wax turned into candles and whatever else rich people need. I waited with bated breath as they inspected the two barrels, but they nodded with satisfaction and went on their way.

We had concealed Motina behind the house. Senelè thought it

best to keep her away from the Hollow Watcher. She'd been sweating, shaking and throwing up – nothing but water, as she'd refused to eat breakfast.

'There's no need to worry,' Senelè said as she shuffled my mother out the door. 'It will pass quickly.'

I don't know what is in Smilte's mead, but it turned my mother into someone unrecognisable. No more of that! I was firm and, to my surprise, as Motina sobered she agreed.

I scan the skyline from the doorframe, and Margusz approaches. 'Austeja.' He dips his head as if bowing to me. 'I want to thank you for your contribution to the church.'

'You're welcome,' I say. Relief sweeps through me like an autumn breeze. We did it. We survived our first harvest.

'May I come in for a moment?' he asks.

I hesitate, glancing back over my shoulder. Danutè's eyes widen, and she rushes to Motina's bedside, pulling the blanket up to her chin as if it will screen the priest from her sins.

'I will continue to pray for your mother, for her to heal,' Margusz says. He stands beside me, watching her. 'To heal in both body and mind.'

I'm not surprised he can see her suffering. It is his job, after all. To read people and guide them, keep them on a righteous path.

'I will call on her in the coming days.'

'Thank you, Margusz.' I am relieved she will have someone to talk with; she misses Tévas so dearly.

Deep in thought, watching the crackle of the hearth, he speaks in a faint voice. 'Does that flame ever go out?'

I swallow. 'Yes,' I say and for once it is not a lie. 'Senelè just rekindled it this morning. A tradition for harvest,' I add.

His eyebrows draw in. 'Even on the warmest of days, like this one?'

'Yes,' I say. 'Even so.'

He dips his head, looks at Motina one last time and then strides out of the house.

'Austeja, will we be okay tonight?' Danutè asks.

I lean into her. 'Yes. Just don't mention to anyone about what happened with Motina, or how Jonas helped us pay our taxes, okay?' I confided in Senelè and Danutè about Jonas's generosity.

'I won't.'

'Good: now let's take the food up to the church.'

She grins. 'I can't wait to eat all that food.'

I laugh. 'Me too. Come on, we must take it now. Senelè and Motina will meet us there.' Whatever was in Senelè's herbal concoction added a little colour to Motina's cheeks as the day wore on.

Danutè and I carry three dishes, which each family is required to bring. Twelve dishes to share for dinner. No meat, eggs or dairy products. It is the time we 'fast' from meat and give thanks for a good harvest and welcome in the next season. We eat rye, fish, grains, field mushrooms and berries. And honey, of course. The best of summer and autumn wrapped up in supper.

Danutè carries the boletus mushroom soup, and I have Senelè's buckwheat cake, rye bread and tasters of our honey in separate pots to gift our neighbours. For without the trees and flowering plants throughout the forest our bees would not have thrived. It is tradition to swap and share honey at the festival.

There is a lightness and liveliness in the church clearing this evening. Cheery chatter and a relaxed demeanour from the beekeepers as they prepare for a hard-earned feast. I join Aldona and Elena, who stand by the table.

'This looks wonderful,' I say.

A long oak tabletop has been brought out for this special occasion, resting now on stumps and laid out with various pots and bowls. Danutè and I add ours to the assortment.

'Oh, girls,' Aldona says. 'You should be so proud of yourselves. This harvest must have been very difficult without your father, and with Marytè's injury.'

'It has been tough,' I say, exchanging a glance with Danutè. She shrugs and runs off to join Elena's children, who are running around the candlelit clearing. 'But I'm proud of what we've achieved.'

'So am I.' She pauses. 'How is your mother?'

'Better. She'll be here soon, but she'll have to keep her leg elevated.'

I've not spoken with my mother about what happened last night. I do not know why she did it, or why she blamed it all on Albertas. He was a nice priest, more friendly than Margusz, but I suppose that's because he'd been here longer. He knew everyone well and he was accepted as part of our community. There was no separation between him and us.

That was how he liked it. But there is separation now. The priest and the Duke and his men on one side, and then there's the rest of us. I suppose this is how it will be from now on.

'Of course. It will be good for her to be here.'

She strokes my arm and smiles and looks to be about to say something else but stops herself. Smilte arrives and Aldona helps her lay out her substantial contribution to the feast. More than her three allotted dishes. Smilte always brings more on account of having three grown boys who eat a lot.

And they are all here. Petras ventures off towards the children, stopping to talk to Elena's oldest boy. Tomas and his father stand apart from the gathering, both watchful, silent.

'Evening.'

My heart flutters as I face Jonas. 'Hi,' I say in a low, shaky voice.

'Did everything go okay with the Hollow Watcher?'

'Yes,' is all I can say, though I want to say a lot more. I pass him one of our pots of honey. 'This is for you and your family. Happy harvest.'

He takes the pot and his fingers brush against mine. I catch my breath. He holds the jar up; it sparkles with hints of gold and amber and chestnut. Honey collected from different sides of the forest, blended as one. There's a little of me and a little of Jonas in that jar.

Our secret.

'Jonas, will you help Margusz bring some things out from the church?' Smilte asks in a pleasant tone.

His eyes flick to me and there's the hint of a smile before he lopes off to the church.

'He's a good boy,' Smilte says, more to herself than to me.

'Yes, he is,' I say.

Smilte chortles. 'Oh, cheer up, Austeja.' She places an arm around my shoulder, and it doesn't feel as comforting as it did when I was wrapped up in her embrace at my father's wake. So much has changed since then.

I have changed.

'Once you're wed to Tomas, everything will all fall into place. It did for me. You can leave behind any troubles and face them as a couple. That is the most rewarding thing about marriage. Someone to rely on. Not everyone is fortunate enough to have that.'

I smile weakly and glance up at the church. There is only one person I can think of on whom I can rely and it is not the man I am meant to marry.

'Those feelings you have, my dear, they will weaken over time.' She dabs the dampness on my cheek. 'Trust me.'

She puffs up her chest with a big intake of air, lets it out in a sharp huff through her nose and then returns to arranging the dishes on the table.

No longer in the mood to mingle, I find myself wandering up to the back of the church, into the clearing where the children play. The sun dips behind the stand of pines beyond and throws shadows on the grassland.

'I've been looking for you.'

My stomach drops. 'Good evening,' I say to the Duke.

'A good evening, indeed.'

277

'I believe it was a very successful harvest for us, which means a successful harvest for you.' I am unable to hide the disgust in my voice.

He chuckles. 'You know, Austeja, I am not here to torture you all. But this is the way of the future. If it were not me coming down here swelling the taxes, it would be someone else. I am merely the conduit for the Duchy. We all have roles in life, some which we choose and some which we do not. We make the best of what we have.'

'Says the Duke, who has more choices than all of Musteika put together.'

He grins and there are remnants of the young man I met in the forest. 'I like your honesty.'

There's a drop in temperature and the forest quietens, lending me its intuition of what is to come. I step backwards.

He studies me. 'I return to Alytus the day after tomorrow.'

'Well, I wish you safe travels.'

His face hardens and the charming young man is no more. He clears his throat. 'I'd like you to join me.'

I glance back at the gathering. 'At the feast?'

His brows draw in. 'No. I mean in the city, as my wife.'

'Oh. Oh.' My mouth hangs open and I can't think of anything more to say. There was a time I wanted to be whisked away to the city but that was the old Austeja. This new one knows the importance of family. Of belonging. Staying connected with the old and the new. Nurturing the forest. And this Austeja has no interest in abandoning the bičiulystė for a dangerous traitor!

'No, I must stay here with my people. I want to stay.'

His eyes narrow and it confirms I am not, and will never be, seen as an equal. To the Duke, I have only ever been an amusement, an outspoken girl from the land of honey. A silly girl under his power.

'You know, dear Austeja, most women would not dare refuse me. I wield a lot of power in these districts. I could take you as my wife, whether it pleases you or not.'

I grip at my chest, for the pressure makes it hard to breathe. As if the forest were embracing me with everything it has. I draw in the forest air, the forest magic, and allow it to expand my lungs, my breath, once more.

I gaze down. 'Of course, Duke, it's just that I am already betrothed.' His eyes widen and I am pleased to have surprised him. 'And to break a betrothal would bring much unwarranted attention from the settlers, who you have so generously honoured as the most successful harvesters in the district. It would be unwise to further upset your hardworking employees.'

'Who is it?' he barks. 'One of those big bear men?'

'Uh, yes. The eldest.'

He smirks. 'Hmm. Interesting choice.'

'How do you mean?' My stomach twists in a knot. He is not my choice at all.

'I just mean you should be careful.'

'Be careful? You mean you don't trust Tomas?'

'Oh.' He guffaws. 'I trust him. After all, we've struck a deal. But you, as a wife-to-be, should keep your guard up.'

'I don't know what you're saying. What deal?'

I hate the hint of panic in my tone, how he has managed to rope me in at the very moment I want to sever all ties with this man.

He looks across at the gathering, people sitting at the table. The feast is about to begin. 'You'll find out soon enough.'

CHAPTER THIRTY-SIX

Austeja

Across the table, there is a forced ease in Tomas's demeanour. He chats to his brothers, but his movements are jerky, as if he is crawling with ants. He imitates someone who is relaxed, but he is very much on edge.

I pick at my food, unable to stomach the mushrooms that only an hour earlier tantalised my nostrils with their rich, earthy smell. The Duke's final words have left me uneasy. What deal did Tomas strike with the Duke?

After the final dish, our buckwheat cake with juniper berries, everyone seems satiated and at peace, except me.

Beside me, Motina looks withered, pallid and weary, but she eases into conversation with Aldona, Elena and Smilte. An occasional hint of a smile. They will think her low mood is purely a result of her knee injury and no more. As her bičiulystė rally around her, I know that she'll be okay.

An involuntary shudder seizes me like autumn leaves rustling in the wind. The Duke and his men have arrived. They didn't join the feast, not after taking half of our collection, but they did not discourage our celebration either. Conversations continue and, other than me and Tomas, no one seems to notice the new arrivals. He stiffens momentarily, and with a deliberate effort he drops his shoulders, feigning a relaxed demeanour again.

The Duke's men approach the end of the table where Krystupas sits. The taller one whispers something into his ear and Krystupas tenses. He throws a look at each of his sons: Petras, Jonas and then he settles upon Tomas with a deep scowl. He stands sharply but says nothing.

Smilte pauses her conversation with Elena and straightens her spine. 'What is happening here?'

Krystupas shakes his head at Smilte as if to quieten her.

'It's okay, mother,' Tomas says, standing to place a firm hand on her shoulder.

She shrugs him off and speaks louder. 'What is wrong?'

Krystupas avoids eye contact with us all and follows the Hollow Watcher and the other man in the direction of the church. The priest waits by the door.

The Duke steps forwards and addresses the table. 'We have discovered the culprit for Stanislaw's murder. We will take him away for questioning.'

Culprit? The Duke warned me something was coming and, as if

reading my mind, he sneers at me.

'I knew it,' Elena mumbles.

Smilte throws her a hard stare. She goes to stand but is urged to remain seated.

There's murmuring and unease around the table. I think back to the day I delivered the news of Stanislaw's death to Smilte's boys and her husband. The way Krystupas looked at his boys, unsurprised. Jonas always says he has been a tough father, that he can't bear to live with him any longer. He is a quiet and controlled man but is he capable of such violence?

'Until then, I'd like to introduce you to the new Hollow Watcher.' The Duke beckons Tomas, who eagerly joins him at the head of the table.

'When I leave with my men for the city, it will be Tomas here who will keep an eye on the hollows. It seems sensible to appoint someone who has knowledge of the region and the people, and of course, the hollows.'

I gasp. Is this the deal Tomas has made with the Duke? To hand over his father, to betray him, in exchange for employment with the Duchy?

Uncertainty rises again.

Now I am truly afraid of the man I am to marry.

CHAPTER THIRTY-SEVEN

Marytè

The mood shifts.

As Stanislaw's murderer is escorted away into the darkness, the celebrations are crushed. Smilte paces back and forth from the table to the church, but they won't tell her anything more.

Until she registered Austeja's shocked expression, Marytè thought her mind was playing tricks on her again. Smilte's husband?! Could it possibly be true? Goosebumps prickle her skin and she rubs her arms reassuringly. More than twenty years. That's how long the four families have been living together in harmony, and now this? Marytè cannot fathom it.

She was nervous about coming tonight, worried her friends would know what she has done. How she lost herself in mead and the past.

How for one frightening day she became her mother. The past and future flashing before her. It may be selfish but she is grateful now for her bičiulystė's' preoccupation.

It seems Jonas has kept quiet about her attack. He was kind to help them. Austeja handled the crisis with admirable calmness, a trait that Marytė has always prided herself on. They are more alike than she thought.

No more time for self-pity. She will not let her daughters down. She will not abandon them the way her own mother did her. She could not do that to them, or to herself. She knows she committed a sin, and she will repent. She plans to confess to the priest – he probably already knows but she will tell him anyway – and she will do what it takes to get back on the righteous path. To become the mother her daughters deserve and a beekeeper deserving of bees.

Marytė was so convinced that Albertas was really there in her house. That he came back for her, to humiliate her, to bare her sins to everyone and ruin her reputation. But it seems none of it was real. It was all in her head. Wasn't it?

Yes, it was suppressed fear, buried secrets stomped down into the depths of her soul along with any painful emotions she ever experienced, the ones she doesn't like to acknowledge or feel. One little trickle dropping upon another, until her body was flooded with so much pain, regret and hurt that there was nowhere else to hide. It seeped out of every crack and crevice.

Baltrus's death has affected her more than she realised. Stanislaw's death was like a niggle of fear threatening to turn into something much larger, and then her knee gave way and it felt as if her life was over. There was nothing left to hang on to, nothing left within her control. Not even her own body! And then the mead took her mind and she let it.

If she's really honest with herself, the stress began long before Baltrus's illness. Because before that was Azuolas's death and before that were four babies who died in the womb or shortly after taking a breath. Even further back, she'd left her mother and the settlement she was raised in to start afresh with her husband. There was her mother's demise. And all the way back at the beginning was her own father's death. The catalyst for it all.

Death, loss, abandonment, change. An interwoven pattern that snakes throughout her life. It has kept her wound up, it has kept her at a distance from the people she loves, it made her push them away when she wanted to pull them closer, hold on tight.

She's made a mess of it all.

She always thought Austeja was the one who had to learn and grow, but now Marytè can see that she does too. The learning and growing never stops. And with each ripple in the stream, each new direction, she is carried along, whether she likes it or not. Austeja has proven she has what it takes to keep her head above the water when life takes a new direction. And Marytè will prove to her daughter she can do it too.

It is time to put it all behind her. No more mead. No more hiding. It is time to face it all head on, and she'll begin by talking with Austeja. There is a lot to clear between them.

She wants to tell her she is proud. That she trusts her to make choices about her future. She rises from her chair, not fussed that she's completely tuned out of the conversation with Aldona and Elena. Her knee is still painful to walk on, but she does it anyway; she doesn't like to lean on others for too long.

'Aldona, have you seen Austeja?'

She glances about. 'No, I'm sorry.'

'Is she with the children?' Elena asks.

'I will look.' Marytè hobbles across the clearing and Danutè runs to her.

'Motina, you should be resting.'

'I'm fine. Where is your sister?'

Danutè points at the forest and frowns. 'She was over there, talking to Tomas.'

'When?' Goosebumps form on her arms again.

Her mouth turns upside down. 'Not long ago.'

'Stay here with the children.'

'Has something happ—?'

'No, just stay with the children.'

There is no sign of Austeja at the beginning of the forest path. It has darkened and it is now impossible to see the bridge. She returns to the clearing and gathers some candles. She pivots on her foot and groans as a sharp pain travels down her leg. Jonas stands before her; he is talking with the Duke. They meet each other's eyes.

'I need you to come with me. Tomas and Austeja are in the forest.'

Jonas swallows, looks past her and clenches his fists. He collects a branch, then another two. Lights the tips with the candles and passes one to Marytè, the other to the Duke.

'Is Austeja in danger?' the Duke asks after looking hard at their faces.

Marytè thinks of that stinger left in Tomas's neck on the day of the swarm. Since that day she's felt the prick of that sting, the regret, the guilt. She should have told Austeja what she discovered: that perhaps he was not the man for her after all. Yes, there were rules and yes, they were bičiulystè, but she would not marry her daughter to a man who was not good. A man who was not respected by the bees. Or by her.

'Let's go,' Jonas says.

'Into the forest?' the Duke asks.

Jonas pauses and glances at Marytè. 'To the hollow.'

And she knows what hollow he means. How can any of them ever forget it?

CHAPTER THIRTY-EIGHT

Austeja

It has all been leading to this.

I knew it the moment the Duke told me a deal had been struck. The moment Krystupas was led away in disgrace. The moment Tomas approached me. I knew.

His eyes twinkled with satisfaction, and he walked with the swagger of a man who'd captured a fat forest beast. All he needed was the corpse of a bison, sprawled out behind him, to add more drama to his arrival.

'I cannot talk to you right now,' I said, unable to look at him. 'I need a moment on my own.'

I did not wait for his response, though he mumbled something and his easy confidence transformed into a deep scowl. As if the crown had fallen from his head.

I wandered into the forest, where my feet always lead me, where my heart is at home.

I arrive at the oak, of course.

The forest chose me to seek the truth and so here I am.

Did Krystupas really take Stanislaw's life?

He's a believable suspect. Krystupas remains on the outskirts of our community, rarely joining the festivities. He is a hard man but is he violent? Could he really have done this?

I lean against the oak and there's a gentle hum from above. I press my ear against the trunk. I may be imagining the vibrations, the busy chatter of a family after being at a feast with my own, because this hollow is burned out. Perhaps it is the voices of my bičiulystė that echo in my mind.

The wind shifts, altering direction. The oak crackles as if puffing up its chest and stretching out its limbs to protect me. Only it cannot.

I am no longer alone.

I knew when I crossed the bridge that it would happen this way. Danger was ahead and yet I came here anyway. Because part of me needs to know, needs to understand what happened here. I do not yet have the truth and I need it. Stanislaw needs it. Isn't it better to risk myself now than marry a violent man – one who may put my family and any children we have at risk of harm?

An image of Stanislaw creeps in, but not one of blood – one of … fear? Bruised and nose bloodied, an arm shielding his face. A shadowy, menacing figure standing over him. I turn and there he is.

'It was you.'

Tomas steps into the moonlight, his face expressionless, watching me. 'What was me?' he says, drawing out every word as if they were each a sentence on its own.

'You killed Stanislaw.'

He raises his chin.

The wind circles me, the forest buoying me with courage. Whispering to me. I am speaking on behalf of Stanislaw. The oak. The forest. We all want answers.

'No. You saw them take him away. It was my father.' There's no concern in his voice, only irritation. 'It comes as no surprise to me. He has always been a cruel man. Belittling me, punishing me when I don't meet his expectations. I was never good enough for him. Jonas was his favourite.'

I shake my head. 'I don't think that's true. Jonas feels the same way about your father as you do.'

A flicker of surprise and then another scowl. 'He always treated me differently, because I am.'

'What do you mean?' I ask, wanting to draw out the conversation. Sensing the tension, the danger, the hairs on my arms standing up, the shiver on the back of my neck. The air and the wind, Vejas, warning me.

He lets out a breath, as if to shake himself free. 'You don't need to worry about any of it. We should be thinking only of our future.' He steps forwards.

'Why? You don't even like me.'

He frowns. 'What does that matter?'

'It should matter in a marriage.'

'My brother likes you well enough so that makes it worth it for me.'

'You're cruel,' I say, and he flinches at the word he's used to describe his father.

His fists close, but he remains still. 'Don't you say that to me again. I do what I must for my family.'

'How does having your father arrested help your family? You did it for no one but yourself!'

'That Hollow Watcher was badgering my father about the mead. He'd sent him on his way, but he was causing trouble for us. Threatening to spill secrets, my mother's secrets. He started on me then. More mead, more taxes. He was greedy. A drunken moron who should never have messed with us.'

'What happened?' I ask. The forest quietens.

'I tried to strike a deal with him. If he put in a good word to the Duke when he arrived, then I'd sneak him more mead. He'd have none of that. Didn't want the Duke to know he'd been striking deals with the settlers.'

My heart thumps in my chest; I know I must tread carefully. Tomas killed Stanislaw because he felt disrespected. He may kill me too.

'He didn't take you seriously.'

'No!' He steps forwards, his face red. 'He said he'd only deal with my father from then on. Didn't respect me at all. Neither did my father, or Jonas. I'd had enough.'

I shuffle back a little to put distance between us. 'What happened then?'

'I took matters into my own hands.'

'You killed him.'

'I didn't mean to.' His shoulders slump. 'We had a fight. He fell back and hit his head.'

Flashes of Stanislaw's last moments come to mind. Him looking up at Tomas, falling. Dark raven's eyes, blood trickling down his face. Insides spilling outwards.

Tension builds in my body; my voice is thick with disgust. 'And then you covered your tracks. Made it look like a theft. Framed your father.'

He storms towards me; a tight grip claims my upper arm. 'I did what I had to and now I have the respect of the Duke. Finally, someone sees me as more than just a beekeeper.'

'There's nothing wrong with being a beekeeper,' I whisper as tears sting my eyes. For the first time I feel as if the beekeeper way of life may be enough. It's enough for me. If I survive this moment, I will be the best beekeeper I can possibly become.

'For a moment there I thought you understood me. But you are just like everyone else.'

'So it was you who killed my bees?'

Tomas spins around and I stumble in his grip. Motina steps out of the shadows, a branch alight in her hand. She hobbles closer. Tomas glances between us, calculating whether she's a threat.

He pulls me closer. 'Why is everyone so obsessed with the bees?'

Motina sighs deeply, her impatience evident.

'What about us?' he continues. 'We've been stuck in this antiquated forest forever. There is a whole world out there. Why should we be stuck here scooping out globs of honey, when people like the Duke are living in castles in civilised towns, devouring our delicacies?'

I realise we are not all that different. We both wanted something more than this place, we both wanted to escape. To be free of the rigid rules and obligations. The only difference is, Tomas was willing to kill for it.

Motina spits at his feet. 'I knew you were a bad person. The bees are wise.'

'The bees know nothing.'

Motina sneers. I attempt to flee to her, but he pulls me back, his arm pressed against my throat, my back against his pounding chest. Grip tightening, my feet lifting off the ground. My toes scratch at the earth, an attempt to stay grounded. Connected to the forest.

'No. I can't let you go and tell everyone what happened.'

'What are you going to do, then? Kill me like Stanislaw? My mother too?' I am short of breath, but a surge of adrenaline inhibits the pain. 'When will it end, Tomas?'

'It won't take much for your mother to look like she's had a fall in the dark. But you: no, I need you. A wife will bring me status. I will finally be considered a respectable man. A husband, beekeeper and Hollow Watcher. I will begin my rise.'

'I will not marry you.'

His grip on my throat tightens.

'I think you should listen to the lady.' The Duke steps out of the shadows, Jonas by his side. 'It's clear she won't be marrying you after all.'

Tomas eyes the men, assessing how much they've heard. 'You have no say in who I marry.'

'We all heard your confession,' the Duke says.

'It wasn't me,' Tomas says and throws me aside. I drop to the ground behind him, digging my fingers into the soil. The cool earth calms me. I take deep, ragged breaths.

'It was her fault.' Tomas growls at me. And I can see it in him now, the rage, the violence. The intent to kill. In that instance I am Stanislaw. Afraid and aware my time is limited. But Stanislaw didn't have anyone to rally around him, to protect him, fight with him. He didn't have bičiulystè.

He leans over me. 'Your grandmother. It is all her fault!'

Senelè? 'How is my grandmother responsible for your behaviour?'

He turns to the Duke now, pleading. 'She's a witch. Everyone knows she is into sorcery. She hasn't let go of the old ways. She put a spell on me.'

'Oh, please,' Motina scoffs.

I crawl backwards, give myself space to get to my feet. My voice barely containing the anger raging inside.

'Are you claiming a spell made you murder Stanislaw?' the Duke asks as his gaze flickers to me.

'Yes! She should be arrested for her pagan ways and so should Austeja. She is just like her grandmother.'

'This is a serious allegation, Tomas. Austeja's grandmother could go on trial for this.' The unsaid words are left hanging in the cool air ... I could be put on trial too.

Jonas shakes his head, disappointment and shock carved into his expression. 'How could you take another man's life?' He has paled.

'I was under a spell,' Tomas repeats.

I find my voice. 'And were you under a spell when you ripped his guts out and tied them around the trunk of this tree? When you covered your tracks and framed some make-believe honey thief? And then your own father! Were you under a spell then?'

'He betrayed the Duke.' Tomas turns to him, trying a new tactic. 'I am loyal to you, can't you see?'

'Stanislaw was trying to help us,' Jonas says with a sideways glance at the Duke. 'You betrayed our father, Tomas. How could you do that?'

Tomas scowls. 'We both know he is not my real father.'

And there it is. The truth of it all.

It comes as no surprise. There are glimpses of Smilte behind his features, and his brothers too, but none of his father. Smilte was heavily pregnant when she moved to Musteika with Krystupas. She's hinted at the truth and so has Tomas. No one questioned the paternity of the firstborn son, not when she'd set up house, among strangers, with Krystupas. Her new husband.

Perhaps it explains his hardness. Had Smilte betrayed him? Had he known of her pregnancy and married her anyway? Or did she deceive him? Whether he knew or not, there was bitterness there. Deep-seated resentment that had never been spoken about. Until now.

Jonas stumbles as if the truth is a physical blow. I want to move towards him, but Tomas pushes me aside. Jonas's large frame deflates, but not from shock. Relief? It makes sense to him now, why his father has always been so hard, controlling. Distant.

The fight has gone from Tomas too. There's no more hiding behind a facade: he is who he is. And so, when the taller of the Duke's henchmen appears in the depths of the forest to march him away, he does not resist.

As he disappears into darkness, I am relieved there will be an end to our betrothal. But intertwined with relief is fear. For I am once again a Marti, a young single woman, and I must still find a husband. Not to mention the allegation of witchcraft and threats of trials over our heads.

'Come,' Motina says. 'Let's return to our bičiulystè.' Away from the oak she guides me, trailing behind Jonas, who trails behind the Duke. As if sensing my fear, the Duke glances back over his shoulder, his face shadowed by the flame in his grasp.

Around me the forest shudders; leaves shiver and the temperature drops.

Even in the half-light, his expression is clear. Watch out, Austeja, it says.

CHAPTER THIRTY-NINE

Marytè

She inhales the sweet scent of stewed fruit, drizzling a little extra honey over the compote to bring all the flavours of autumn – apples, gooseberries, raspberries and vibrant red bilberries – into a cold, sweet soup. A special treat for them all. Austeja collected the assortment from the woods and Marytè placed them in the hot pot on the hearth and crushed the fruit with a spoon as it heated and softened, juices oozing, colours transforming. The smell, delicious. The heady scent of autumn is what she needs to pull herself out of her stroppy mood once and for all.

With the benefit of hindsight, Marytè recognises just how low she let herself fall. She permitted an injured knee to keep her immobile, to drown her in her past; and then glugging down the mead just pulled her under deeper, quicker.

Well, no more of that. Her mother had been lost forever. Marytè was only lost for a few days: she took the wrong path but found her way back again. She knows to be careful where she treads now.

The arrest of Krystupas sobered her quickly, and then the frightening ordeal with Tomas. Marytè will not allow herself to think about what could've happened if she'd not been clear-headed enough to follow her instincts. That niggling feeling she had about Tomas. The one she shared with the bees. Imagine if she'd not gone into the forest? What then? Her daughter, her beautiful strong daughter, would've married a tyrant, she would've sacrificed her happiness to protect the family. Or worse, he could have ...

Marytè breathes in the fruity scent, stirs, focuses on the task at hand. She is not deluded: she knows she has some work to do, to stay on the right path. Austeja has done so much for the family and now Marytè must do her part too.

As if on cue, a knock on the door drags her gaze from the rainbow-coloured stew to the priest's face.

Margusz.

She blinks, focuses her vision. Yes, definitely Margusz. Here to keep her on the righteous path.

He clears his throat and Marytè sees his attention drifts to Senelè, breathing deeply through her nose and the air catching in her throat. Her chest shakes and rattles as she emits a phlegmy cough. As if in sympathy, Marytè's own throat thickens and huffs. A cacophony of coughs vault across the insulated walls of the house. They are little forest creatures in a hollow, and the walls are the trunks muffling the sound for the outside world.

Margusz remains at the door, concern etched into his forehead. She takes the pot from the hearth and sets it aside to cool. Hmm. Shall the soup be dessert or the main tonight? She'll leave it up to the girls to decide.

Outside, they stroll along to the Scots pine and sit upon the bench underneath its shaded canopy. There was a time when she spent hours sitting here with Albertas. No matter what happened with Albertas, she misses their conversations. She's always been a reserved person, but she's been able to keep her emotions in control for so long and not go off path, because she had the regular, safe space to explore what was in her head and mind. She wants that again.

'What would you like to talk about today, Marytè?' Margusz asks. He speaks in a gentle but firm tone. She has come to see he is not as naive and detached, or too much the creature of the Duke, as she once thought. He is kind and he is here for their people. He is here for her.

Margusz apologised, on behalf of Albertas, for what transpired between them. She told him she's forgiven his predecessor; they were both to blame. Margusz is pleased with her progress, her desire to let go of the anger and resentment, to focus on the future.

'I suppose I've had to adjust my expectations of my work,' she says, massaging her knee, which remains tender and vulnerable to sudden movements. She's been forced to slow down and be mindful of the way she uses her body.

'Ahh. In what way?'

'I believed I must be able to do it all to be a beekeeper, but now I see

300

there are many aspects of this profession, and I do not have to perform them all. At least not in the way I thought.'

'Hmm.' He doesn't prompt her further. Allows her mind to wander to other possibilities.

Jonas has told her about the log hives. What a revelation. No more climbing! He says he'll help her collect logs before winter to store in the threshing barn so she can carve the hollows while the bees hibernate. She is thrilled with the prospect of tasks to keep her mind and hands occupied when the temperatures drop.

Austeja is capable of caring for the hollows, the ones high up that Marytè will not be able to reach until she's made a full recovery, and a full recovery may not be for some time, or at all. Her body no longer springs back the way it once did. This thought should send her deeper into despair, but Austeja is here to take the reins. Marytè, at a similar age, took over the care of her family hollows, and Austeja will now do the same.

It might be that the only way Austeja has been able to flourish is through Marytè taking a step back. Perhaps this is how it has to be.

'Perhaps this was God's plan all along,' Margusz says, as if he has read her thoughts.

Marytè soaks in the sun's rays, which warm her face. There will only be a few more weeks of warmth before the forest prepares for winter. 'You know, Margusz, I think you are right.'

CHAPTER FORTY

Austeja

There's balance in the forest again. I can feel the change as I walk along the forest path. Negative energies are drawn out and cast aside. It is not exactly peace, but there's comfort in truths being unearthed and the seeds of hope scattered among the pines.

When families pass through to make trades, the anxious city parents warn their children not to venture too far into the woods alone. There's no logic to it. I know that now.

We only have each other to fear.

The forest protects us. It protected me. It warned me of danger, of Tomas, and it showed me the truth. I've slept soundly, deeply and dream-free every night since. No flashes of Stanislaw behind heavy lids. He is free, and so is the oak and so am I. For now, at least.

Tomas, I suppose, is free too. No one can live fully with such a heavy heart.

The Duke waits at the bridge for me. The ease I've felt since Tomas's arrest is thrown aside. My skin tingles, the forest wavers.

'Austeja.'

'Hello.' I cross the bridge and pause when I've passed him, so that the forest is behind me, like eagle wings rearing up behind, ready to take flight.

'I wanted you to know that Tomas insists Stanislaw was the one who damaged your hollow.' He pauses. 'And then he delivered the punishment on behalf of the settlers.'

'But you heard him confess.'

He presses his lips together. 'Yes, and I will be called upon as a witness at the court. I am a respected Duke and make generous contributions to the Duchy. He has no hope against me.'

No, nor do I. It is a reminder that Tomas may have been a threat, but he is a small threat in comparison to the Duke. I may be free of the nightmares and the Hollow Watcher's pleas for justice, but I am not free of the Duke.

Another pause. My limbs twitch, eager to be on my way, to be with the oak. I want to check whether there really is new life living inside. I suspect Jonas had something to do with that.

'With Tomas's arrest, I am in need of a new Hollow Watcher.'

I stand up tall. Perhaps the Duke does not intend to threaten me. Could it be me? Could I be made the first female Hollow Watcher in the Grand Duchy of Lithuania? I swell with pride, unexpected pride, as being a beekeeper, let alone a Hollow Watcher, has never been how I envision my future.

I look up and see that I am a tiny speck among pillars of pines. Instead of making me feel small, it is empowering. The watcher of the hollows. The eyes of the forest. I can think of no one more suited than me for the job.

'Oh, it won't be you, Austeja.' He laughs and draws himself up taller, as if to mimic the surrounding pines. 'I cannot trust the settlers; Tomas has taught me that. No, I will summon someone from Alytus. Someone I trust. Someone unafraid to take charge and who will not be swayed by bribery as Stanislaw was.'

'I would expect nothing less, after everything that has happened here – you would not want the Duchy to find you incapable of operating such a valued asset.' I grit my teeth.

'No,' he agrees, and I realise I do not have the upper hand at all. 'There's one more thing. Given Tomas's accusation of sorcery was made publicly, we are obliged to investigate this further. The priest would like to speak to your grandmother.' He pauses. 'I'm sure it will come to nothing, but I wanted to warn you, especially, since you were also the target of his witchery accusations.'

Before I can reply, he dips his head and exits the bridge, his confident gait taking him briskly along the forest path towards the church.

Heart pounding, I walk further into the forest. My breath is laboured but I walk on, walking off the tension before I return home and warn my family.

If there are any suspicions about the old ways, we could be in serious trouble. I must speak to Senelè. She's been a little confused lately. She sleeps often, and coughs, and rambles. She's been asking me about the bees. Have the bees been following you? They sense your power. They look up to you, Austeja.

It's all rather strange. It's usually Motina who is obsessed with the bees.

I tread lightly upon the earth, but creatures scatter in all directions anyway. Lizards lapping up the last of the autumn sun, rabbits gorging on grasses, and a dormouse fleeing with a crimson-coloured berry in its mouth. The last chance to fatten up before winter.

I know the feeling. We're all preparing for winter, the creatures, the settlers and even the bees. They'll be narrowing their hive entrances to keep out wind and pests. They'll take flight one last time over the coming weeks and then settle in for hibernation. We'll be pulling up the last of our beets, onions and cabbage. Stuffing ourselves with berries and savouring the perfect round of curd cheese Dominykas brought back from his trades for us. Drizzled with fresh honey, it is divine.

I collect mushrooms and berries, filling my pockets along the leaf-strewn path. Acorns snap and crunch underfoot. And I am here, at the oak. I do not need to climb it to see the bees buzzing around the hollow entrance, but I do anyway. I perch myself on the lowest limb, and as I settle, leaves in shades of yellow, amber and red rustle and drift in the cooling breeze. They fall past my dangling legs, skidding in one direction and then another, before dropping to the earth below. The oak sheds old growth, its old way of being.

The wind shifts direction and clouds hover overhead. The hollow entrance is a buzz of activity, bees retreating from the flower groves to the safety of their homes. The clouds are tinged with dark edges, but there's no scent in the air of rain. Something else has them spooked. The wind whips around me and then stops altogether. The coolness retreats and a warmth rises through me.

A cuckoo calls. Hoo woo. Hoo woo. A shiver trails down my spine.

The forest quietens. Bows to the broadcasting bird. Whispers reach for me, and although the words are tangled like the roots of the oak tree, I read their meaning.

The forest reawakens, it breathes again, but now something vital is missing.

My heart swells with grief.

And a little relief too.

Now there will be no one for the Duke and priest to interrogate.

CHAPTER FORTY-ONE

Austeja

She's gone.

Up on the High Hill, the breeze circles. Weaving in between bodies, familiar faces in mourning. A cuckoo calls. Hoo woo. Hoo woo. People glance about anxiously.

Senelè gave me the gift of trusting my instincts, leaning into my connection with the forest and, most importantly, trusting myself. I will hold her wisdom within me; it'll strengthen my bones, direct the blood flow through my body, sharpen my senses. I will keep hold of the old ways so they don't fade as Senelè feared. I owe her this.

I must be careful. Now that a seed has been planted in the Duke's mind about witchcraft and sorcery, those seeds will not perish with Senelè. Out of fear, paranoia grows, and if I am not careful, this little seed will flourish into a forest. I cannot bring more harm to my family.

I will carry on the old ways for Senelè but I will also be cautious like Motina.

Senelè is where she wants to be. From the moment Tévas's soul flew away, so did hers. We have all mourned his loss, but Senelè never recovered. She inhabited her son, cough and all, succumbing to it in her very last breath.

She'll be at peace now.

'Are you ready?' Motina asks.

'Yes,' I say, stepping forwards to join her and Danutè. The three of us are draped in white scarves again. Two funerals bookended by two winters. Just the three of us.

For now.

The Duke and his men have escorted Tomas to the city, and Margusz too has left after delivering a sermon for Senelè, so only the settlers remain in Musteika. We have all changed, though, since the arrival of our new overseers last winter. No doubt there will be more change to come.

Smilte and Krystupas stand separate from the gathering, on the surface mourning a member of the bičiulystè, but underneath mourning their firstborn, and nursing the humiliation and horror of his actions.

In time, we'll be able to look towards the future, instead of the past. Because in the past lies hurt and pain. The future is tantalisingly hopeful.

My stomach flips. I can sense his gaze upon me. At Senelè's graveside, I glance over my shoulder and our eyes lock. As Jonas watches me, he tells me everything he wants to say but cannot in this moment.

I am sorry for your loss. I am sorry for everything. I am here. I am waiting.

I smile but it fades quickly as the Duke's threats in the forest linger. I can only hope Tomas's accusations have swayed his interest away from marrying me. The Duke is ambitious and will not be associated with any real – or imagined – sorcery. It would damage his reputation.

The coffin is made of both conifer and spruce, as I insisted. One to keep the positive energy in and one to keep the negative energy out. The way Senelè would have liked it.

Senelè's body will lie in peace in the earth surrounded by forest, and her soul will float about the High Hill, telling stories to Tévas and reuniting with her long-lost loved ones.

'It's your turn,' Motina says, prompting me to step forwards.

I study Senelè's wrinkly, scarved head and I blink to imprint her on my mind. So I can carry the image of a peaceful death and let go of the haunting images of Stanislaw. I fall to my knees, sinking into the dampened earth.

I make offerings for Senelè's afterlife.

A chunk of rye, a sprinkle of salt and ashes from the hearth.

Now she can look after Gabija, and our family, as she lives alongside us.

Thank you. Thank you for being in my life, Senelè. For teaching me to be myself, for helping me to embrace the old ways. I will take this with me, and I will be open to the new ways. Because we must adapt if we are to survive.

To survive, we must let go of some of our ways, to protect our family from threats. I'm sorry, Senelè, but we must let the eternal flame go out. I will relinquish the practice but not the memories.

The tears flow and my voice cracks, but I part my lips and succumb to the sorrow. My last parting gift, my lament, to Senelè.

'Oh, my dear grandmother, why did you have to leave us? Oh, why did you have to take a trip up to the High Hill? If only you had a look at your two granddaughters, If only you stayed here and cared for us ...'

I am joined by the women, falling to their knees, at one with the earth. Motina and Danutè either side of me. We unite with our voices. Weeping, singing, pleading, processing, releasing.

'If only you hadn't flown away to the High Hill! Ask the earth to let you go, to open the windows and let you fly. Travel back along the high road and come back to us. Follow the bright sun, she will show you the way ...'

The cries muffle words and I draw in a deep breath to ease the shudder in my rib cage. I pull a handkerchief from my pocket and dab my eyes. As I pull it away a distinct buzzing sound catches my ear, followed by a light tickle on my hand.

A bee.

It has been happening with increased frequency since Senelè left. They must be confused. My salty tears should repel them. I may be one with the forest, but I am not cloaked in pollen. It flutters its wings and rubs its tiny hands together. A little pollen sac sits on its leg.

It is beautiful.

I catch Motina's eye, and she beams back at me. I know what she's thinking. A bee does not sting a bad person. Bees choose their keepers.

She is right, and so was Senelè. I do have a special connection with the forest. One that cannot be described with words because it is felt in my heart.

The bee flutters away and my heart swells with a renewed sense of self. Of who I have become.

I am a good person. An agent of the forest.

A beekeeper.

I am Austeja.

I am goddess of the bees.

Acknowledgements

[to come]